Praise for the Natalie McMasters Mysteries

Stripper! A Natalie McMasters Novel (2018)

***** – Extremely well written. The plot was very entertaining and the characters were well developed and likeable. Told from the first-person perspective of Natalie McMasters – the book is a real page turner. Great read! – Amazon review

***** – Excellent crime/mystery story, kept me turning the pages. Burns has created a fascinating lead character--Nattie McMasters. She's young, sexy and courageous. – Amazon review

Revenge! A Natalie McMasters Mystery (2018)

***** – A fast-paced story, Intriguing true-to-life characters with an explosive ending. Looking forward to the next book! – Amazon review

***** – This was an unexpected gem. I was fully gripped from page one to the last word as the pace was fast without much down time. Natalie was the type of character I appreciate, with dimension. While hard, and often crass, there is also a vulnerability to her that makes her more than the average cardboard sassy heroine. – Amazon review

Trafficked! A Natalie McMasters Mystery (2019)

***** – Bluntly put, this ain't your average mystery book. It's gritty, raw, and "human" in the worst way possible. And I enjoyed it every dark minute of it! – Amazon review

**** – There was blood, whipping, love making, sewer stench, a tour of Manhattan and Kosher food, honor, despair, and a healthy dollop of deceit and mystery solving. Burns is a good writer and is on to something good with his Natalie McMasters Mysteries. Amazon review

Venom! A Natalie McMasters Mystery (2020)

Sniper! A Natalie McMasters Mystery (2020)

Killers! A Natalie McMasters Mystery (2021) - Winner of the Silver Falchion Award for Best Action Adventure of 2021 from the Killer Nashville! International Writer's Conference

series with these characters stands alone even though the characters continue to change and evolve throughout the series. Publisher's Weekly Booklife Review

***** - In the new Natalie McMasters mystery, KILLERS!, that petite powerhouse heading Thomas Burns's series is back with a powerful opener that never lets go. This time she's determined to find the killer of her therapist friend and surrogate mom. Natalie has a complicated history, and is currently one third of a throuple. That leads to interesting complications and subplots while the twists escalate in several directions. Chasing clues and serial killers, stumbling across more dead bodies, there will be gunfights and a look into the world of BDSM before it's all finished. And how does the murder of an aged Chinaman from Alabama fit in? Burns explores it all, as Tai Chi and southern culture collide with a maniacal killer, a sexual sadist known as The Marquis. But he's not the only sicko Natalie and her team will encounter. Graphic and all too real, Killers! explores a vastly different world with non-stop action. Amazon Review from Anthony and multiple Award-winning author M.K. Graff

***** - Ripping good read! Thomas Burns returns with another Natalie McMasters winner. Action explodes off the first page, when Natalie attends her friend's funeral, only to see her friend's murderer watching from the edge of the crowd. In that instant, Natalie knows she's next on this serial killer's list. Accompanied by an unlikely series of friends, she sets out to find and destroy this man known as The Marquis, before he can complete his destruction of those she loves. Burns builds the atmosphere and suspense through a variety of well-depicted, isolated settings. The headlong pace is relentless, rarely stopping for so much as a breather. Strong character development and a plot that doesn't disappoint grab the reader from the first page and won't let go. Let's hope this isn't the last Natalie McMasters mystery. This reader couldn't put the book down. Amazon review from Betsy Ashton, author of the Mad Max Mysteries

***** - Wham Bam! Killers! takes off like a rocket and never slows its pace. The story begins with Nattie McMasters at the funeral of her friend. While at the graveside, she sees the serial killer who murdered her friend. He's watching her and Nattie knows she's next on his list. She does her best not only to protect her family and friends, but to hunt down the evil villain known as The Marquis. Author Thomas Burns takes the reader on a wild ride, complete with non-stop action and intensity. Amazon Review from Brenda Donelan, author of the University Mystery series.

Sister!

A Natalie McMasters Mystery

Thomas A. Burns, Jr.

Published by Tekrighter LLC 2022

The Natalie McMasters Mysteries by Thomas A. Burns, Jr.

Stripper! (2018)

Revenge! (2018)

Trafficked! (2019)

Venom! (2020)

Sniper! (2020)

Killers! (2021)

Sister! (2022)

Dedication

To my mother, Myrtle, the only other woman who loved me for me.

Sisters never stand a chance to be friends. We're pitted against each other from the moment that we are born.

Mary H.K. Choi

Prologue

Bobby Ray Samples hates his stupid job.

Four fucking years of college, and now I'm wasting my life behind the counter of a convenience store owned by some fuckin' rag head who wasn't even born here. It just isn't fair!

An electronic chime beeps and Bobby Ray turns his head to the front door.

Sheeit fire! Now that's what I'm talkin' about!

A twentysomething babe in a leather jacket over a frilly top and faded black jeans, her mussed blonde hair falling over her shoulders, giving her that just fucked look.

A job where I get to meet somethin' like this doesn't seem so bad after all.

She goes straight to the coolers in back while Bobby Ray changes his position behind the counter so he can keep an eye on her in the convex mirror mounted high up in the far rear corner of the convenience store.

Fuckin' A! Check out that tight ass in those jeans!

As she opens the cooler door and reaches in, standing on her tippy toes, to snag a pint can of Colt 45 off the top shelf, he imagines slipping the bone growing in his boxers between those plump cheeks. She slithers up the walkway toward his register, snagging a bag of chips on the way. He fixes his eyes on the end of the aisle where she'll emerge, intending to give her that patented boyish grin of his that almost always gets him laid.

I just have to make a play for this shit or I'll never forgive myself.

She meets his eyes with her ice blue gaze, returning his grin with a dazzling smile.

Holy fuckin' shit man, I might actually get lucky here!

Walking up to the counter, she lays down the can and the bag of chips as he frantically runs through his litany of opening lines. He's only got the one chance—that opener will make or break you, every time.

She reaches into her jacket pocket, extracts a folded cloth pillowcase, then tosses it on top of the beer and chips. Reaching back under her jacket, she produces a small, flat black semiauto pistol. She brings her other hand around to close around the grip so she's holding the gun with two hands, and a scarlet light flashes from beneath the barrel and dances in the center of Bobby Ray's chest.

With the same glittering smile, she says, "Fill the bag, shithead, or I'll blow a hole in your heart."

Bobby's hard-on deflates like a balloon leaking air, and a warm dribble runs down the side of his leg as he snatches up the bag. The Ayrab who owns the store has a .357 in the drawer under the register, but Bobby Ray doesn't even think twice about it.

No fuckin' way I'm gonna risk my neck for another man's money.

He pops the register drawer and pulls out handfulls of cash, stuffing the bills into the sack. The door chime sounds again as he hands the bag to the girl, and the dribble becomes a stream.

Oh no! Nothing like another customer walking in on her heist to get this crazy bitch shooting!

He looks left and sees a young man and woman, who've stopped dead in their tracks at the sight of the gun.

The blonde pulls the trigger twice, grinning as a crimson rose blossoms on Bobby Ray's chest. As he crumples to the floor, she wheels and fires twice at the fleeing couple. A 9mm round catches the hapless young man in the back of the head, blowing out the front of his forehead as it exits.

Above the register, a little red light blinks on the top of the security camera catching the whole thing.

The frightened girl madly dashes for their pickup truck, parked beside the gas pumps. As the gunwoman bursts through the front door of the store, the girl throws it into gear without even closing her door and burns rubber out of the parking lot.

Tucking her gun back into the rear of her pants beneath her jacket, the shooter carries the pillowcase containing the cash to a dark blue Range Rover parked on the opposite side of the pumps from where the pickup was. Opening the passenger door, she slides in.

A mature, elegant dark-haired woman behind the wheel turns to look at her.

"Everything go well, Dear?"

"I'm sorry that I let one get away, Ma'am."

"These things happen, Dear." The driver puts the car in gear, cautiously pulls out on the main road, and slowly drives away.

Chapter 1

The Tao Te Ching says, "When you recognize the children, and find the mother, you will be free of sorrow." It lies!

My name is Natalie McMasters. I'm twenty-four, blonde (OK, it's bleached), and this afternoon, I will graduate from State University with a Bachelor of Arts degree in Humanities. But right now, I'm standing beneath a tin-roofed pavilion by a lakeshore, just breathing—eight seconds in, eight seconds out, four breaths a minute.

A warm May breeze blows off the lake, carrying with it the scents of green leaves and marine life. Frogs croak—a muted splash signals a fish breaking water to seize a bug from the surface.

Breathe from the abdomen; draw it in, let it out. Feel the *chi* rising from Mother Earth, through your feet, up your legs, into the *dantian* where it forms a warm, comforting ball. Ye-ye says that the practice of *qi-gong* attunes you to life itself. He's not wrong.

Next to me is Maribeth Woodrow (we call her M.B.), a fiftysomething FBI agent who's been a frequent visitor of late because she's sweet on my Uncle Amos. He's now living with me, my wife Lupe, and my husband Danny at Hyacinth House, our home. Uncle was reluctant to move in with us, because he's fundamentalist Christian who didn't cotton to two women and a man living together as a family. But since he's paralyzed from the waist down, it was getting more and more difficult for him to be on his own and run the 3M Detective Agency too, which he founded. It was M.B. who convinced the old goat to move in with us and to grudgingly accept our throuple, and to run the agency from the mansion as well.

Beside M.B. is Vivian, our most experienced student. She's about my age and as dark as I am light, wearing her black hair in a skullcap and dressed in a black tank top and loose-fitting black pants. I've tried to vibe with that girl, but it's her 'tude for me—I just can't even.

Leading the group is Ye-ye. He's a Tai Chi master in his eighties with white hair hanging half way down his back. I met him a couple of years ago when I was looking to learn self-defense. He's wearing only a pair of white duck pants that comes to his ankles. His hairless upper body could be that of a man in his thirties, with well-sculpted pecs and a distinct six pack. He also wears a white cloth around his eyes, because he was blinded a couple of years ago by a maniac who was gunning for me. Vivian has moved in with him to do the things he can't do for himself.

Sister!

He finally told me that Ye-ye is not his real name—it's Chinese for grandfather, and that's what he's become to me. I can tell that man anything. If he was sixty years younger, I'd marry him too!

"*Yù bèi*," says Ye-ye, bending his knees slightly, and rotating his hips as he steps out with his left foot to assume the *wújí bù* stance; feet shoulder width apart, knees slightly bent. The rest of us mirror his movements. "*Yù bèi shì*," he says, using his whole body to raise his arms chest high, rotating his hips to draw them back, dropping them to his waist again before pivoting left into the *gōngbù* stance—his left foot extended, right foot back. He then goes into the first posture in the form, known as *zuǒ péng*, or ward off, left.

It takes nearly forty-five minutes for us to do the 108 postures of the *Wudangshan* form. When I started *Tai Chi Chuan*, I couldn't believe that I would ever know them all by heart, but now I can perform them without even watching Ye-ye, or do them backwards, or go into any one he calls out in any order. The form simulates a hand-to-hand battle with multiple attackers, so each posture has several martial applications that can be used for attack or defense. At the beginning, I never thought that *Tai Chi Chaun* was anything but exercise for old ladies, but now, little ol' me at five-one and ninety-eight pounds can easily take out a two-hundred-and-fifty-pound guy. It's all in the waist.

After completing the form, we take a water break, then Ye-ye pairs us off for push hands—himself with M.B., since she's the least experienced, and me and Vivian. We stand in *gōngbù* facing each other, our forearms touching, then begin moving back and forth, each one trying to read the flow of *chi* in the other to anticipate her movements, countering any attack by neutralizing and redirecting the energy before it is released. The loser of an exchange is the one who goes off balance first. When I was first learning, I couldn't beat Vivian at all—now I can win about a third of the time. Anybody who knows me will tell you how much I hate losing. A loss triggers me to double down and try harder, but that is exactly the best way to keep on losing at push hands. To win consistently, you have to detach your mind from your movements, feel the opponent's *chi* flow and let it drive your reaction. Tai Chi's been a great tool to help me control my temper and accept what life gives me instead of continually fighting it.

But today is not a good day. Maybe it's nerves about my impending graduation, but I just can't seem to read Vivian at all. She frowns as she knocks me aside for the third time in five minutes. "Come on, Nattie. You're better than this!"

It's nearly noon when we call it quits. We still have to get back to Hyacinth House and shower before heading to campus. My wife Lupe and my husband Danny will be in the audience to see me walk. Mom and Uncle wanted to be there too, but I was only allowed two tickets for guests. State has set up venues across campus where others can watch the ceremonies on CCTV, but Uncle's wheelchair would make that difficult. "Y'all can show me your diploma when you get back," he said. I know he's proud of me as the first person in his fam to graduate college.

We head to our cars. As I'm getting into my Jeep, I suddenly think that maybe Ye-ye would like to come and listen to graduation on CCTV, so I hop out again and head over to the tiny house at the forest's edge where he and Vivian live, to ask him. I'm a frequent guest of his, so I don't knock. I just stroll into the great room and stop, staring with my jaw on the floor. Ye-ye, his white duck trousers beside him, is laying on his back on a futon, his hands on Vivian's hips. She's as bare as he is, and perched on his erection, humping for all she is worth!

Chapter 2

A man and a boy are kneeling in the center of an expansive emerald lawn behind a rambling, glass-walled A-frame mansion.

The man, solidly built with short blond hair and dressed in a white t-shirt, camo pants and combat boots is Danny Merkel, Natalie McMasters's husband. The boy is Eduardo Ibáñez, the biological son of Lupe, Nattie's wife, and he just turned ten last week. With his great shock of black hair and dark Latin eyes, he's big for his age and could easily be mistaken for a sixth or seventh grader.

They are fussing over a small object on the ground, or rather, Danny fusses while Eduardo watches. Over his mother's strenuous objections (she doesn't want to spoil him), Danny bought him a birthday present—a drone, complete with a video camera that will transmit pictures back to a PC via the internet. Danny, nothing but a big kid himself, spent over $500 on the thing, though no one in the fam but him knows that. The only difference between men and boys is the size and the price of their toys.

The drone is remarkably compact—less then a foot long and only a few inches wide and deep. Danny extends four folding legs, equipped with propellors that tightly hug the sides of the body, then removes the protective cover from the camera and inserts a memory card in a slot near the front. He places the drone on the ground and retrieves the controller from its carrying case. It's the size and weight of an overgrown cell phone. It opens into two parts to reveal a couple of fold-down joysticks on either side of a text screen, and a video screen that comprises the entire upper half. Danny presses and holds down a button on the lower half and both screens flicker, then flash to life.

Wow! You can program this thing's flight path and time, maximum height, and it will automatically return to its launch point when the flight is over or the battery starts to weaken. It will fly for one hour before you have to replace the battery. Danny remembers the radio-controlled, gasoline powered airplane his dad got him when he was about Eduardo's age. It took him about ten minutes to crash it into the house, earning him a terrific beating from the old man. The plane never flew again afterwards. That's not going to happen with this drone—it's even got sensors to warn it when it gets too close to an obstacle, and it will take control from a user flying it manually to avoid a wreck.

Danny looks at Eduardo's handsome Latin features, the joyful smile the boy can't help but wear, his dark eyes brimming with wonder. Even if Eddie was his own son, he could never lay hands on him like his dad did to him.

6

Danny doesn't even know if the drunken old bastard is still alive, and he cares less. On his eighteenth birthday, he walked out of the house and went straight to the Marines recruiting office, never to return.

"We'll do one flight on automatic, just to be sure everything works," says Danny. "Next, I'll try a manual flight, then I'll show you how to run it? Copy that?"

"Aye-aye, sir!" Danny has taught Eduardo well.

Danny sets the parameters on the screen, then hovers his finger over the start button. "Ready?" Eduardo nods enthusiastically. "In three. Two. One."

"Go!" shouts the boy.

Danny hits the button and the propellors begin to spin, first vaporizing into an amorphous grey mass, then vanishing entirely. Holy shit! The thing is absolutely silent as it soars straight up into the powder-blue sky. Danny has set the height for 100 meters—by the time it reaches that altitude, it's nearly impossible to see. It hovers a moment, then takes off in the direction that Danny set, away from the house. Too late, he realizes that it's flying towards the sun, so now he can't see it at all, then he remembers the video screen and presses the button on the controller to activate it. He and Eduardo are treated to a view of the green lawn rolling by below. Danny presses an arrow on the keyboard to change the direction of the camera, and the scene shifts to show the nearby woods rushing up under the craft. Reaching the trees, the drone changes direction by forty-five degrees and flies along the perimeter for a while, before executing a ninety-degree turn. Now it's heading straight for the house, but it's still high enough so there's no danger of hitting it. Finally, when it's above the circular drive in front, the little drone spins to complete the quadrilateral before returning to where it started. It's suddenly back on the ground like it popped in through a wormhole—Danny and Eduardo never even saw it descend.

Danny kneels down in front of Eduardo, holding his arms above his head and his hands open. The boy enthusiastically slaps him ten.

"Ohmigod! Was that great or what?" Danny says.

Eduardo is so excited he can't even get out the words to answer.

Danny flies the same route one more time, manually controlling the drone with the joysticks. It almost gets away from him over the woods, but when it comes too close to the trees, it immediately overrides his control and returns to a safe height. When he's landing it, it again controls itself when it's near the ground, touching down like a feather.

Danny is going over the programming procedure with Eduardo when the warm breeze brings a sweet spicy aroma to his nose. Both boys turn to see a short, raven-haired woman approaching from the direction of the house—it's Lupe, Eduardo's mom.

"Time to come inside," she says. "We have to leave for Nattie's graduation soon."

Two voices ring out. "Awww, Mom!"

"Just one more flight! Please?" Eduardo whines.

"No. Eduardo, I want you in your room, doing your homework." Her nose wrinkles and her eyes travel to Danny. "And Danny, you said you were going to take a shower before we go. I will not ride in that truck with you if you do not."

Danny inspects his sodden t-shirt. "I am pretty ripe," he agrees. "Look, Eddie, we'll be home in time for a few more flights after supper. It is daylight savings, you know."

Looking at the ground, Eduardo answers in a low voice, "Okay..." He casts a sidewise glare at his Mom, which Danny picks up on.

"Don't be that way, Chief. We got all weekend to fly." Eduardo manages a feeble grin. "You know I love you, right?" The grin becomes a smile again. "Go do what your mom says."

***

Eduardo's scowl returns as he follows Mamà Lupe and Daddy Danny to the house. Daddy puts the drone up on top of the wardrobe in the mudroom, then goes into the kitchen. Eduardo looks at the carrying case longingly. Damn Mamà Lupe! She never lets him have any fun! But they'll all be gone to Mamà Nattie's graduation soon, and he has plans...

Chapter 3

Two hours later, I'm sweltering in State's basketball arena (go Centaurs!).

The peoplestink in the cavernous room, a mixture of body odor and perfume with some old food smells from the closed-down concession stands thrown in, passes right through the surgical mask they're making us wear because Miss Rona. I have on a t-shirt and cut-offs under my international orange gown, the coolest undergarb I could think of, but my skin is still totally slick with a sheen of sweat. At least the stupid electric blue cap on my head is keeping it from running into my eyes. We've already had a couple of people who had to be carried out of here because they passed out from the heat, and maybe a lack of oxygen, too.

It's been over an hour already, and we've heard speech after speech from everybody but the dean's dog. We still haven't walked. As the time wears on, more and more people are removing their masks—finally, I take mine off too. There's an announcement that masks are required by order of the chancellor, but everyone seems to be ignoring it.

They've just given honorary degrees to a politician and an activist, but nothing yet to anybody who's earned anything. The last speaker, a student no longer called the valedictorian because that ain't woke, spent twenty-five minutes trying to convince me that I've never really earned a thing in my life; I'm just the beneficiary of the labors of the proletariat, to whom I must now spend the rest of my life giving back. The bastards running this thing know we're outta here just as soon as we walk. They don't even give you your diploma on stage—you have to pick it up at your department.

I still can't unsee Ye-ye and Vivian.

WTF were they thinking?

In the throes of their passion, they didn't even notice me!

C'mon Nattie! It's no big deal—it's just sex. I totally can't blame Ye-ye—he's just a horny old guy who prolly don't get much anymore. As for Vivian, she's always been jealous of me, the first student in Ye-ye's new Tai Chi school.

She's prolly fucking him to make herself more important to him than me—she has more Tai Chi experience I do and wants to be his favorite student.

I did the same thing with guys when I worked in the strip club—gave 'em what they wanted so they'd give me anything to get it. It's all about control. Except it won't work with Ye-ye. I've never seen anyone more in control of himself than him.

Then why is he fucking somebody sixty years younger?

Because he can, Nattie.

I look down at my program in an attempt to get the pic of the two of them out of my head. Great, only one more speaker coming up.

A stout black woman in full African dress wearing a leopard-patterned mask steps up to the mic. She taps on the diaphragm and waits for the crowdbuzz to die down before speaking.

"I'm Esther Miller, and I have the honor to be your chancellor. I want to remind you once again that masks are required at this event." She stops speaking and surveys the crowd. So do I, and I don't see a single mask replaced.

Her expression says she's pissed, but she apparently decides to accept reality and not to make it an issue any longer.

"I'm here to introduce our keynote speaker today. He's our distinguished alumnus Mr. Jerome Ellis."

Never heard of him. From Miller's tone, I can tell she doesn't like the dude much. That may be a point in his favor.

"He's asked me not to share any personal details with you because he prefers to do that himself. So, without further eloquence, I give you Mr. Ellis."

Yay.

The dude who takes the mic isn't wearing any academic regalia. In fact, he's dressed in a navy track suit with a white stripe running down the arms and legs. He a fiftysomething and he's smoking—I can tell he's got a bod like an NFL jock under that athletic suit and he's sporting a totally sexy buzz cut and five-o'clock shadow. Even as far back as I'm sitting, I can see his sheepish grin. Or is it a sneer?

"Good afternoon, ladies and gentlemen. Now I know that addressing you as ladies and gentlemen is controversial in this day and age, but I will say a lot of controversial things today, so I wanted to start off on the right foot. And by the way, I don't know why Mrs. Miller referred to me as an alumnus, because while I did go to State, I never graduated. Come to think of it, I can't really figure out why they asked me to talk to you at all today. Hmmm. Maybe it's that two or three billion dollars they say I'm worth. Ya think?"

A titter rolls through the crowd.

"Now I'm going to tell you the truth today. Many of you won't like it, but trust me, it's for your own good. I'm really happy that you're going to get your worthless degrees in a little while. A few billion like I have, that will take a little longer. Oh right, I forgot, I'm not supposed to talk to you about money. I'm supposed to talk about giving back, like that other kid did..."

He drifts into a rambling rant about how he was neglected growing up, but how by hard work and diligence, he showed everybody what he was made of. His delivery is snarky and irreverent, and I actually find myself liking him. I wonder along with him why State even asked him to speak— he's got to be one of the most unwoke guys I ever heard.

The scene with Vivian and Ye-ye pops back into my head.

Why am I so shook?

When I fell in love with Danny while I was married to Lupe, the world tried to tell me I had to pick one or the other. But I said fuck that! The heart wants what the heart wants. Now I've got them both, and I've taken quite a bit of shit for that from some people. So why can't I give Ye-ye the same freedom I have?

Because he picked her over me. He could have asked me if he wanted to get laid, but he ghosted me.

On the stage, Jay Ellis is saying, "Now some people have said that I'm filthy rich. You know, like having money makes you dirty. But if you don't want to make money, why the fuck are you even here?"

The crowd grumbles.

Why does he think? They're just here to get their paper.

"Me, I know exactly who I am. I have a lot of cash, so I can do exactly what I want all the time. And you know what? That pisses some people off. It makes them mad because they think if they can't do what they want, why should I be able to? But here's something I've never been more sure of— anybody can do exactly what they want, if they have the brains and the guts to. You don't need anybody's permission. You don't need no goddamn degree. You just need brains and guts. Do you have the brains and the guts to do exactly what you want?"

The audience beaks into spontaneous applause.

Holy shit, where has this guy been all my life? He's absolutely on fleek. If Ye-ye wants to fuck Vivian, more power to him! It's just sex—it don't mean nothing.

"So here's my message to you. Don't pay attention to the bastards who want to tell you what you can and can't do. They're just trying to drag you down—they're envious. You can have it all! If you're intelligent and ambitious, the only excuse for failure to succeed at life is lack of effort. Do what you want, when you want and apologize to nobody! Nobody! That's what I did, and I'm one of the richest men in the world. You can be too if you want to. And if you don't, I really don't know why you wasted your last four years here."

A few boos arise, but they're drowned out by another, even louder round of cheering. Ellis has apparently struck a chord with the graduates. He basks in the ovation for a while, then gives a tight-fisted salute and leaves the podium.

Wow. Another great thing—he only talked for about ten minutes. Chancellor Miller returns to take the mic, saying, "Well, I'd like to thank Mr. Ellis for sharing his somewhat unique point of view with us today. And I've just been informed that he's generously endowed a new building for our business school in the amount of fifty million dollars! May we have another round of applause for him, please?"

After the applause dies down again, they finally begin the walk. It's gonna be row-by-row. I'm squarely in the middle of the alphabet, I have a while to wait. At last, the usher reaches my row and motions us to stand. As we begin moving out, something catches my eye. A group of people coming up from the back of the auditorium—a man, a woman and two policemen.

Wait a sec, I recognize that blond-haired woman...

The group reaches our row at the same time I'm ready to step out into the aisle. The blonde is Detective Julia Sykes, whom I met a couple of years ago. She looks me in the eyes, saying, "Natalie McMasters?"

Puzzled, I nod.

You know who I am. And WTF are you doing here, now?

The man grasps my shoulder and pulls me out of line. "Turn around," he says, spinning me so my back is towards him. Cold steel encircles my wrists.

Sykes says, "Natalie McMasters, you are under arrest for the murders of Robert Samples and Frederick Young. You have the right to remain silent..."

I try to keep my head high and avoid looking at the people in the audience as I get perp-walked out of my college graduation.

On the way, my eyes meet those of an older, dark-haired woman sitting on the aisle. Is that a smirk I see on her face?

Chapter 4

Perched on an overturned five-gallon bucket that used to be white, Eduardo places a cigarette between his lips and applies a flame from a disposable lighter to the tip.

He inhales a lungful of smoke with nary a cough—unknown to his fam, he's been smoking for a while—and lets the smoke slowly dribble out his nostrils like he saw a guy on TV do, closing his eyes in bliss as the nicotine surges throughout his body.

Plucking the smoke out of his mouth, he holds it with the lit end up so his friend Freddy Hall can take it. Freddy takes a deep drag and passes it to Arnie Schultz, who gives it to Shannie Flynn, the only girl in the group. When the smoke comes back to Eduardo, there's only one drag left, so he finishes it off and flips the butt into the nearby stream.

This Saturday afternoon, Eduardo and his friends are down in a ten-foot-deep cement culvert that serves as a storm sewer. It's about fifteen feet across with a ditch full of oily brown water running through the center. The culvert is accessed by metal rungs embedded in the concrete wall every hundred feet or so. For a kid, it's a great place come to do those things that you don't want adults to see.

Freddy sits directly on the cement floor paging through a copy of *Penthouse* the kids found in the trash. He gets to the centerfold and holds the magazine high, letting the page flop fully open so he can ogle this month's pet, who's sitting on a bed with satin sheets, her mouth open and her legs splayed.

"Shit, you can see her pussy and everything!" Freddy says with a big grin, pointing at the model's crotch. "She's got it shaved!" He turns to Shannie. "Hey, Shannie's a girl. She's got a pussy! Hey Shannie, show us your pussy, will ya?"

Eduardo rockets to his feet, overturning the bucket, which rolls into the stream. Rearing back, he pops his fist into Freddy's left eye, sending the other boy ass over teakettle. Before poor Freddie can even cry out, Eduardo is straddling him, repeatedly punching him in the face. He grabs Freddy's shirt and hauls him to his feet, then turns him to face Shannie, who's just standing there looking puzzled.

"You say you're sorry to her!" Eduardo yells. "Say it, or you'll get some more!"

Sister!

By this time Freddy is crying so hard he's gulping for air and can't say anything. Eduardo gives him a hard shake and tells him again. Finally, he stammers out, "I'm sorry, Shannie, I'm so sorry!"

Eduardo takes Freddy's face in both hands and looks him right in the eyes. "You ever do anything like that again, I'll kill you," he says. He gives Freddy a hard push, sending him stumbling into the stream, where he falls, soaking his clothes. Then he goes to Shannie and puts his arm around her.

"He didn't mean nothing," he says. "He won't do it no more."

As Freddy slinks off for the safety of home, Eduardo basks in the glow of Shannie's smile.

The kids spend the rest of the day playing, talking and smoking. *Mamá* Lupe and Daddy Danny won't be home from graduation until late, so Eduardo doesn't have to get there until just before dinner. Home is not a place he wants to be much anymore. Ever since he saved *Mamá* Lupe and *Abuela* from that bad man a couple of years ago, *Mamá* Lupe has really gotten on his case. *Even about my birthday present! I just can't do anything right anymore.* They all treat Eduardo like a kid, except maybe Daddy Danny. *But I'm a man! Kids don't kill bad guys, do they?*

Chapter 5

The picture on the TV in the interrogation room is black-and-white, grainy, but clear enough.

A young blonde woman who looks an awful lot like me shoots a convenience store clerk twice in the chest, then spins around and shoots another man who just came in the door in the back of the head. But it's not me! I only knew one other person in the world who looked that much like me, and it's not her either. I'm sure, because she's dead.

"What have you got to say for yourself, McMasters?" asks Detective Julia Sykes. "Come clean with me about why the hell you decided to do something like this on your graduation day, and maybe I can get the D.A. to take the death penalty off the table."

I'm in a gnarly little room at police headquarters downtown, which smells like a cross between a gym and a ladies' room. Still wearing the orange graduation gown the cops wouldn't let me lose, I've got both hands cuffed to a metal bar that runs the length of an oblong table bolted to the floor. I'm bent over, sitting in a hard plastic chair with hot fluorescent light glaring down on me. Sykes sits across from me in a similar chair. She's a thirtysomething, hard blonde woman who I met a couple of years ago when she worked for the campus police. Now she's apparently come up in the world as a detective for the city cops.

"It wasn't me." Sykes looks at me like I'm something on her shoe. "When did this happen?"

"You know damn well when."

"Humor me."

She rolls her eyes, but complies. "This morning, around ten-thirty."

Excitement courses through me. "I wasn't there. I was doing Tai Chi with my fam. They'll tell you."

"Family members don't make the best alibi witnesses, you know."

"My *sifu* will tell you, too. And his assistant." Her expression doesn't change. "I've even got a real-life FBI agent who'll vouch for me."

She raises her eyebrows. That got her attention.

"Her name is Maribeth Woodrow, and she's staying with us for a few days. She'll tell you."

Sister!

Sykes tilts her head and her jaw drops a little—she doesn't like what she's hearing but she knows she can't ignore it. Getting up from the table, she says, "Stay put."

Like I've got a choice.

She goes outside, and the door clicks behind her.

The other woman I knew who looked so much like me was named Becca Chapman. She was a State student I met on campus about four years ago, and we became besties. Then she got murdered. I tracked down the mofo who did it and killed him. The cops don't know that, though.

An eternity later, a welcome blast of cool air washes over me as the door opens and Sykes returns. She's got a sour look on her face as she reaches over and unlocks the handcuffs. "Okay, McMasters, SSA Woodrow confirms your story. I guess you do have a doppelganger out there."

Rubbing my wrists, I grumble, "Don't I even get an apology? I ought to sue you for false arrest and for ruining my graduation!"

"Sorry, it was an honest mistake. She looks just like you. Do you have any idea who she is?"

"No, I don't."

I have a pretty good idea who might know, though...

***

"Mom, she could have been my twin! Is there something you need to tell me?"

My mom, Judy, lives in the guest house on our property. After leaving police headquarters, I went straight to her place and told her what happened. Now she's perched on the edge of the sofa in her living room ignoring the glass of wine in front of her, sitting straight up with a stricken look on her face. I'm in the easy chair, facing her. There's an upside down shot glass and a bottle of Heineken on the small table next to me.

"Nattie I'm so sorry this happened to ruin your graduation. But I swear I have no idea who this woman who looks like you could be!"

"Then you and Daddy didn't have triplets and give two of them up for adoption, or anything?"

"Of course not! And what do you mean, triplets?"

16

I realize that I've never told Mom about Becca. Her death was a dark event in my life that I've only shared with Lupe and Danny. Even now, I don't want to tell her all of it. "A few years ago, I met another woman who could have been my twin. Her name was Becca Chapman."

"Well, where is she now?"

"She died, Mom. Don't ask how."

"Oh!"

We're silent for a moment. I sense that Mom is uneasy. "What are you not telling me?" I ask her again.

Her eyebrows drop and she frowns, then she looks straight at me as if she's decided something. "Maybe it's time you knew," she says.

It's suddenly cold. "Knew what?"

"It's nothing bad," she says, apparently sensing my distress. "It's just that you weren't born like most people."

"What does that mean?"

She lets out a breath and settles back on the sofa. "Daddy and I had a really hard time getting pregnant," she says. "We tried and tried, but I could never catch. He got very upset—he said he thought it was his fault, but I could tell that he blamed me. It was really putting a strain on our marriage. I told him that it really didn't matter why it wasn't working—the thing to do was go and get some help. So, we finally did."

"What did you do?"

"We contacted this place in New York City. It was a fertility clinic; one of the best in the country, according to everything we could find out. They took eggs from me, sperm from Daddy and fertilized them in a test tube. Then they implanted an embryo back into me, and eight and a half months later, you came along. Just you."

"I'm a test tube baby!" I say, astonished. "How could you not have told me that?"

Mom shakes her head, her mouth a thin line. "Because it didn't make any difference. You were our daughter, and we loved you. That's all that matters." She's quiet a minute, then continues, "Your uncle doesn't know either," she says. "Because of his religious beliefs, we thought it best not to tell him. It really isn't any of his business, anyway."

I say nothing for a bit, digesting what she said. She's right—it really doesn't matter. It's not like I was adopted or anything. Then a thought strikes. I know what must've happened. "They made other embryos from you and Daddy," I say. "They must've implanted them in other women."

Sister!

"No," says Mom. "I specifically asked about that. Our doctor told me that they did have more embryos, and that they were going to freeze them in case I had a miscarriage, so they could try some more. But I didn't, and after you were born, the doctor asked if I wanted more children. Daddy and I talked it over and decided that I was getting older and we didn't want to tempt fate. So, the doctor said that the extra embryos would be destroyed."

How could she be so clueless? "Oh Mom, that's the easiest lie in the world to tell. They had to have kept them and used them in other women. What other explanation for two other people who look exactly like me can there be?"

Mom's face is a mask of apprehension, making me totally sorry that I ever brought this up. Finally, she says, "Maybe you're right. But what difference can it make after all this time?"

"It can help the cops find the woman who killed those people," I say. "My sister."

Chapter 6

Eduardo clambers over an eight-foot grey brick wall and approaches Hyacinth House.

The house overlooks a landscaped circular driveway and has two, single-story grey brick annexes on either side, and a matching detached two-car garage. It's ringed by beds of the pink and blue flowers that give it its name, and their heady scent reaches Eduardo as he nears them

The sun is sinking behind the pines that surround the property. Eduardo pulls out his phone and holds down the button to turn it on. Even though *Mamá* Lupe has told him not to, he turns it off when he leaves the house so she can't call him or use the tracking app to tell where he is. The phone powers on and he checks the time: 7:36 p.m. Bad news. The 'rents usually park in front of the house, not in the garage, so Eduardo can see who's home. More bad news—*Mamá* Lupe's yellow VW bug is there. So is the pickup that *Mamá* Nattie and Daddy Danny left in after lunch, *Mamá* Nattie's red Jeep, *Señora* M.B.'s little car and *Señor* Kidd's Lincoln. He'll avoid the front door on principle, so it's best he go in through the side door into the south wing. If he uses the back door, he'll prolly run into *Mamá* Lupe in the kitchen. She's been giving him hell lately about everything—school, his friends, his attitude, everything!

The living room, dining room and kitchen comprise the rest of the first floor, with the offices of the 3M Detective Agency in the north wing and bedrooms in the others. If Eduardo can just make it upstairs to his room, he can claim he was here all afternoon. The house is so big that it's quite possible nobody would have seen him. As he exits the south wing into the foyer, he can hear voices in the living room: *Mamá* Nattie, Daddy Danny, *Tío* Amos, *Abuela*, *Señora* M.B. and *Señor* Kidd—everyone is there. Quiet as a cat stalking a squirrel, he creeps across the tiled floor to the spiral staircase and up to the second floor. From the stairs, he can see them in the living room, but they're too busy talking to each other to notice the likes of him. He steps away from the edge of the balcony. He's safe! He trots down the hall into the north wing and his room. Opening the door, he slips inside, then a ball of panic grows in his belly as he catches her spicy aroma. *Mamá* Lupe clicks on the light next to his bed where she's been sitting and says softly, "Where have you been?"

Her low voice is full of menace—he's busted! Lying will just make it worse. "Out. With *mi amigos.*"

"Speak English!" she spits. "Before we left, did I not tell you to stay home and work on your lessons from school?"

Sister!

"Yes *Mamá*."

She glares at him, her hot Latin eyes burning with fury. The cold ball in his tummy expands. Her expression tells him something else is wrong. She should not be this mad just about him disobeying her order to stay inside.

"I had a call this afternoon. From Mrs. Hall."

¡Oh, dios mio!

"She told me that you beat up her son, Freddy. Badly. She said that she had to take him to the urgent care."

"No, *Mamá*, no! It was not that bad. He say some dirty things to my friend Shannie. I could not let him get away with that!"

Lupe reaches behind her on the bed, and when her hand reappears, she's holding a doubled-up leather belt about two inches wide. "Take off your pants," she says.

"No, *Mamá, por favor...*"

"It will be worse if you make me do it." Lupe threatens.

Sobbing now, Eduardo undoes his belt, unsnaps his pants and lets them fall to his ankles.

"Take them off, I said!" Lupe barks. "Your shorts, too! Then come over here!"

At ten, Eduardo's old enough to be embarrassed to be naked in front of his mother. As he approaches the bed, he gives it one more try. "*Por favor, Mamá!* I am sorry! I will write a letter to *Senora* Hall and Freddy and tell them so! *Por favor!*"

Lupe rises and grabs her son by the nape of the neck, pulling him towards the bed, then pushes him down so he's bent at the waist with his bare butt in the air. She grips his wrists behind his back so he can't use his hands to protect his ass, rocks her arm back, and whips the belt down across his buttocks with all her considerable strength.

Crack!

Eduardo lets out a wail of pain.

"Do you know what I went through to come to the United States so you could have a good life?"

His voice breaks as he screams, "No, *Mamá*, no! *Por favor!*"

Crack!

"Now you hurt American boys so they have to go to doctor!"

Crack!

"Aieee!"

"How you like it when somebody hurt you?" Lupe gets madder and madder with each swing of the belt.

Crack!

Crack!

Crack!

"You think this is bad? Wait and see what happen to you when the *policia* come for us and we get sent back to Mexico!"

Crack!

A rumble of running feet arises in the hallway, then the door bursts open. *Mamá* Nattie's voice shouts, "Lupe! What the fuck!" Eduardo's hands are suddenly released, but the pain shooting through his bottom and legs momentarily freezes him in place. Then he tumbles onto the floor as Lupe stands up.

"Give me that!" Nattie hollers, and Eduardo rolls over to see her reaching for the belt in his mother's hand. But Lupe doesn't give it up. Instead, she whips the leather across Nattie's forearm.

"Motherfucker!" Nattie shouts, pain etched on her face. She plants her feet and rotates her hips as she thrusts her open hand forward into Lupe's chest. The force of the blow takes Lupe off her feet, and the belt flies off as she tumbles backwards onto the bed. Nattie cocks her fist back for a good old-fashioned sock in the jaw, but Danny grabs her wrist before she can deliver it.

"Dammit Nattie, calm down!"

"Fuck her, Danny! She hit me with a belt!"

Lupe abruptly rolls over on her belly, crying furiously, and seeing his mother's distress, Eduardo wails all the louder in concert. He was the cause of all of this! If he had just done what he was told...

***

Later Saturday night, Danny and me are in bed in his room. We all have our own rooms so we can have privacy when we need it, as Lupe obviously does tonight.

21

Sister!

"I'm worried about her, hon," I say. "She's been getting worse lately, and Eduardo's behavior is not helping."

"She should take him to a shrink," Danny says. "A lot of adults can't handle having taken a human life, much less a kid."

He's right. I should know, having taken more than a few myself.

"She's scared to death that the government will take him away from us again if they find out he's killed somebody," I reply. "I've told her a hundred times that a doctor will have to keep it confidential. Besides, the kid killed a serial murderer in self-defense. There's no crime there."

Danny's quiet for a moment, then he says, "You're right. So why don't we take him to the doctor?"

"What? She's his mother. She said no."

"So are you. You did legally adopt him, with her blessing, right?"

"Sure, but that was only so he'd have a legal parent if something happens to Lupe. I've always said that her wishes should dictate his upbringing."

"Even when they're causing him harm? And her too? Lupe's a recovering addict, you know. She can only take so much. Her behavior today was over the top."

I can't argue with that.

"Okay, I'll have a talk with her tomorrow. I have to patch things up after that fight."

"No, you don't Nattie. Lupe was the one in the wrong. She owes you an apology, and you should insist on that. I'll back you up. And she owes Eddie one, too. Sure, maybe he should have been punished for what he did, but not that way. Maybe if we can make her feel guilty enough about beating him, she'll agree to let him see a psychiatrist."

I cock my head and look at him wide-eyed. "Since when did you get so conniving?"

"Since I married into this crazy family." He rolls over and turns out the bedside light. "Go to sleep. We'll talk to her in the morning."

Chapter 7

I **wake up at 8:30 on Sunday morning.**

As usual, Danny's eyes pop open as soon as I stir, but when he sees the time, he rolls over to go back to sleep. It's eerie how quickly he can wake up and fall asleep—he tells me it has to do with being a Marine.

Downstairs, I find M.B. in the kitchen at the breakfast bar, watching the news. She's made coffee, so I pour myself a cup. There's no sign of Lupe yet, for which I am grateful. I don't feel up to dealing with her yet.

M.B.'s eyes travel to the dull red welt on my forearm. She certainly heard the fracas last night but she's way too polite to bring it up. Muting the TV, she asks instead, "How does it feel to be a college grad?"

"I'm way pissed that I didn't get to walk," I say, "but I guess I get why Sykes did me like she did. When I saw that vid, I almost thought it was me killed that guy." I told M.B. about the video after she alibied me.

"Have you got any idea who that girl was?" asks M.B.

I open my mouth to answer her but I'm not sure what to say. My eyes drift to the TV screen, and I see a tall, elegant-looking black man in a police uniform standing at a podium, getting ready to speak. I know him; his name is DeAndre Trevelyan, and he's the acting police chief. "Hey, turn that up." M.B. obliges.

"...first time since the sniper attacks that we've had a multiple homicide here in Capital City," he's saying. "I want to assure you that we're working several leads and expect an arrest very soon."

A reporter speaks up. "Darren Murphy, WTCD News. Chief, a source tells me that the police have a security video of the shooting. Why has that video not been made public? Don't you think that would help you track down the perpetrator?"

OMG! While I've not been in the news for a while, my face is pretty well-known in this town, especially to the Press. I'm screwed if the cops release that vid!

"There are privacy issues with that, which we are working on," Trevelyan says.

"Do you or do you not have the shooter's face on tape?"

Sister!

"The short answer is yes," the chief says. "That's one reason we expect a quick arrest."

A familiar female voice is next. "Betsy Kiefer, *The State of State*. What can you tell us about the police activity at the State graduation ceremony yesterday? Who was arrested? Did that arrest have anything to do with the shooting?"

I groan inwardly. Betsy Kiefer has been salty with me for years. If she gets hold of my name...

"That action is no longer relevant to this discussion," the chief answers.

Kiefer seizes on his words. "No longer relevant! Then it *was* relevant! Who did you arrest, chief?"

Trevelyan ignores her and picks on another reporter. M.B. mutes the TV again and looks at me expectantly. I'm trying to think of a polite way not to rehash ancient history with her when Lupe saves me by walking into the kitchen. Seeing her, M.B. picks up her coffee cup, saying, "You know what? It's a beautiful day. I think I'm going to have my coffee out on the patio this morning." She rises and goes out the back door. Damn! I was intending to quiz her about what's going on between her and Uncle.

Dressed in a frumpy robe, Lupe looks like cold shit warmed over. Her thick, black hair is a rat's nest and her reddish face is puffy like she's been crying. I know I'm supposed to say something to put her at ease, but goddamnit, I'm still totally ratchet with her. She fucking hit me! I opt for, "So, have you been in to see your son yet this morning?", hoping to make her feel guilty about what she's done.

Now she does cry, and I feel bad. Her tears have always had that effect on me even when I'm mad at her. "No," she answers. Then, "I'm sorry I hit you." She doesn't sound like she means it.

"I'm not the one you need to say sorry to. Poor Eduardo! He's going to have marks from that beating for weeks. You better hope they don't see them in school, or Child Services will be back here again." They took Eduardo out of our home once before, largely because of our lifestyle. We managed to get him back, but if they take him again...

Lupe's raised voice shows her frustration. "But he cannot keep on doing what he has been doing! They will take him away from us for that, too!"

"I'm so glad to hear you say that," I tell her, meaning every word. "We need to talk about getting him some help."

For the next twenty minutes, we go back and forth about taking Eduardo to a shrink. Because she was abused in Mexico as a child, then for many years as an undocumented immigrant, Lupe has a deep distrust of authority. But after last night's debacle, even she can see that we just can't keep on like we have been. "OK," she says finally, "You can take him to the doctor."

I'm thinking that Eduardo's not the only one in sore need of therapy around here, but I decide to take the W and leave the discussion of her treatment for a different day. About that time, Danny comes into the kitchen, looking smoking AF in a pair of gym shorts and flippies. He casts a sour look at Lupe, presumably because of last night, then meets my eyes and asks, "Where's Eddie? I want to tell him we can play with the drone today."

"Still in bed, as far as I know," I answer.

"Uh uhhh," he says. "I looked in his room before I came down. He's not there." A pause. "And the bed was made."

Woah. That does not sound like Eduardo. "He must've got up early. Maybe he hurt too much to sleep in," I say.

"No," says Lupe. "I give him Tylenol last night before he goes to his room."

"It wears off," Danny says mercilessly. "And a beating like the one you gave him can hurt for a week. I should know. I've had a few myself."

"I said I'm sorry, OK?" shouts Lupe. "He's been getting in lotsa trouble lately and I'm afraid they gonna kick him outta school..."

"Let's not rehash this again, Danny." I say in a firm tone. "Lupe's agreed to let me take Eduardo to a doctor to get his problems addressed."

Danny brightens immediately. "Great! Well let's find him, and maybe I'll make pancakes."

Fifteen minutes later, we're back in the kitchen. There's no sign of Eduardo.

"I'm gonna kill him!" spits Lupe. "The last thing I told him before sending him to bed was that he was grounded for a week. He just won't do what he's supposed to."

"He's prolly mad AF about the hiding you gave him," I say. "I sure would be. Cut him some slack. He'll prolly be back for dinner."

"And when he does come back, I'll..."

"...do nothing!" I finish for her. "Beatings and other punishments aren't working Bae. What's that NA saying you keep telling me? 'If you keep on doing what you're doing...'"

Sister!

"'...you'll keep on getting what you're getting.' You're right, Nattie."
Now she has a look of resignation, which is what I wanted to see.

At about 3:30 pm, Lupe, our usual cook, lets it be known that she's
totally not up to it tonight, so M.B. volunteers, with me as *sous chef*. After a
look at the pantry, M.B. says she needs a grocery run and conscripts me to
tag along. We return in an hour with the fixins for country fried steak,
collard greens in the pressure cooker and mac and cheese. Uncle will be in
hog heaven, and I'm sure that M.B. knows it. By six, it's ready, and
everyone gathers at the oblong table in the dining room. Everyone but
Eduardo, that is.

After dinner, Lupe tries to track Eduardo's phone, but gets no sig—he's
prolly got it turned off. She starts calling around to his friends, and her
anxiety increases with every "haven't seen him today." Finally, she says,
"I'm gonna go and check his room."

"What good will that do?" I ask. "You know he's not there."

"I'm gonna check," she says again, and goes upstairs.

Five minutes later, she's back, her face as white as a dead man's eyes.
In her hand is her purse, and Eduardo's phone.

"Two hundred dollars is missing from my wallet," she says, "and
Eduardo's backpack is gone."

26

Chapter 8

Only a couple of miles from Hyacinth House early Sunday morning, the forest is thick, shadowy and interlaced with briars.

The only sounds Eduardo can hear are the rustling of leaves, the snapping of branches and his own muttered curses in Spanish as he forces himself through the underbrush—any animals in his vicinity have long since fled or wisely remain hidden. He has been following a well-marked game trail when he decides he can reach his goal much quicker if he goes cross-country, but he doesn't count on the obstinacy of the southern woods in the springtime. He also does not realize that he does not have to stray far from the trail before everything around him looks the same. True, he can find his way back to the spot where he left the path by following the track of churned leaves and broken branches, but that would be giving up. A real man, a man who has killed somebody, he does not give up.

Stopping, he scratches his neck where the sweat runs under his collar, allowing an itchy coating of crumbled leaves to stick to his skin. Perhaps the orange and blue State University hoodie he wears was not the best choice for a woodland outing on a morning in May. His fingers encounter something hard and round that does not move much when he tugs on it. He digs in his nails and pulls hard, feeling a sharp pinch, then examines the thing between his fingers—a tick, still alive, mindlessly crawling about, seeking another place to latch on to drink his lifeblood. He shakes his hand with an oath and the tick flies off—no matter though, because there are probably dozens more attached to him. He peels off the sweatshirt and ties it around his waist before going on.

Eduardo is hunting his friend Shannie. He knows she lives in a homeless camp nearby. He found out because he followed her into the woods after school one day. After a while she spotted him, and she asked him not to follow her home because there were people there who wouldn't understand.

Staring at the woods ahead, he thinks he sees a patch where it seems lighter, and he catches the sharp odor of woodsmoke on the breeze. He pushes forward once more, and after a few hundred feet, he emerges from the briars onto another trail. This time he's wise enough to stay on it instead of plunging back into the underbrush again. He follows his nose and the odor of smoke strengthens and becomes intermingled with food smells. He spots a flash of orange ahead—as he stares at it, it slowly morphs into a tent. He sees another, then another, then a few ramshackle sheds built from whatever materials their owners could scavenge. Old packing crates. Corrugated metal. Entire windows removed from abandoned houses, with walls put up around them so they'll fit. All of this carried over considerable distances and punishing terrain. Everything is camouflaged with pine boughs and leaves to render the camp nearly invisible unless you're right on top of it.

As Eduardo moves further into the settlement, he sees that trees have been cut down inside to provide space for a central shanty, with a large firepit in front of it. Indigenous shrubs have been trained to grow around and over the structure, so from a few feet away, it more strongly resembles a thicket than a house. Half-a-dozen people laze about, sitting on stumps or old crates. A carcass, which Eduardo thinks might be a large dog, hangs from a tree near the firepit.

A deep voice, threatening and repulsive, barks, "Hey you, kid! What do you think you're doing here!" and Eduardo nearly jumps out of his skin. He wheels around to see a man wearing a filthy pair of coveralls that used to be lime green and a red-and-white Bush Hog ball cap advancing on him aggressively. The dude is over six feet tall with a scraggly beard, a crazy light in his eyes and some bottom teeth missing. Eduardo backs away from him, but that takes him into the camp itself, where the others are rising from their seats near the fire.

Oh, dios mio, I'm in trouble here!

Another voice, high and shrill, hollers, "Eduardo! Thurmond, leave him alone. I know him!"

It's Shannie! The ugly man stops advancing, but he's still glaring at Eduardo with a look that says he wants to do great bodily harm.

The boy looks around and spots Shannie coming out of one of the tents. "Eduardo, what are you doing here?" She runs to him and throws her arms protectively about him.

"I have run away because *Mamá* Lupe whipped me. I want to come and live in the woods with you!"

At his words, Shannie hugs him all the harder. Thurmond, who heard, says "Oh fuck no! I got enough mouths to feed without a little greaser too."

Eduardo stares up at the big man still hovering over him and Shannie. "I got my own food," he says.

Thurmond's eyes light up. "You got food? Where? In your backpack?" He reaches for Eduardo, who tries to push Shannie off and back away, but Thurmond snags the front of his shirt. He pulls the boy to him and strips the pack off his shoulders, opens the flap and roots round inside, coming up with an opaque white plastic container with a red top. He pops off the lid and erupts into a wide, toothless grin at the contents. Eduardo all but forgotten, Thurmond scarfs down a pound of Lupe's cold enchiladas with his fingers, licking the inside of the container when he's done. Tears come to the boy's eyes; he was counting on those to feed him for a couple of days, at least.

"You just bought yerself a room fer the night, kid," says Thurmond.

Shannie tugs on Eduardo's sleeve. "C'mon, before he changes his mind." she whispers, leading him to a tent. After getting him settled on a cheap sleeping bag, she tells him, "Nobody here is going to share food with you, you know."

"That's okay. I have some money."

Her eyes suddenly become full of fear. "Oh shit! If Thurmond finds out, he'll take it. How much have you got?"

"Almost two hundred dollars. I get it from *Mamá* Lupe's bag. If that man tries to take it, I kill him! We can use it to buy bus tickets, go somewhere where nobody knows us. We can get jobs and make more money!" Despite herself, Shannie rolls her eyes. "What?" says Eduardo.

"You haven't got a clue." she says. She tells him the sad details of her life—how her father deserted her and her mom a couple of years ago before Covid hit and put a moratorium on evictions, how they lost their house because her deadbeat dad cleaned out all the accounts before he skedaddled. She was in public school at the time, so nobody asked questions about her residency when the time came to transfer to middle school. Then the 'Rona killed her mom, and now Shannie has to get by on free breakfasts and lunches from the year-round school and what little she can steal.

"Gimme that money before Thurmond thinks to search you," she says. Eduardo produces a battered canvas wallet and extracts some bills, which Shannie tucks into an inside pocket in the tent.

"I can prolly talk Thurmond into letting you stay here for a few days," she says. "After that, you're going to have to go unless you give him money or food and think of some way to get more."

"But we can get bus tickets..."

"No. Eduardo, it's good for me here. I have a warm place to sleep and I get food at school. If I leave, I lose all that. You have a home and people who love you. You should go back to them."

"*Mamá* Lupe does not love me anymore, or she wouldn't have beat me like she did. *Mamá* Nattie and Daddy Danny love me, but if I go back, then they all will fight and *Mamá* Lupe will take me and run away."

"Well, you can stay for a few days. Tomorrow there is school. Are you going to go?"

"I cannot. They will find me if I do."

Sister!

"I have to, to get some food. I will take some of your money and buy more, and try to use some of it to pay Thurmond to let you stay. But you must think about what you are going to do after he makes you leave."

Later, Eduardo lays snuggled up to Shannie in the sleeping bag, listening to the soft buzz of her breathing as she sleeps. His ass still hurts, but not as bad as before. He thought he had everything figured out—a new city, a new life, like he and *Mamá* Lupe did many times before. He's beginning to realize that life is way more complicated than he can figure out.

Chapter 9

We discuss whether to call the cops and report Eduardo missing.

Natch, Lupe is opposed, I am for it. So Danny is the deciding vote.

"I say no. The cops are obsessed with this double murder right now. How much time you think they'll give to looking for a ten-year-old? Besides, I think we're a bunch of sorry-ass detectives if we can't find him ourselves. Lupe, get that student list from his school and call his friends' homes. If he's not with one of them, they might know where he would go. Nattie, you and I can drive around and look for him. We'll take two cars. I'll print off a couple of pix of him that we can show people. We can check the parks and playgrounds and fast-food places—he's gotta eat. It might even be a good idea to check the school too—he could be holed up over there waiting for it to open tomorrow. If we don't find him, we can call the cops in the morning and get them to put out an Amber Alert."

Lupe makes her phone calls and strikes out—none of Eduardo's friends admit to seeing him today. Me, Danny and M.B. spend a couple of hours before dusk driving around, following Danny's program, but we find no sign of him. I'm beginning to get way triggered. We live in an upscale hood but there are predators everywhere. What if Eduardo has run into one?

We meet back at Hyacinth House as darkness is falling. Lupe is seriously starting to lose it, so she decides to head for a NA meeting. The rest of us console ourselves with the idea that even if Eduardo's gotta spend the night outside tonight, it won't kill him. The weather's been pretty warm. And he might come slinking back later, after he thinks that everyone has gone to bed.

Unfortunately, Eduardo's not my only concern. I'm still way ratchet about my doppelganger, and itching to try to find her. I'm sure she's my sister. And if the cops release that vid or Betsy Kiefer finds out it was me who was arrested, the shit will totally hit the fan.

What I really want to do is go to New York and check out that fertility clinic. I think it will be better for me to fly up there instead of trying to do shit over the phone—people tend to respond better to someone in their face. Danny, Leon and M.B. can handle hunting for Eduardo. Lupe might get salty about my going away, but hey, if she hadn't whipped him, we wouldn't even be here.

When Lupe gets home, she says that she's going to sit up in the living room, all night if need be, in case Eduardo comes home. Danny and me try

31

to talk her out of it, but that ain't it. So Danny, trying to be the good husband, says he'll wait up with her. Me, I'm going to bed, because I'm gonna try to get a flight out of here tomorrow.

Monday morning comes and still no Eduardo. Lupe calls the school and they agree to let her know if he comes in, then Danny calls the cops about an Amber Alert, but that's a no go—they say they have to confirm that an abduction has occurred and that Eduardo must be at risk of severe injury or death. A runaway ten-year-old simply doesn't qualify. But they ask us to fax them a pic of Eduardo and say they will mention him as missing at roll call, so that's something.

After breakfast, Lupe wants to hit the streets again and look for him, but Danny and me put our foot down. "You were up most of the night, Bae. You won't do him any good if you wrap your car around a tree because you fall asleep at the wheel."

"I won't be able to sleep even if I try."

"Maybe not," says Danny, "but you will get some rest. Let me, Nattie, and the others keep looking."

Obviously, there's something I need say.

"Hey, y'all, I hope you don't mind, but I have something else I need to do. I had a talk with Mom the other night..." I go on to tell them about what Mom said about my birth. "So, I might have a sister out there I hate to think that was her in that vid that Sykes showed me, but it's possible."

Danny says, "Hold on a minute, Nattie. Even if you had a sister, she wouldn't be an identical twin, right?"

"I don't know. We've all seen siblings who are not twins who look an awful lot alike, haven't we?" Lupe nods. "And remember Becca? Her resemblance to me was eerie."

"So, what are you going to do?" Lupe asks. I can hear the tension in her voice.

"Mom said that I was conceived at the New Horizons Fertility Clinic in Manhattan. I'm going to find out if they'll release my records to me." I hesitate, then I come out with it. "I'm thinking about flying up there today."

Danny's jaw drops and Lupe's looking daggers at me. "What about Eduardo?" she says.

"What about him? Y'all are looking for him. The cops are looking for him. Me staying here and driving around in the Jeep ain't gonna help much."

"That's true, but..." Danny begins.

"No buts, Danny."

"I was gonna say that I'll bet the clinic won't release the records to you."

"Why not? They're mine."

"Not necessarily. They could claim that they're your Mom's property."

Looking sideways at Lupe, I can tell she's so mad she's speechless. Tough. She's the one responsible for Eduardo running off, not me. To Danny: "I'll talk to Mom about that right now."

Lupe turns and stalks out of the room. Danny watches her go, then says, "Maybe you better go talk to her some more."

"No, Danny. She doesn't want to hear it. She'll cool off once Eduardo is back. And I know either he'll come back or y'all will find him." A pause. "This is just something I have to do."

Danny's lips form a thin line and he shakes his head, knowing better than trying to argue. He follows Lupe out of the room.

Guess I've got everybody salty with me again. Oh well...

I pull out my phone and call down to the guest house.

"Oh Nattie, why don't you just leave it alone?" Mom says after I tell her what I want. "I don't want to go to New York."

"You don't have to, Mom. You can give me a letter that says to release the records to me. Uncle Amos is a notary, so you can sign it in front of him as a witness."

"OK..."

"Great!" I kill the call and head for the 3M office to get on my PC and see about a flight out.

***

That night, I'm dragging my suitcase along West 35th Street between 9th and 10th Avenue in Manhattan, in the neighborhood known as Hell's Kitchen. A light mist accentuates the sweet sewer smell of the City, bringing with it a strong sense of *déjà vu*. It's approaching midnight, and compared to the South, it's chilly.

Sister!

This is a place I've been before. A few years ago, I stayed in the apartment building at the end of the block—a fifth-floor walkup above a Kosher restaurant called Winogradsky's. Today, since my fortunes have changed, I'll be at the Four Points Sheraton across the street.

The lights from the hotel lobby cast a triangle of light on the dirty sidewalk. As I approach, a couple of guys step out of a doorway, blocking my path. They're youngish, twentysomethings, and their ill-fitting clothes mark them as street people. More *déjà vu*, as I remember a dear friend who I met here last time who was also a street person, who's no longer with us. The sentimental memory doesn't stop me from reacting, though. My right hand drifts down to the front pocket of my jeans, but then I remember that New York City doesn't want women to protect themselves—my pistol is back home since I'm not allowed to carry it here. So I let go of my bag, letting it stand straight up beside me and step into *gōngbù*, with my open hands held in front of me palm out, my wrists low and my fingers slightly spread.

"Watcha got for us, babe?" one of the guys says.

"*Nada*," I say, looking past him to the door to the hotel. At this hour in this neighborhood, it's locked—I've got a numerical code to punch into the keypad next to the door to get in. Unfortunately, I can't do that in a hurry and I'm sure these guys know that. "I don't want trouble. Get out of my way."

The speaker looks at his friend. "She don't want trouble," he mocks. "Well, we don't neither. We just want a little lovin'..."

Okay, this just escalated hundo-p. Let's get it over with. "You'll have to come and get it," I tell him. I've shifted my breathing to my *dantian*, slowly inhaling on an eight-count, perfectly calm.

He smiles nastily, thinking, I'm sure, that little ole me will be *no problem* for a big macho dude like him. He takes a step forward, reaching to grab me. I bring my hands up to meet his wrists just like in push hands, rotate my hips, and use his energy to pull him forward and behind me. I raise my empty front foot, kick his leg out from under him as he goes by, and he does a face plant on the sidewalk ten feet away. I swear I can hear his teeth break.

I step toward the second guy, rotating my hands in front of me to confuse him. He decides he wants no part of me and bolts toward Tenth Avenue. Casting a look behind me and seeing my opponent on his knees struggling to get up, I grab my bag, run to the hotel door, punch in the code and slide inside before he can follow.

The desk clerk, a fortyish Indian guy, looks questioningly at me as I approach.

"Two guys out there just tried to grab me," I say. "I've hurt one of them. We need to call the cops."

The clerk's face assumes a disbelieving look. "Oh, dear!" he says. "I do hope you haven't hurt him too badly. Those two are harmless—all bluster."

"All bluster my ass! One of them tried to sexually assault me!"

He tries to deescalate the situation. "Do you have a reservation with us, Miss?"

I'm not having it. "Are you gonna call the cops or not?"

He's silent a moment, then, "No, I'm not. Since all this 'Defund the police' has been going on, it would take them twenty minutes to get here, and those guys will be long gone by then. Tell me your name, and let me get you to your room. Everything will be fine by morning."

I don't like it, but I know he's right. I give him my information, and in fifteen minutes, I'm letting myself into my fifth-floor room. The clerk upgraded me from a queen to a king to make up for my trouble. I hoist my bag onto the luggage stand and look out the window, finding myself staring at the fire escape of the building across 35th Street, which triggers a memory of me and Danny standing out there at midnight, frantically wondering how we were going to get away from the cops.

Yeet! Remember why you're here, Nattie.

Tomorrow I'll visit the New Horizons Fertility Clinic and get some answers.

Chapter 10

"**H**ow could she just leave like that when Eduardo has run away?" Lupe says for the thousandth time.

Danny mentally rolls his eyes, while maintaining a calm expression—a skill he learned from dealing with many a drill sergeant in the Corps.

"Nattie's only one person, hon. She's trusting the rest of us to find him. And we will."

During their marriage, Danny has come to love Lupe very much, but he surely doesn't like the nagging personality that emerges when she's worried. And with Eduardo acting out lately, that's been happening more and more.

"So what are you going to do?" Lupe challenges.

"Like I said before, I'll go to his school, ask them to let me talk to his friends. Find out what his favorite haunts are. He's just a kid; I'm sure that's where he'll go. Heck, if we do nothing, he'll probably come home in a day or two when his food runs out or if it rains on him." Seeing the look of alarm that appears at that last, he says hurriedly, "Don't worry; I'm not going to do nothing." Her face relaxes, and Danny thinks that it's a good time to bring up something else. "Look Lupe, when he does get home, you need to apologize to him for that whipping you gave him. If you keep on treating him that way, he's just going to run off again."

"No, he won't! I'll lock him in his room..."

Danny smiles. "You can't do that, darlin'. He has to come out sometime, to eat, to go to the head, or to school. He'll just wait you out. I don't think I've ever told you, but my dad thought he could raise me with whippings. So, I took off at eighteen and joined the Corps. But you know what the worst thing is?"

Lupe shakes her head.

"I don't care if I ever see that sonuvabitch again as long as I live. You want Eddie to feel that way about you?"

"No!" she shouts.

"Then make it up to him when he gets back. We'll take him to the doctor and address the fact that he killed that man who was going to hurt you and Judy. We'll get him better, hon, but it's gonna take time." He opens his arms. "C'mere."

Lupe steps into his embrace, and he buries his face in her long, dark hair, holding her close as she cries softly into his shirt.

***

Later, Danny is at the locked front door of Blue Ridge Road Middle School. He remembers a time when a parent could just walk into his child's school, but in this time of school shootings, those days are long gone. He presses a button mounted between the two sets of double doors, and after a moment, a voice squawks from a box mounted below the button.

"Yes?"

"My name is Daniel Merkel. I would like to talk to someone about one of your students, Eduardo Ibáñez."

"Are you his parent or guardian?"

Danny isn't sure how he's listed, but he is on the list to pick Eduardo up after school, so he says, "Yes."

The door buzzes, and Danny opens it and steps into the lobby. There is another set of glass double doors across the room, with a pair of metal detectors in front of them, and an office to the right, closed off with a half wall topped by a sliding glass panel. Inside, a young man sits behind a counter and a girl student is running off copies at a machine.

This place has more security than a bank.

He steps over to the office and the young man presses a button. A tinny voice comes from a speaker on the wall. "Can I help you?"

Danny repeats his request about Eduardo. "He's missing. I'd like to talk to his teachers, and some of his friends if I can, to get an idea of where he might have gone."

Because he's looking at the receptionist, Danny does not notice the girl at the copier cock her head toward him.

"Perhaps I can see if the principal or the vice-principal has some time to speak with you, sir," the receptionist says.

Danny keeps his distaste for bureaucracy off his face. He says, "That would be fine, sir."

The girl takes her copies out of the hopper on the machine, taps the stack on top to align them, then puts a rubber band around the sheaf. Tucking it under her arm, she goes out the door into the lobby next to Danny, and the receptionist buzzes her through the double doors.

Sister!

Danny cools his heels in the lobby for ten minutes until a fortysomething African-American lady arrives. "Mr. Merkel? I'm vice-principal Anna Drayton." Danny takes her offered hand and explains his mission. When he's finished, she frowns. "Of course, I'm sorry to hear that Eduardo has run away. However, I simply cannot allow you to speak to any of our students without their parents present. And our teachers are all holding class right now."

Don't raise your voice.

Danny forces a smile, saying, "When will I be able to speak with Eduardo's teachers?"

Ms. Drayton purses her lips. "Well, the procedure is usually for the parent to contact the individual teacher directly and make an appointment..."

He just can't help it—Danny lets some of his impatience show on his face.

Ms. Drayton looks at a clock on the wall. "Our first lunch period is in twenty minutes. I'll see which of Eduardo's teachers might be available to speak with you for a few minutes."

"Thank you so much, Ma'am."

***

In the school building, Shannie drops off the stack of copies she made for Ms. McCurdy at her classroom, then asks permission to go to the bathroom.

"Can't you wait fifteen minutes until class is over?" Ms. McCurdy asks.

"No'm. I really gotta go."

"All right then. Hurry back."

Shannie is torn.

If I go before lunchtime, I'll have to leave today's food behind.

But I really need to tell Eduardo that the cops are on his trail. That big blond guy looks like a bull if I ever saw one.

She finally opts to stay for lunch—breakfast tomorrow is way far away.

She goes back to the classroom and takes her seat, and doesn't hear a word that Ms. McCurdy says until the bell rings. Then, walking as fast as she can to the cafeteria (running in school is a no-no), she gets in the lunch line.

I'm in luck—today is bologna and cheese sandwich day.

She also grabs an apple and a container of milk. Totally portable. She stuffs it all in the front pocket of her hoodie and goes out in the hall just in time to see Ms. Drayton usher the blond cop into the teacher's lounge.

Five minutes later, an alarm goes off (as she knew it would) as she opens a back door and slides outside. If anybody bothers to come and check, they'll never notice the small girl in the parking lot among all those cars. She hides between two of them for a couple of minutes just to be sure, then disappears into the woods behind the school.

***

Anna Drayton conducts Danny to the teacher's lounge, which is tastelessly furnished with unmatched pieces that could be cast offs. He wonders if the teachers brought them in from home. Ms. Drayton's directs him to take a seat on an uncomfortable plaid sofa that looks like it belongs in somebody's beach house.

Checking her iPad, Ms. Drayton says, "Eduardo's supposed to be in Ms. McCurdy's class this period. She'll be along in a few minutes."

"How will I know her?" Danny asks.

Ms. Drayton does something on the tablet screen then turns it so Danny can see a picture of a twentysomething woman with dark, curly hair and large black glasses.

In about five minutes, the bell shrills, and the sounds of talk and laughter arise in the hallway outside the door. It opens, and a group of teachers enter, Ms. McCurdy among them.

Danny rises and approaches her, hand extended. "Ms. McCurdy?"

Danny is a six-foot two, blue eyed hunk. He's got on a tight camo t-shirt that shows off his pecs and shoulders superbly. Ms. McCurdy turns and gives him a look he's seen from many other young women—her eyes widen, a sheepish smile appears and she raises her breasts slightly in his direction. "C-can I help you?" she stammers.

"I hope so," he says, looking into her rheumy eyes and smiling. "I'm Danny Merkel, Eduardo Ibáñez's dad. Eduardo's gone missing, and I was hoping you could tell me who he hangs around with. They might know where he is or would go."

Sister!

It's obvious that Ms. McCurdy is still flustered. "Oh wow, that is, I'd totally like to help you, Dan..., I mean, Mr. Merkel, but..."

"You can call me Danny. I can't talk to the kids without their parents' permission. But you can."

"I don't know..."

Danny gives her a little-boy-in-distress look. "Please. Eddie has been gone from our home since Saturday night. We're worried that something might have happened to him. Can't you just ask some of his friends if they've seen or heard from him? I'd be so grateful." He gives Ms. McCurdy his best sincere smile. That does it.

"I'll see what I can do, Mr... er, Danny. I'll be right back."

Danny takes his seat on the lumpy couch again as she leaves the room. Several other of the young female teachers cast surreptitious glances, but he ignores them. He's worried about his boy.

Ms. McCurdy returns after about ten minutes and takes a seat next to Danny on the sofa. He catches a strong whiff of perfume she's probably just applied. "I've spoken with two of his friends," she says, "and they tell me they haven't seen him. I tried to find his best friend, but apparently, she did not go to lunch."

"Who is she?"

"Oh, I'm sorry, I can't give you names of our students."

"Well, can you catch her before her next class?" Danny flashes the winning smile again, and Ms. McCurdy sidles a little closer to him. Danny moves a little to, so they're touching.

"I can certainly try," she says, "if you don't mind waiting. Lunch will be over in fifteen minutes."

She tries to make small talk, and Danny reluctantly goes along, though he's consumed with worry about Eduardo. Despite what he told Lupe, he's apprehensive about Eduardo having been outside overnight.

The bell trills again, and Ms. McCurdy, a hungry look on her face, reluctantly leaves along with most of the other teachers in the lounge. It's not five minutes before she's back, obviously puzzled.

"I tried to talk with Shan..., I mean, Eduardo's friend, but she wasn't in her next class. That's odd, because I know she was present in my class. I actually sent her to run off some copies for me..."

Danny remembers the girl in the front office. Had she heard him mention Eduardo's name?

"You said she was Shan something?" This time Danny gives her an imploring look. "If you can't give me her name, perhaps you can help me get in contact with her or her parents. I wouldn't ask if it wasn't really important."

Ms. McCurdy is clearly troubled. "All right," she says finally, "but you didn't hear it from me. Her name is Shannan Flynn. She and Eduardo have been thick as thieves since the semester started. I'll get a phone number for you."

Danny takes her hand and presses it gently. "Thanks so much, Ms. McCurdy. I'll let you know what I find out."

Gaping at him with wide, milky eyes, she says, "You can call me Agnes."

Chapter 11

When I wake up Tuesday morning, I've forgotten where I am.

My face is buried in a pillow, and a fruity odor mixed with an undercurrent of my own b.o. fills my nose —I didn't bother to wash off yesterday's travelsmell before crawling into bed. Turning over, I open my eyes and an electric blue headboard, beige walls, and a four-foot wide window comes into view. Oh yass!—the Sheraton, New York City. I check the alarm clock on the nightstand.

08:30. That's Gucci—I'm planning on hitting the NHFC around ten or so.

I put on my nice jeans, a white blouse like I'd wear to work and a pair of white Nikes, then grab my backpack and head downstairs. As I exit to the sidewalk, I look both ways to assure myself that my friends from last night are gone. I can see a brownish smear where my attacker's face left part of him on the sidewalk.

I walk up to 10th Avenue and cross 35th Street, heading for Winogradsky's. Its façade is composed of many glass panes about a foot square, framed in dark wood, giving the place a total Euro vibe.

I open the door and the aroma of coffee that engulfs me makes me salivate and my eyes water. The crowd is sparse, but most people will be at work by now. The waiter and cooks are masked, but none of the patrons are. To my right is a counter with five empty stools. I recognize the big guy in white behind the bar (I'm sure he doesn't remember me). He fills a mug with coffee from one of those big metal pump containers and places it in front of me. I pick it up in both hands and take a long swig—the temperature is perfect.

It's as good as I remember.

I don't even look at a menu—I just order the lox and bagels.

Half an hour later, all I want to do is go upstairs and back to bed. Maybe that big breakfast wasn't such a great idea after all. I check my phone for directions to the clinic at 52 Laight Street, then leave the restaurant and walk down to Eighth Avenue. It's a bussin' day; bright sunshine, not a cloud in the sky and a strong east wind keeps the citystink down. I step up my pace to help walk off breakfast and in ten minutes I'm at Penn Station.

Going downstairs to the main concourse with its glass ceiling, I look up for the sign that directs me to the subway on the lowest level. The further underground I go, the more decrepit the station becomes.

That's New York City for you, totally iconic on the outside, but God knows what you'll find if you look too deep.

The subway platform is pretty full even though rush hour is over. About half of the people, including me, wear masks—the threat from Miss Rona is low these days, but zero it ain't.

Between the virus and the current anti-cop vibe, random violence in the City is at an all-time high, and the masks make it hard to tell what's on people's minds.

I wish I had my Sig.

I don't have long to wait before a glowing yellow orb appears the down the tunnel and a moment later, the C-train rumbles in. It's standing room only, so I grab me a pole for the short ride downtown. These trains sure haven't gotten any quieter since I was here last; the air reverberates with creaks and groans as the train judders into the tunnel. I feel something brush my ass and I look over my shoulder; there's a couple of male straphangers behind me that pass my quick vibe check, both in business suits and looking up at the ads where the ceiling of the car meets the wall. I turn back, and after a minute I feel it again, harder this time.

Shit. I didn't come up here to get groped on the subway.

I decide to leave things on read unless it gets way worse. The perv strokes me a few more times before the speaker squawks "Canal Street next" and I'm able to get away from his sorry ass.

I don't know who it was, but I hope he came in his pants.

Checking my phone as I come out into daylight, I see I'm on Varick Street in TriBeCa, short for Triangle Below Canal Street. Once a produce market and commercial center, TriBeCa morphed into a mecca for artists and other creative types in the 20th century. By 2000, the neighborhood was a high key residential district that included businesses such as art galleries, boutique shops, restaurants, doctors' and dentists' offices and bars.

A fenced-off highway on my right prevents me from directly walking to Laight Street, but I spot a pedestrian bridge a block away that will take me over it. I put number 52 Laight Street into the iPhone's search box and hit Enter, then follow the route up the stairs, crossing the highway beneath a grilled canopy that prevents losers from throwing shit on the cars below. I descend onto a cobblestoned street on the other side, Laight Street. My phone says number 52 is about a block and a half west.

The building turns out to be a five-story red brick structure with a green wood and gray stone façade on the ground floor. There's a defunct furniture warehouse here, which throws me for a sec, then I see that that's number 50. A doorway on the far side is number 52.

Sister!

I go in, inhaling the scent of wood and lemon wax as I check the wall directory—the NHFC is on the top three floors of the building.

A new-looking stainless-steel elevator silently whisks me up to three. The doors open onto a large reception room with white walls done in sleek curves, lit by fluorescents so bright it's almost eye-hurting. The walls are adorned with wood-framed brown and orange blobs on a white background—abstract artwork carefully chosen to offend no one.

A twentysomething redhead dressed in a tight white dress more appropriate for clubbing than work sits behind an arc-shaped counter across the room. She looks up when the elevator doors part, favoring me with a ravishing smile that makes me tingly.

"Can I help you, Miss?" she says in a breathy voice.

Approaching, I see a plaque on the counter.

Brianna Marsh.

"I hope so." I tell her the cover story I made up during the flight. "My name is Natalie McMasters, and I was conceived here about twenty-four years ago. I'm hoping to get some documentation about that for a genealogy project."

"You'll have to talk to Dr. Thistlebottom," she says.

Thistlebottom? She's kidding, right?

"I'll see if he's available." She picks up a white phone. After a moment, "Doctor, there's a woman here asking about her birth records." She listens a moment, hangs up and points to the right. "Just go all the way to the end of the hallway and he'll meet you."

Glass partitions on either side of the hallway enclose offices where white-coated workers labor in front of computer monitors. I would hate working here—no privacy whatever, and all the lights would give me a headache.

I notice a dude behind the glass with curly blond hair, wearing round, wire-rimmed glasses, look up at me, then abruptly back to his monitor when my gaze meets his.

Hey man, I don't bite.

I turn my eyes toward the end of the hall. An older man in a doctor's smock waits on me in front of an open, solid white door.

Apparently, the boss doesn't have to be under constant scrutiny like the help does.

44

He's fiftyish, not bad looking, with white hair down to his shoulders and wears a t-shirt under his lab coat. As I approach, he extends a hand, saying, "I'm Doctor Pierce Thistlebottom, the director here. And you are?"

"Natalie McMasters."

He waves me into his office. "Come in, come in."

He follows me in, shutting the door behind us.

The office is rectangular, only about fifteen feet deep but nearly twice as long, with bright white walls and a matte black desk in front of two windows overlooking Laight Street.

"Please sit," he says, indicating a black leather chair facing his desk.

I slide out of my backpack and do so, letting the pack sit on the floor beside the chair.

The rest of the office has white file cabinets along the walls and a circular glass table surrounded by more black leather chairs in back.

The doc takes a seat behind his desk, rocking back in his chair with his hands behind his head. "Now, how can I help you, Ms. McMasters?'

I repeat my cover story about the genealogy project. He leans forward, resting his arms on his desk and frowning.

Oh, oh! Bad vibes.

"Ms. McMasters, it pains me to tell you that we give no one outside of the company access to our files. However, if you want documentation beyond your mother's word that you were indeed conceived here, I would be happy to provide you with an affidavit attesting to that fact. I can even include your parentage, if that would be helpful."

I hesitate, then take the plunge. "I guess what I want to know is whether or not any more embryos from my parents were used to produce any kids. In other words, do I have a sister somewhere?"

"What does your mother say?"

He's holding something back.

"Of course, she says no, or I wouldn't even be here. And I believe her. I guess the question is really whether my parents' embryos were implanted in another woman without her knowledge."

Now he seems shocked. "Of course not! That would be unethical, to say the least."

No shit, Dude.

"Why would you think you had a sister?" he continues.

Sister!

Again, I hesitate.

Shit, go for it Nattie!

I tell him about the shooting back home.

His look becomes thoughtful. "You say this woman looks exactly like you?"

"She could be my twin."

"I don't know what to tell you," he says. "We wouldn't have used your parents' embryos in another woman without your mother's permission. Besides, it's highly unlikely that a different embryo would have produced an identical twin anyhow. Identical twins arise from a single embryo during the same pregnancy."

You're trying really hard to convince me, dude.

Reaching for my pack, I say, "My mom gave me a notarized letter with permission to look at her file..."

He makes me talk to the hand. "It doesn't matter. The files are the property of NHFC. Permission is not hers to give."

"She can't see her own file?"

"That's right. Not without a court order."

This is bullshit!

"Now, do you want me to get you that affidavit or not?"

You could put anything in that affidavit that you want to, Hunty.

"I guess so. When can I get it?"

"Just give your address to Brianna on your way out and we'll get you a copy in a few days."

As Uncle Amos would say, there's no sense sitting here beating a dead cat against a barn door. Getting up, I tell him, "OK, I'll do that." I sling my pack on my shoulders and wait for Thistlebottom to play the gentleman and open the door for me to leave.

As I go toward reception, I see the dude behind the glass eyeing me again, so I throw him a smile. He blushes and looks back at his screen once more. I give Brianna my address, not expecting to hear a goddamn thing from these asshats, then take the elevator down. Outside on the sidewalk, I check my phone.

Shit, it's only a little after eleven.

My flight home doesn't go until tomorrow after lunch, so now I've got to figure out what the fuck to do in New York City by myself for most of a day.

A voice calls from behind me. "Hey, Miss!"

I turn. It's the blond dude from upstairs. He's lost the lab coat and is wearing a blue-and-white striped polo shirt and gray plaid pants. Yeet!

He walks toward me, his hand extended. I take it—it's like touching a dead fish, cold and stiff. "I'm Irwin," he says. "Old Thistledouche screwed you over, didn't he? I can see it from your face."

I want to tell this simp to swerve, but I'm trying hard to be not me so much these days, so I say instead, "Yass, but I'm used to that. I'll get over it."

He's looking at the sidewalk as he says, "He's a total prickosaurus. Why don't you let me apologize for NHFC by buying you a drink?"

"Aren't you supposed to be working?"

"I can take an early lunch."

His vibe is way cringy, not my type at all, but then I think maybe here's a way into those files. It totally can't hurt to sip some tea with this dude and find out. "Sure. What's bangin' around here?"

He walks me south about five minutes to the corner of Hudson and Moore Streets where a dive called Bubby's has outdoor seating under a canopy. We grab a table and order—I get my usual Heine and Turkey, and he asks for a hard seltzer—I think those things taste like piss.

"So what did you talk to old Thistledouche about?" Irwin asks.

I have to decide how much of my personal business I want to let this dude in on. What can it hurt to be honest? "I was conceived at the clinic," I tell him, and see his eyebrows go up. "I just wanted a look at the files related to my birth for a genealogy project. Thistlebottom says they're proprietary. So I'm hosed."

He gets right to the point. "What's it worth to you to see that file?"

"Oh, I don't know. A hundred, maybe?"

The tip of his tongue snakes out and he licks his upper lip. He's got a wispy little blond 'stache that gives me the creeps. His eyes fasten themselves to my tits. "I wasn't talking about money," he says.

"What are you talking about, then?"

Oh shit! I know where this is going.

Sister!

He looks right in my eyes with his watery ones. "How 'bout a hookup?"

The words *Fuck no!* want to explode from my lips, but I swallow them.

How bad do you want to see that file, Nattie?

I worked in a strip club for months and I lost count of how many lap dances I gave dudes slimier than Irwin—more than one dropped his pants and his shorts so I could get him off rubbing my pussy on his schlong. I even fucked a dude I didn't want to one time, to save my life. What's another one? The pic of Vivian and Ye-ye pops into my head again.

Hey, it's just sex—everyone's doing it.

"I guess."

An evil little grin appears on his face. "Kewl! I can call in sick, take the afternoon off..."

"Hold on there, dude. I wasn't born yesterday. You ain't gettin' nothin' until I see that file."

That wipes the grin away—now he looks pissed. Tough shit. "How do I know you'll keep your side?"

"You don't. But you can count on no file, no pussy. So what'll it be?"

"You Stacys are all alike," he says sourly. Then, "OK. Meet me out front of NHFC at eleven tonight. Everyone will be gone by then."

"See you then." I down my shot and chug my beer, then get up and go. I don't want to spend any more time with this asswipe than I have to.

Chapter 12

Thurmond Jordan knows that most people think he's a bum.

That's fine with him. He thinks that most people have their heads up their asses anyhow, with their holier-than-thou attitudes, just because life didn't shit on them the way it did on him.

He grew up on a sharecropped farm in the eastern part of the state, his daddy sinking every dime he made into 'shine and meth. Finally, his Mama had enough of her husband's beatings and carried Thurmond and his brother to the big city, but it wasn't long before she got herself killed by one of her johns and he and Jody ended up in the system. Life was a little better then, but the worst thing about the group homes was that nobody there loved you—all they did was take care of your physical needs—which was better than nothing, he supposed. Thurmond was a big kid, and he found out real fast that it was much better to be the bully than the bullied. He ruled the roost in each home they put him in until he got hisself kicked out for fighting, and when he turned eighteen, they put him out on the street with no skills to support himself. It didn't take long before he did a stint in jail for shoplifting. When he got out, he graduated to a dime in the joint for armed robbery.

He could have liked prison if it wasn't for the lack of sex and the abuse from the screws, all of whom seemed to be clones of his Daddy. So, when he got out, he made a vow never to go back, but that was easier said than done—a man has got to find a way to live on the streets. He took up begging, and that turned out all right, because he learned to pick marks he could intimidate. His 6'6" frame and the lack of dental care that cost him two of his lower front teeth turned out to be a blessing, because it gave him a truly terrifying appearance when he leered at a mark.

Eventually Thurmond learned about the homeless encampment in the woods, so he went over there and deposed the reigning monarch. He instituted his own rules—if you wanted to stay, you had to give him a cut of your daily take, whether it was money, food, smokes or whatever. Some of the women were even pretty enough to fuck—Thurmond liked them young, before the ravages of their way of life turned them into hags.

These days, Thurmond doesn't have to go into town but a couple days a week because he's selective about who he lets into camp. He's keeping Shannie around because he knows she's gonna be of fuckin' age in a couple of years—he's spent many a night choking the monkey thinking about what he'll do to her when she's ready. But now she's brought in this new kid—a greaser, no less. She really seems to like the little peckerwood, so Thurmond is worried that if he kicks him out, Shannie will go with him. Besides, he's getting a vibe that the little beaner's got some bucks. He made him turn out his pockets the other day and found nothing, but the two of them could have hidden it. He decides to wait a couple days and see what the kid brings him for rent, then he can always go rifle their tent and see what he finds.

His reverie is interrupted by the sound of a car engine. A dirt two-track off the main drag leads into the campsite, and sometimes those goddamned four-wheelers in their fancy-ass Rubicons find their way down here. It usually doesn't take Thurmond very long to run their skinny white asses off. He opens the drawer of an old bureau he's got in his shack and removes a large revolver, which he sticks in the back of his pants, letting his shirt flop down over it. He's never had to draw the thing yet, but he'd rather have it and not need it, than need it and not have it.

He goes outside and over to the spot where the road ends. It's mid-afternoon, so everybody but him and the two kids are in town, earning. He takes them in a battered van each morning, dropping them off at busy intersections, freeway ramps and other places that get a lot of traffic, then picks them up around sunset. For this service, he gets half their day's take. It's a sweet deal—he spends most of his days here, smoking and drinking, and he always has plenty to eat.

He's mildly surprised to see that the visitor is not a Jeep; it's a royal blue SUV, a Range Rover. The windshield is deeply tinted so he can't see inside, but when the door opens, a pair of low-heeled black boots appears. A woman! She's older, maybe in her 40s, with short black hair swaddling her head like a skull cap, wearing a white blouse over black slacks and a matching designer windbreaker. Spiral silver earrings dangle next to a well-sculpted face, and she's sporting a matching silver necklace. Thurmond licks his lips, not sure if her sexiness or the aura of money attracts him more.

"Good morning," she says. "Mr. Jordan, I presume."

Holy shit! She knows his name?

She holds out her hand. "I'm Ms. Atwater, and I'm pleased to make your acquaintance." She's got a foreign accent; English, Irish, Thurmond isn't sure. What he is sure of is that it's raising the hackles on his neck. Fuckin' foreigners!

His conflicting emotions raging in him make it hard to speak. Finally, he gets out, "How do you know me? What do you want?"

"I've come to make you a business proposition, Mr. Jordan.

He gets bolder. "You have, have you?" Now he's thinking seriously of drawing his gun, getting this bitch on her knees and giving her the business. Then she reaches into her pocket, and when her hand reappears, she's holding a little silver pistol. His belly goes suddenly cold.

"You'll pardon me if I ask you to raise your hands and turn around, Mr. Jordan. You needn't worry—this is just a precaution to make sure that our negotiations go smoothly." She runs her hand over him and finds the revolver of course, which she plucks from his waistband and tosses in the bushes. Taking a step away from him, she says, "Now you may turn around again."

She's put away her pistol, but the expression on her face tells Thurmond she's not afraid of him, which makes him scared to death of her. It's a feeling he detests. "What do you want?" he asks her again.

"I work for a local philanthropist. He has a desire to help indigent children, and he sent me to enquire if you have any in your camp. If so, I'm willing to compensate you if you'll allow me to take them away with me."

"Compensate me how?"

"Oh, let's say two hundred dollars per child."

Two hundred! He tries not to let his excitement show on his face, but he's sure he fails. Nevertheless, he says, "Well, I dunno. They're under my care, you know. What does your boss want with them?"

"Simply to remove them somewhere they can be properly clothed and fed, and given a chance at a better life. Can you help me?"

"I dunno," he says again. "I might have a couple here, but they're part of our group and they earn their keep."

"Hence the compensation I offer. Since you have only two, I can go to three hundred each, but that's all."

Strictly speaking, the greaser isn't his kid, but she doesn't know that. He raises his voice. "Shannie! Get out here, and bring your friend." After a moment, Shannie emerges from the tent, Eduardo following. "Come here," Thurmond says. "There's somebody I want you to meet." When the kids are close enough, Thurmond takes them by the shoulders and holds them in front of him like a protective father. "This lady wants you to go with her. Says she'll give you a place to live, food and clothes."

Shannie has fear on her face. Eduardo, on the other hand, looks puzzled.

"Shannie, my name is Geraldine. Who is your friend?"

"I'm Eduardo. What is it you want with us?"

Sister!

"It's like Mr. Jordan said. The man I work for wants to give you a home. He'll care for you, send you to school, see to it you have everything you need."

A smile lights up Eduardo's face, and he turns to Shannie. "That's great! It's just what we're looking for–isn't it, Shannie?"

"I don't know..."

"Then why don't you go and get your things, while I talk to Mr. Jordan some more," the lady says. "Then we'll be off."

Thurmond gives the kids a push toward their tent. He whispers to Shannie, "If you fuck up this deal for me, I'll whip your ass, and his, too!' When they disappear inside, he holds out his hand. Geraldine reaches into a pocket, then counts six crisp hundred dollar bills. He briefly considers grabbing her wrist and overpowering her, but his innate survival instinct tells him that would be a really bad idea.

Shannie and Eduardo come out of the tent, both carrying backpacks, and run over to the adults. "Go on and get in the car, you two," says Geraldine. "Back seat, and buckle up." The kids hasten to obey.

She extends her hand to Thurmond again, and he takes it this time. Her grip is surprisingly strong for a woman.

"This never happened, Mr. Jordan. Do you take my meaning?" Her deep umber eyes bore into his watery blue ones.

"Yes, Ma'am."

She takes a couple of steps back while facing him, then turns and gets in the car. She fires it up and turns around in the clearing, then it disappears into the woods.

Too late, Thurmond thinks, *Damn! I should have asked her for a ride into town.*

He's got some money to spend.

Chapter 13

L aight Street has no restaurants or bars, so it's mostly deserted at 11 p.m.

As I cross Hudson Street, a fresh wind blows up from the Battery, bringing the smell of fish and salt air with it, but it immediately cuts off, blocked by buildings as I continue west on Laight. Some have apartments, so a few windows are lit—I doubt anyone notices that I am here though. I remember a news story from a few years ago where a woman was raped in an area like this. Many of the residents heard her screams and some even looked out their windows and saw the attack, but they all did nothing, assuming that someone else would call the cops. I'm not too worried to be alone on the street though. Two years of *Tai Chi Chuan* training with Ye-ye has done wonders for my ability to defend myself against untrained opponents, even big dudes.

I still wish I had my Sig and my knife though.

I see no one as I walk toward number 52, and I briefly wonder if Irwin's chickened out. His vibe told me that he's not way comfortable around women. The thought of clapping cheeks with him makes me cringe, and I briefly think about ghosting him, but that's not me. I'll do him if he gets me what I want.

But he's gonna wear a rubber, that's for sure.

I jump as he steps out of the doorway of number 52. Gimme a break! He's got on a dark gray windbreaker and a black stocking cap, looking like a tough guy from a bad TV show. He gives me that creepy little smile of his, saying, "You came!" as if he didn't believe it was gonna happen.

"Facts." I motion toward the door. "Let's get this bread."

He punches a code into the keypad, and there's a click and a low buzz as it unlocks. Opening it, he pulls out his phone. "Just a sec." His thumbs dance over the screen. "OK. I've disabled the video cam. Hurry up before somebody notices." Once inside, he closes the door, then goes to the elevator and hits the button. White light streams out as the door opens, lighting up the whole lobby, which makes me jump. We pile in and he works his phone again, then we ride up to three. Again, the entire reception area is illuminated as the door opens. He fiddles with his phone once more, then nudges me out of the elevator. When the door closes, only a soft light from the city outside the windows remains. We go down the glass corridor to Thistlebottom's office and Irwin punches in another code.

Sister!

"There's no cam in here," he says. "I guess Thistledouche doesn't want anybody to see him beatin' off while he's watching porn."

Once inside, he removes a flashlight from his windbreaker. "I'd rather not turn on the overhead light," he says. "Now, what is your mom's name and your birth date?"

I tell him, and he quickly locates the right file cabinet. I get the idea that he's been in these files before. "How come all this isn't on computer," I ask him. "Aren't paper files pretty much yesterday?"

"You're right, but you were born twenty-four years ago. We're in the process of digitizing, but it's slow. Takes away from the current workload." He grunts. "Here it is."

He brings the file folder over to the table. I see the name McMasters on the tab. He opens it, and begins sorting through the papers inside. There must be twenty pages in there! "Why so much paper?" I ask.

"The file documents the entire *in vitro* procedure," he says as he riffles through the pages, and I see black-and-white photos of cells under a microscope. It's totally uncomfy to be looking at myself before I was me.

"This is weird," he says. "It doesn't look like a standard IVF."

"What do you mean?"

He flips through the photos again, slower this time. "Look here. This series shows a normal fertilization sequence," he says, running a finger over the pictures.

"If you say so."

"But now..." He flips a page, "Holy shit, they split the embryo. They split that motherfucker into four parts! Look!"

Now I'm getting a really bad vibe.

"What does that mean?" I ask.

"Sometimes they implant more than one embryo in the mom, just to be sure one takes. But those are usually independently fertilized."

"What do you mean?" I ask again.

He makes an impatient huffing sound, prolly 'cause he thinks I'm less savvy than he is. "Look. They stimulate the woman's ovaries with a hormone to promote the growth of the follicles containing the eggs because they want her to produce a lot of them. They monitor the ovarian response with ultrasounds and blood tests, and when they think she's ready, they collect as many eggs as they can. They get Dad to jack off on the same day. They mix the eggs and sperm together *in vitro*, incubate them until 60 to 70

54

per cent of the eggs are fertilized, then track them microscopically until the embryos are mature enough to implant. You follow?"

"Yes."

"Then they generally implant one good embryo into Mom." Sometimes they'll do two or three if they have reason to believe she'll have a problem. They'll freeze the embryos they don't implant in liquid nitrogen in case the pregnancy doesn't take and they have to do it again. But they didn't do any of that here."

"What did they do?"

"It's called an Intracytoplasmic Sperm Injection, or ICSI. It's when they inject a single spermatozoa directly into a single mature ova, *in vitro*. Usually when they do that, they let the embryo develop like normal, then implant it into Mom when it's mature enough. But here, they let it grow, then split it into four parts."

"Why four?"

"Probably to get the same number of cells in each embryo. Then all four of them would continue to develop at the same rate." He scans the pages again, his lips moving as he reads. "But they only implanted one embryo into your Mom."

Now that bad vibe is getting a lot worse.

"What happened to the other three?"

"It doesn't say."

We're both quiet for a moment, thinking. Then I ask him, "Can you look up another file for me?"

"I guess. Whose file?"

"The kid's name was Rebecca Chapman."

"I need the mother's name."

"I don't remember it." I tell him, exasperated. "How many Chapmans can there be?"

"We'll just see." He jerks a drawer open and riffles through the files. "There are three. The mothers are... Marilyn...Theresa...and Sylvia." He looks at me expectantly.

Shit! "No, I don't think it's any of those." Something is nagging at the back of my brain. Wait a minute. I remember now. "Rebecca Chapman was an alias. Her real name was Hines. Fiona Hines. That's H, I, N, E, S."

He opens another drawer. "Aha! Only one Hines, name of Bridget."

Sister!

"That's the one! I'm sure of it! Let's see if they did the same thing."

He pulls the file, lays it on the table, and shines his light on the contents. I don't even have to look hard to see that the files have the same thickness, and the pictures are similar. "Yep," he says. "These pix are dups of the others."

A cold ball suddenly blossoms in my belly and my knees buckle. I'm barely able to push a chair back from the table and collapse into it before I break down in tears.

"Hey, Natalie! What's the matter with you?"

I open my mouth to speak, but nothing comes out but a great wrenching sob. I try again, and manage, "Fiona was my sister! My twin!"

He's still looking through the file. "Yep," he says. "Sure looks like it."

"She was my twin sister, and she was murdered!" I wail.

Now it's his turn to stand speechless. Finally, he says, "What happened?"

I have neither the time nor the desire to get into it with him. "I don't want to talk about it."

His face tells me he's not satisfied with my answer, but fuck him. He doesn't need to know.

It takes a couple of minutes for me to get myself back under control. Finally, I say, "Can we find out who the sperm and egg donors for me and Fiona were?" I know I must have another sister out there. One who murdered a man in cold blood. I've got to find her and ask her why she did that.

"For that, we'll have to go to the computer," he says.

At the PC, he jiggles the mouse, then types in a password. "I stole Thistledouche's login info a while ago," he smirks. "It will take me a couple minutes to get into the archives."

I go to the copy machine and start making copies of the material in the files. Irwin pays no attention, engrossed with his own work.

A few minutes later, he says. "Here we go." Having finished the copies, I bring the files over to his desk, then pull up a chair and sit beside him. He's got a spreadsheet on his monitor. He asks, "What's your mom's ID number? It's on the first page of her file." I find it and give it to him. After a minute, he says, "That's odd."

"What?"

"Look here." He points at the screen. *Sperm donor: 001*, it reads. Beneath is *Egg donor: 001*.

"The sperm and egg came from the same person?" I realize how stupid that is as soon as I say it.

"No, you nitwit. The sperm and egg donors have two different registries. These people were number one in each."

"Can we find out who they are?"

"I'll check the registries." His fingers fly over the keyboard and another spreadsheet flashes on the screen. "Hmmpf."

"What?"

"There's no name for sperm donor 001. Let's try Mom." The keys rattle again, and the screen blinks. "Woah. Same thing." He sits back in his chair with an air of resignation.

My mind is going a million miles an hour. One thing I'm pretty sure of—sperm and egg donors 001 were not Sean and Judy McMasters. Damn! My parents are not my parents! I have another idea, "Is there a way to see who else these donors parented?"

"Maybe." The keys rattle. "Holy shit!"

"What!"

He's scrolling down a long list on the screen. "There's nearly a thousand names here," he says.

I can't even! "You mean I have almost a thousand twins?"

He gives me that look like I'm stupid again. "Not at all. There were only four embryos from that ICSI. But the rest of these would all be your sibs."

I look at Mom's name, noticing that the font is red. "Scroll back to Bridget Hines," I tell him. Yep, it's in red too! "Are any other names in red?" He scrolls through the list, stopping at another name. "Abigail Dupont. Is there an address for her?"

He clicks the name and another screen comes up. "Bay Street in Sag Harbor. That's in the Hamptons. Rich bitch," he says.

I think I've just found the mom of one of my other twins!

Chapter 14

Danny calls the phone number that Agnes McCurdy gave him and gets a recorded message that it's been disconnected.

Hmmph. Shows you how much contact the schools actually have with parents these days.

He makes another call to Mrs. Hall, the mother of the kid that Eddie beat up, and gets zip again. She tells him that she's forbidden Freddie to have any more contact with Eddie. So he calls the school and leaves a message for Ms. McCurdy, informing her that the number she gave him was no good.

He goes to the 3M Detective Agency office on the first floor of the north wing. Amos Murdoch, Nattie's uncle and the founder of 3M has his bedroom there, so he doesn't have to cope with getting upstairs in his wheelchair. The rest of the bedrooms have been converted to offices and a conference room. The other partner, Leon Kidd, is in the field on a stakeout, but Danny peeks into Amos's office to see if he's there. He is, and he's not alone. M.B. has a chair pulled up next to him, and the two of them are staring at his monitor with their heads an inch apart like two kids watching a cartoon show. Danny clears his throat, and the two of them jump like he caught them making out on the sofa.

"Hey Danny," says Amos, "what's going on?"

"Still looking for Eddie. He hasn't come home yet and Lupe's past frantic."

"He's likely awright," says Amos. "Hell, when I was a kid, we'd go campin' in the woods for a week and our folks never worried a lick."

"It's a different world now, Amos." Turning to Danny, M.B. says. "Let me know if there's anything I can do. I can use some bureau resources and apologize later."

"Maybe if we don't find him by tomorrow," says Danny. "I don't want you to get in trouble."

"It's no trouble to help family," she says.

Danny raises an eyebrow. Last he knew. M.B. was a good friend, but family she wasn't.

"I think it's time we told y'all," says Amos. "Me and the little woman here are gettin' hitched."

M.B. gives Amos a look that clearly says "the little woman" is a sobriquet which she definitely does not appreciate.

The old goat has such a goofy smile on his face he probably doesn't even notice.

"Hey, that's great you two! When's the date?"

"We're not in a big hurry," M.B. says. "I'll be spending most of my weekends here while we get things worked out."

"I take it y'all haven't told Nattie yet?" says Danny.

"Nope," Amos replies. "Y'all are the first to know,"

"Well, you should let her know ASAP. It will be better if it comes from you than me."

Danny goes to his office and fires up his computer, Just because the phone number he got from McCurdy is non-functional doesn't mean that it's useless. He opens a reverse directory that will provide a name and an address to go with the phone number. In a minute he's looking at a Bertha Flynn, whom he assumes is Shannan's mother. There's also an address, but when he runs it in another directory, the name of the current resident is different. OK, Bertha must've moved or something. Danny does a deep search on Bertha Flynn, looking for a current address.

Woah! A newspaper article pops up. It seems a woman named Bertha Flynn was one of several addicts who died from Covid-19 last year. The piece mentions nothing about the victim's families. Is it possible that Shannan has a foster family? If that's the case, why does the school have an expired phone number for her? Surely, she can't be living on the street?

Names and addresses of foster families aren't available even to licensed P.I.'s, but like any good detective, Danny still has contacts at the police department. He phones one now, trying to find out if there's a Shannan Flynn in the system. Half an hour later he has his answer. She isn't registered with child services.

Danny's deep dive revealed no info on family for Bertha Flynn. He does a quick check of divorce records to see if there's an ex, but it's no go.

Danny does a quick scan of a city map, trying to locate major intersections or beltway exits where professional panhandlers are likely to be. Then it's time to hit the street.

Sometime later in his pickup, Danny takes the beltway exit for the largest shopping mall in the city. Predictably, there's a panhandler at the light at the bottom of the ramp. Danny slows to ensure that the light will turn red before he gets there, earning the ire of the driver behind him, who leans on his horn. As the pickup comes to a stop, he watches the guy begin walking up the line of stopped vehicles, displaying a cardboard sign that details his sad tale. The panhandler is dressed in cammies, a khaki field jacket and an army patrol cap, probably to garner sympathy by giving the impression he's a vet. Sure enough, when he gets to Danny's truck, Danny sees that his sign says Afghan vet in big letters. Danny is as compassionate as the next guy about folks down on their luck, but a vet who's begging always leaves a bad taste in his mouth. He likes to think that if he ever found himself in such a situation, he'd go volunteer at a soup kitchen or a shelter. or do something to help somebody else instead of just expecting the world to support him. Whatever. Right now, he needs intel from the guy. He holds up two twenties fanned out and the dude's eyes get big as he grabs for them. Danny pulls them back, saying, "Nuh-uhh. I need to talk to you first. Get in the truck."

The beggar's expression changes to wariness. "Can't do that, boss," he says.

"Look, I won't hurt you. I just want some intel."

The light goes green and the guy behind Danny leans on the horn again. Danny wiggles the bills, and the guy gives up. He dashes around the front of the truck and hops in on the passenger side. The aroma that comes with him makes Danny sorry he didn't find another way to interview him. Danny lets off on the brake, drives through the intersection and down the road to parking lot for the mall. He turns in, finds a space far from the mall entrance and pulls in, taking the truck out of gear but leaving it running.

"When were you in the 'Stan, man?" Danny asks. "I did a couple cruises myself. Last one was with the 2nd Recon in 2012."

"I got back a couple of years ago," the guy says. Danny figures he's lying—the guy indicated no unit, and he knows that the U.S. pulled most of the combat troops out of Afghanistan by 2014. But he's not here to bust the dude for stolen valor. Holding up the twenties again, he says, "I'm looking for a kid who might be in your community." He then proceeds to give the guy a pretty accurate description of Shannie based on the quick look he got at her while she was at the copy machine. "Know where I might find her?"

The guy's got that distrustful look again. "What do you want her for?"

Ah, so you do know where she is.

"Just want a word with her, is all." Danny reaches into his front pocket with two fingers and withdraws his wallet, then adds another twenty to the first two. "My final offer," he says.

The guy grabs for the bills again and this time, Danny lets him have them. "She's at our place, dude," he says.

"And where's that?"

"In the woods. I'd have to show you."

Danny puts the truck back into gear. "Let's go."

The guy directs Danny onto the freeway, then down a couple exits to a rural road. "It's just up here on the right," the guy says.

"Woah!" Danny brakes as a car emerges from the road that the beggar pointed out—it's dark blue, a Range Rover, with deeply tinted windows and a black roof.

Danny can see neither the driver nor the passengers. *An expensive ride,* Danny thinks. *Must be some rich kids out four-wheeling.*

"You can let me out here," the panhandler says. "Thurmond will be pissed if he knows I brought you here. Can you gimme a ride back where you found me when you're done?"

"We'll see," says Danny, as the guy hops out of the truck.

The guy is standing there, mouthing "What do you mean, we'll see?", as Danny throws the truck into four-wheel drive, turning onto the two-track. The road's not smooth, but it is worn enough so he can tell that it gets plenty of use. The pickup jolts along for about five minutes, the bushes on the roadside making squealing noises as they scrape its sides, until the road finally widens and a bright spot looms ahead. Danny emerges into a clearing of sorts, where there's a smoldering central fire pit surrounded by several motley shacks, with multi-colored tents scattered throughout the woods that envelop them like Mother Nature is reclaiming her own. The Marine gets out of the truck and looks around, spying a figure in the bushes, rooting around as if looking for something. Danny assumes this must be Thurmond.

"Yo, Thurmond!" Danny hollers, and the searcher flinches, then begins thrashing the shrubbery even more anxiously. Danny suddenly has the feeling that he doesn't want the dude to find whatever he's looking for. He lets his right hand drift back towards his hip as he approaches the fellow, ready to draw his 1911 if the guy shows any sign of producing a weapon.

Thurmond stands up straight and faces Danny, apparently giving up his search. What an ugly motherfucker—buggy eyes, missing teeth and a patchy beard sprouting from a filthy face.

Reminds me of the Predator from the movie.

Sister!

The guy is a head taller than Danny and his overcoat flaring out makes him look twice as wide. He balls up his fists at his sides and stalks out of the undergrowth, snarling, "Yew jest get back in that fancy truck of yourn and haul yer ass outta here, mister!"

Danny brings both hands in front of him. He has no need of a weapon to deal with this asshole. "Look, partner, I just need a little intel, might even be a couple of bucks in it in for you."

Unfortunately, Thurmond is spoiling for a fight. Danny's offer of remuneration doesn't even slow him. Once his feet are clear of the shrubbery, he lowers his head and comes at Danny like a charging rhino. Between his Marine training and Tai Chi, Danny has so many ways to take him out he almost feels sorry for the fool. Almost.

Apparently, his rush was a ploy, because as Thurmond reaches Danny, he suddenly stops and rears up before the Marine like a grizzly, ready to pummel him into submission with those massive fists. Danny puts an end to that shit by the simple expedient of grabbing his ears, pulling his face down and head-butting him in the nose. The wail that arises from the wounded giant is truly pathetic as he goes down like a felled tree. On the ground at Danny's feet, he claps both hands to his ruined face, crying, "My dose! Jew broke my fuckin' dose!"

Yes I did, and now you're even uglier than you were before.

He takes a couple steps back. "You brought this on yourself, sailor. I just wanted to talk."

All of the fight gone out of him, Thurmond struggles to his feet. "What the fuck do you want? I ain't got nuthin' fer ya."

"I'm looking for a little girl, about ten or so. Name of Shannan. I heard that she might live here."

"Who tolya that?"

"Never mind. Does she stay here, or not?"

"Not anymore," Thurmond says.

"What do you mean, not anymore? Did she used to stay here?"

Thurmond simply glares at the Marine as he vainly tries to staunch the red river gushing from his crushed nose. As much as it pains him to do it, Danny reaches for his wallet and withdraws a couple of twenties. "I'll pay you if you can tell me where she's gone."

"I dunno," says the big guy. "They just left. Didn't say for where."

They? "Was somebody else with her? I'm also hunting a young boy. Mexican, ten years old."

"He was here. Put him up for the night."

Dammit! "When did they leave?"

"You just missed them."

Holy shit! The Range Rover! "Somebody took them? Who?"

"I dunno, man! Rich bitch. Never seen her before." Thurmond's right hand leaves his nose, dropping protectively toward his front pants pocket."

Danny now knows exactly what happened and he's pissed beyond words. "You sold them, didn't you? You sold them to the woman in the Range Rover." Thurmond's expression is all the answer that he needs.

Danny puts the twenties back in his wallet and the wallet back in his pocket. For two cents, he'd beat the snot out of the guy and take whatever the woman gave him. He turns on his heel instead, silently hoping that the son of a bitch will take the opportunity for a sneak attack. But Thurmond has had his fill of Danny Merkel, so he gets to keep his cash.

Getting back in his pickup and turning around in the tight space, Danny runs over the fire pit in the process. He checks his side mirror as he pulls back onto the two-track, seeing Thurmond just standing there with his hands clasped to his face. He doesn't feel sorry for him in the slightest.

Chapter 15

My mind is still reeling as we get off the train at Astor Place.

My parents ain't my parents! I've got over a thousand brothers and sisters! And possibly two more identical twins!

We come out of the subway to street level at Cooper Square, with its mix of modern and vintage buildings. This is a busy neighborhood—a fair-sized crowd is still out at this hour, taking advantage of the East Village bars and restaurants. Irwin's got my hand, tugging me along Astor Place with the ferocious intensity of a dude who's gone unlaid for way too long. We cross 3rd Avenue and enter the tree-lined St. Marks Place, packed with bars and squatty brownstones.

Now that we're out of the noisy train, I can ask Irwin the question that's been on my mind. "Just how many eggs can they harvest from one woman?"

He looks over his shoulder at me with an expression of disbelief. "What?"

I repeat the question.

"Thousands, I suppose. Who the fuck cares?"

He leads me to a metal door with a rectangle of wired glass in the center, in a painted brick wall next to a body-piercing shop that's still open after midnight. The unhinged side of the door is covered by a metal plate so no one can pry it open with a crowbar. Irwin wields a key, and the stench of bleach and old eggs hits me in the face as he half-shoves me into a black hole at the bottom of an unlighted stairway. He steps inside after me and pulls the door shut, closing out the remaining light from the street.

Giving a push in the center of my back, he orders, "Upstairs."

Claustrophobia makes my throat begin to constrict as I stumble up the steps. Irwin follows. The corridor at the top is nearly pitch black with only a small glimmer of light seeping in through a window at the far end. The apartment doors are blacker holes, spaced at even intervals.

"It's the second door on the right," Irwin says. He follows me and uses his key again, pulling the door open to reveal a short hallway leading into a larger room. It's brighter in here, because the two windows in the far wall overlook the street. Irwin flips on a dim light as he comes in behind me, so I can see that the flat is essentially one room with doorways to a tiny kitchen and bathroom. The place is sparsely furnished with an easy chair, a divan, a huge TV hanging on the wall, a bureau and a large wardrobe with double doors. A small round table and two stools with backrests near the kitchen serve as a dinette. The walls are sparsely decorated with posters—one shows an upraised white fist clutching a lightning bolt and another is a line drawing in black ink on a white background, of a bald man with a gloomy look, captioned *TFW*. A confederate flag is draped on another wall. I'm getting a creepy vibe. WTF have I gotten myself into?

Irwin perches on the divan and tells me to take off my clothes.

"Can't it wait a few minutes?" I ask him. "I want to talk about what we found at the clinic." I hold out the overstuffed file folder containing copies of everything we found.

"Later, Stacy," he says. "I got you what you wanted. Now it's time to pay up. Strip!"

I wonder who the fuck Stacy is as I turn around to put the folder on the table, then face him again. OMG! He's already got his pants and his underwear down around his knees and he's playing with himself. "C'mon, do it, do it!" he says.

It's not like I haven't done this before when I worked in the strip club. It's just sex—it doesn't mean anything. I reach down between my legs and start stroking myself, pumping my hips at him. I bring my hands up and slowly peel up my t-shirt, showing him my navel and my belly before pulling it over my head. I pull off one cup of my bra a titty pops out before I reach behind to undo the clasp. Irwin's eyes are a big as dinner plates, his mouth is gaping and he's drooling slightly like he's never seen a naked woman before. I feel the familiar rush I get when I strip for a john—give me five minutes and I'll have this asshole kissing my toes. I pull the bra off and bend over to take off my shoes and socks, taking my time, letting my tittles dangle and sway in front of his gaping eyes, then I straighten back up and thrust my breasts at him. I undo my belt and slide my jeans and panties down together, giving him a peek at the top of my bush before covering it again. Gradually, I ease the pants down further and further—now Irwin's eyes are laser-focused on my dark triangle. Finally, I step out of the clothes and kick them away.

"C'mere," he says, his hand still working furiously. With any luck he'll do the job for me and I'll be able to get away without fucking him. I step towards him and he stops playing with his dick and reaches for my shoulders, pulling downwards. "Suck it, Stacy," he says.

Yuck! A sour smell floats up from his crotch as I lower my lips, barely brushing the tip of his dick—I hope it's enough to get him off. No such luck! As I open my mouth to take him in, his hands go to the back of my neck and

Sister!

I pull away, saying, "Nuh-uhh! If you want this, keep your hands at your sides." No way I'm letting him shove it down my throat. His eyes are full of loathing as he does what I tell him—too bad, Hunty. I take him in my hand, licking him until I feel a weak pulse, then I pull away and pump him quickly. A drop or two hits my face, but all-in-all, I've accomplished what I wanted.

I expect him to go limp after he's finished, but he surprises me—he's still hard. "Slipped me a Cialis before!" he smirks. Getting up and kicking his pants away, he motions toward the divan. "Down there on your belly," he orders. "Now it's time to get real."

I reach over and pick up my pants instead, and take a condom out of the pocket. "Put this on," I tell him.

"A rubber? No way, Stacy."

"You want pussy, you wear it," I say. "Come here. I'll put it on for you."

He glares hatred at me, but comes over. I take the rubber out of the package and roll it down his length, stroking his balls when I finish.

"OK. On your belly," he orders. Great. I don't have to smell his breath.

I assume the position, and he grabs my hips and slides inside, none too gently. I wince—I'm not turned on by any of this, so I'm not very wet. The rubber is lubed, but it still smarts as he begins pounding, then my body gradually compensates and it gets somewhat easier. I only hope he'll be done again soon—I don't think there's going to be any satisfaction for me tonight.

His strokes speed up and his breathing becomes more rapid as he wheezes like an old steam engine—maybe the sumbitch will have a heart attack. He's gripping my hips hard enough to bruise—I might have some explaining to do when I get home. Abruptly, he pulls out. A moment, and the rubber lands on the couch near my face. Then I feel his dick pressing against my other opening.

"No!" I shout. "Not there!" Of course, he doesn't listen, and searing fire lances through me as he forces himself in. I shout "No! No! No!" over and over.

Now he's holding both my wrists behind my back and shoving me relentlessly into the divan. An overwhelming sense of helplessness engulfs me—my years of martial arts training are worthless in this position because he's a strong man with leverage from a superior position. I try to relax to lessen the pain, but I just can't. Waves of agony ripple through my thighs and my belly as the assault goes on. I've never felt so powerless and abused in my life! Suddenly, he explodes and the agony abates somewhat as his wetness spreads.

The weight on my back lets up as he pulls out, but he's still holding me down. I roll sideways and he lets go, and I fall off the divan onto the floor on my back. He looms over me, still erect, his eyes shining as he ogles my nakedness with an evil grin.

"Man, oh man!" he exclaims. "That was something!" He takes a step forward and reaches down for me, saying, "Time for round two!"

I prop myself up on my hands and feet and scuttle backwards out of his grasp like a crab until I hit the wall, then push myself up until I'm standing with my back against it. He follows and reaches to grab my wrists again, thinking to use his manly strength to overpower me once more. He totally has no idea what's coming.

I let him take my wrists, then I use his energy to pivot us parallel to the wall, sinking into *gong bu* and emptying my front leg. As he tries to pull me forward into his embrace, I snap a kick into his dangling testicles.

His mouth forms a perfect O as he lets go of my wrists, his hands fly to his hurt, and his cry of pain fills the room. Hitting his nose with the heel of my hand to get him to take his hands off his nuts, I kick him again in the same spot, grab the back of his neck as he doubles over, then break his nose on my upraised knee. A spinning elbow strike in the eye lays him flat on his back on the floor, his hands clutched between his legs again. Holy shit, his dick is still rigid!

That's got to hurt, motherfucker.

He just lays there bawling like a child who's gotten his fingers crushed in a car door.

A red rage still overwhelms me. I want nothing more than to stomp the shit out of him as he lies helpless, letting him know what it's like to have someone else dominate him, but a voice of reason tells me that I could kill or seriously injure him.

That's the idea.

The voice replies, *That would certainly get you in trouble with the law, rape or no rape.*

The voice is correct. But he surely did rape me. Should I report him to the cops? Fuck no! He'll just turn it into a he said, she said, and I'd have to testify in open court about what he did to me.

Who's even gonna believe a former stripper?

No thanks. Time to cut my losses and get the fuck out of here.

Sister!

I move around the room, collecting my clothes and getting dressed. It's agonizing—every step I take is punctuated with bolts of pain in my butt, my belly and my upper thighs.

Irwin's screams have turned to curses. "I'm going to fucking kill you, you fucking Stacy"—seems to be his favorite line, which he intersperses with other equally quaint sayings. He's struggling to get up—he's let go of his nuts and his arms are at his sides as he tries to prop himself up on his forearms. I step between his legs and put my heel on his swollen balls, pressing down just hard enough to show him what I can do if I choose to use my full weight. He lets out another keening wail and his expression changes from anger to terror.

"You just lay right there till I'm gone, asshole, or you'll never have kids," I tell him. Another press with my heel brings another screech of anguish. "You get me?" A frantic nod.

Looking down at the groveling bastard, hatred fills my soul. His curly blonde hair, his misshapen teeth, his hairless torso hung with rolls of fat, everything about him disgusts me. Fuck it! I throw my weight forward, grinding my heel down on his testicles. I swear I can feel them pop as his ragged scream fills the room.

I gather up my files from the table and slip out into the hallway. I can still hear his moans and curses after I shut the door, so I assume his neighbors can too. I guess the reputation of New Yorkers for not giving a shit is true, because no one looks out into the hall to see what's wrong. Or maybe they just love Irwin as much as I do. I hobble downstairs and out into the night.

Chapter 16

As soon as he opens the front door to Hyacinth House, Lupe is on Danny like a bug on flypaper.

"Did you find him?"

Danny hesitates, unsure about what to tell her. Finally, he says, "I've got a lead."

"A lead! What is it? Do you know where he is?"

"Let me run it down, sweetheart. Then we'll talk."

Danny curses mentally as he walks down the corridor in the north wing of Hyacinth House. He'd managed to talk Lupe out of following him to his office, but he had to promise that he'd let her know as soon as he found something. If only he'd gotten the plate number off that Range Rover! In his defense, he had no reason to believe that Eduardo was in that car, or even at the homeless camp. But now he needs to find the owner of that vehicle ASAP.

There's no one else here, so Danny can work undisturbed. Sitting down at his desk, he fires up his PC and navigates to the Land Rover website. A few clicks and he's looking at Range Rovers.

Wow! I had no idea that they could be so expensive!

Some run well over $100K, and even twice that much. There are a ton of different options. Tracing the specific car he saw may well prove impossible.

Maybe narrowing it down might be all I can reasonably expect.

He looks again at the different options shown on the website, noting subtle differences, then closes his eyes and tries to visualize the moment when the car emerged from the woods. The vehicle was dark blue with a black roof and deeply tinted windows. He was sure it had a black stripe on the front of the driver's door where it met the front of the vehicle. He decides to use the Build Your Own feature on the website to see if he can reproduce the car he saw, hoping that a picture will jog his memory. He goes step-by-step through the build—yes, the black stripe is an option, as are a black roof and the tint. The most expensive model has a distinctive grille and bumper. Closing his eyes again, he becomes certain that is the one he saw. And it had matte black wheels; he finds an option for that and adds it as well.

Sister!

Soon he's finished and he's studying a near duplicate of the car from today. Yikes! Over $250K! Can't be too many of those babies running around in the city.

Danny opens a database that will allow him to search for car owners by make and model. He finds four of those Land Rovers in the area.

That's a million bucks worth, people!

All of them are registered to the same person—Jerome Ellis.

Isn't that the moneybags who spoke at Nattie's graduation?

It doesn't take long to come up with an address for the billionaire. He's got a walled estate on Green Lake, not far from Ye-ye's pavilion.

Danny keeps on digging for more intel about Ellis. What he finds is troubling. Some articles say the billionaire has a penchant for young women, as young as the early teens, definitely illegal. However, Danny knows that he might find similar stories on just about any man with that kind of money—when you're rich, moochers, con artists, and blackmailers come out of the woodwork, some seeking to damage your rep out of sheer envy and spite, others hoping to cash in with a quick settlement. As far as Danny can ascertain, no charges of sexual misconduct made against Ellis have ever stuck, whether they involved teens or anyone else. And the guy has some really powerful friends—two former presidents, several senators and congressmen, captains of industry, a cardinal, and a member of the British royal family have all been seen at functions he's organized. Danny comes across a video news story dated just a couple of weeks ago. The headline reads, *Local Billionaire Donates Advanced Technology to Local Police Department.* The gist of it is that Ellis has given the CCPD a software package that does facial recognition, computer-aided dispatch, and interfaces with various public records and state and federal databases. He's also given the city money to increase its traffic cam coverage and install a gunfire detection system downtown. Somehow Danny doesn't think that a call to CCPD telling them Ellis might have his son at his estate is going to get much traction.

But there's really nothing to prevent me from simply driving out to Ellis's estate and asking, is there?

Danny sneaks out a rear door to avoid Lupe, who would surely insist on coming along. He thinks about Nattie, wishing that she was here, instead of chasing her own demons in New York City. Nattie has an almost magical ability to calm Lupe down. Danny could sure use some of that about now. He loves Nattie very much, but he can't deny that she's just plain selfish sometimes.

He fires up his truck and gets off the property without Lupe noticing. Ellis's compound is only about a ten-minute drive. Soon he's cruising next to a grey stone wall eight feet high, with outward pointing spikes along the top. The spikes don't really provide much of an obstacle, but they do indicate that trying to scale the wall may be a bad idea. Danny is sure that there are plenty of electronic security devices on the other side.

He comes to a T-intersection, where a break in the wall is barred by a wrought-iron gate, and pulls up to a little guard shack on the left. Inside is a large fellow all in black—jeans, t-shirt and beret. He's got a patch on his shoulder depicting a swooping eagle with lightning bolts for wings and the initials QRF. Danny is familiar with the patch from his time in the 'Stan. It's the logo for the Quick Response Force company, a defense contractor. It's odd to see them stateside doing a routine security job, but then again, Ellis has got enough coin to hire anyone he wants. Hell, maybe he even owns the company.

The guard steps out of the shack as Danny pushes the button to bring down his window. "Can I help you, sir?"

"Last time I saw you boys was in Kandahar with the Marines," Danny says, and the guard grins.

"When was that?"

Danny tells him, then follows up with, "Hey, I've come by to see your boss."

Checking a tablet, the guard says, "I don't see an appointment here."

"I was kinda hoping he'd squeeze me in."

Now the guard looks sus. "No can do, jarhead." Normally, a Marine does not like to be called jarhead, especially by someone from another service branch, but Danny tries to squelch any visible sign of anger.

Looking at the road past the guard shack, Danny sees a series of skinny, rectangular trap doors in the concrete. He knows that the guard could push a button and they'd spring open in seconds, ranks of wicked spikes popping up across the road, which would shred his tires like cole slaw, stopping his truck dead. He'll have to find another way in—maybe it would be best to come clean with this guy.

"Look, friend, I have it on good authority that a woman from this compound found my son this morning. He's ten, and he ran away from home. I just want to find out if he's here, and to take him home if he is."

"Haven't heard nothing about anything like that. I've got strict orders that no one passes this gate without leave from the boss. Mean my job if I let you in. But if you'll leave your info, I'll see what I can do for a fellow serviceman.

Danny fishes out one of his business cards and hands it to the guard, who takes it. He raises an eyebrow. "You're a private detective?"

"Yes, but that has nothing to do with this. I'm just looking for my boy."

"I'll see that this gets up to the main house, and I'll mention your son," the guard says. "I'm sure they'll get back to you if someone found him."

Or not.

He pulls forward into a U in the road and turns around, going back out on the main drag. He decides to circle the place just to get the lay of the land. After about a quarter mile, the wall takes a 90-degree turn into the woods, with a guard tower in the corner, while the road continues straight. *Yikes! I've seen prisons less secure than this place.*

He can think of nothing better to do than go back to Hyacinth House. Again, Lupe is waiting for him as he enters.

"Where were you? Did you find him?"

"No, Sweetie, I was chasing a lead but it didn't pan out."

"What lead? Where is my son? Where is Nattie? Why has she not called? Does she not care about Eduardo?"

Danny is getting seriously worried about Lupe—she sounds like she's going off the deep end. He gathers her into his arms, pressing her face to his chest and kisses the top of her head as he shushes her. "Of course she cares, Hon. She's just trusting us to find him. Why don't you go and fix dinner? Cooking always seems to calm you down."

"How can you even think about food..."

"I'm not. I'm thinking about you. You can't go on like this."

She dissolves into tears again. Finally, "You are right. Let me go and see what's for dinner. You find out how many are eating, and let me know." Danny releases her and she walks unsteadily to the kitchen.

Great! She's given Danny just what he wanted—a chance to go to the office to talk to Amos or Kidd. He can't let Lupe know about Ellis's compound yet. She'd go storming over there and maybe get herself shot.

He's in luck. Amos, M.B., and Leon are all in the office. Danny asks them to come down to the conference room for a powwow.

Once there, he tells everyone about the homeless camp, the Range Rover, and explains what happened this afternoon. When he's finished, Amos asks, "How sure are y'all that the boy is in there?"

"Where else would he be? Jerome Ellis is the only person in the city who owns cars like that."

Leon Kidd, a black retired Marine lieutenant who looks more like a linebacker than a detective, speaks up. "I met Ellis when I was on the Job," he says. "He's a police buff. Likes to hang around the house, go to cop bars, listen to the guys swap stories, that kinda thing. He's helped the department out a lot over the years with donations for equipment and such. I'm sure if Eduardo is at his place, he's feeding him ice cream and cake, and he'll send him home soon."

"Want me to call over there and see what I can find out?" M.B. asks. "The letters FB and I usually persuade folks to talk."

"Sure," says Danny. "The sooner I can tell Lupe that he's OK, the better."

"I'll make the call from Amos's office. Be right back."

A few minutes later, she returns with a puzzled expression. "They say that they haven't seen him," she says.

"Who did you talk to?" Danny asks. "The security guy I asked didn't know squat."

"I got a receptionist when I called."

Who has a receptionist to answer the phone at their house?

"Once I told her I was with the Bureau, she put me over to a woman named Geraldine McCauley. I think she's the lady of the house. She said that she hadn't seen Eduardo."

"But Thurmond said he was in that car!" Danny explodes in frustration.

"You didn't see the driver or the passengers?" Kidd asks.

"Nope. The tint on the windows was too dark. But why would Thurmond lie?" A bolt of fear passes through Danny as the answer comes to him.

Because he'd done something to him!

"Y'all need to talk to that Thurmond feller again right now," Amos says.

Chapter 17

Geraldine McCauley goes to the drive-through at McDonald's and buys Big Macs, fries and chocolate shakes for Eduardo and Shannie.

"You can eat them now," she says, handing the bags back, "but if you get food on the upholstery, you'll have to clean it up when we get to the house."

"*Señora*, we shall be very careful not to get your *muy hermoso* car dirty," Eduardo replies, his mouth filling with water as the aroma of the burgers saturates the vehicle. And he means it. He has certainly never been in such a beautiful car in his entire life.

The food serves as a good distraction during the fifteen-minute drive. The kids are just finishing up as Geraldine briefly stops at a black, metal gate and lowers her window, nods to a man in a black uniform, then drives inside after the gate opens. She proceeds along a tree-lined road with wide, sprawling lawns behind the trees and takes a right onto a curving road at a fork. Looking out the window, Eduardo is excited to see a large black helicopter sitting on a concrete pad in the middle of a field—he wonders if he'll be able to get a ride on it someday, if this place is really to become his new home. A sudden sadness wells up inside him that he will not see *Mamá* Lupe, *Mamá* Nattie, or Daddy Danny any more. But then he hardens his heart. He would not have run away if *Mamá* Lupe had not beaten him like that.

Geraldine turns a corner and pulls the car in front of a three-story house with a peaked black roof, a little steeple rising from its center. The lower floor is grey stone and the second floor has powder-blue shingles all around. Two columns support a wooden balcony over the front double doors. Flower gardens chockfull of multi-colored blossoms flank the entry—their pungent sweetness brings tears to Eduardo's eyes.

Getting out of the car, Geraldine says, "We're here. Bring your things and we'll go inside and meet everybody."

The kids comply, meekly following her as she opens the door and ushers them into a large room that smells of books and chalk. The walls are decorated with summery pictures, some featuring the upcoming Father's Day holiday. It looks like a classroom to Eduardo, but one like he's never seen before, with several round tables and chairs randomly placed, and shelves on the floor, easily reachable by kids, all around the perimeter and scattered about the inside space too. The shelves contain all sorts of toys, pictures, geegaws, baskets and boxes—Eduardo spies several interesting items and his palms tingle in the anticipation of messing around with them. He wonders if they have a drone. Several tall windows evenly spaced on all four walls admit enough daylight so the fluorescent lights above do not need to be turned on. The tables are occupied by other children, all of whom seem to be a little older than Eduardo and Shannie. There's a white, red-headed girl dressed in a frock who's absorbed with removing stamps from a box and pasting them into an open book. A black girl sits at another table, trying to fit multicolored puzzle pieces into a wooden frame; another white kid of about sixteen with dark, curly hair and oversized glasses sits with her, looking like he wants to help, but she gives him a look that says "Don't even", and he backs off. A Hispanic boy, maybe a year or two older than Eduardo, occupies a third table, busily engaged in building a model car. A pretty blonde girl who looks to be sixteen or seventeen is standing in the center of the room, observing each of the children in turn and making notes on a clipboard. Spotting the newcomers, she lowers the clipboard and says, "Class, we have visitors."

The two girls and the curly-haired boy look up at the newcomers, but the Hispanic boy acts like he hasn't heard, still focusing his attention on his car. "Pepe, I said we have company. Please put the car down and say hello," the teacher says. Turning to the Eduardo's group, she says, "Welcome! My name is Cheryl. Who are you two?"

"I am Eduardo Ibáñez, and this is my friend Shannie."

"You should let Shannie speak for herself, Eduardo," Cheryl chides. To the class, "Please tell Eduardo and Shannie who you are."

"My name is Evelyn," the white girl says, "but everybody calls me Eve."

The black girl says, "I'm Tabitha, but people call me Tabby. I'm pleased to meet you."

The curly-haired boy's voice is so soft it can barely be heard. "My name is Lex."

Pepe doesn't speak.

"Pepe, introduce yourself," Cheryl says.

"Why? You already told them who I am."

"Because I asked you to," Cheryl sighs.

"Okay, okay. I'm Pepe." He turns his attention back to his car.

Geraldine motions to Cheryl and leads her away from the kids to the far side of the room, then speaks to her in a low voice. Eduardo is unsure of what to do next, then decides he'd like a closer look at Pepe's car, so he goes over there, Shannie following.

Sister!

"That's a cool car," Eduardo says.

"Yeah, but don't you fucking touch it man, or I'll break your face."

Pepe is a head taller and older than Eduardo, but Eduardo bets that he's never killed a man before. "Don't be an asshole, *amigo*. I wasn't going to."

Pepe puts the car down very deliberately and turns to Eduardo, glaring into the smaller boy's eyes. "Did you just call me an asshole, *maricón*?"

Eduardo realizes he may have just bitten off more than he can chew, but it's too late to back down now. "No man," he says. "I said don't be one..."

Pepe jumps up from his seat and cocks a fist back, aiming straight at Eduardo's nose. Eduardo now wishes that Mamá Lupe had let him take those fighting lessons from Ye-ye.

"Pepe!" Geraldine's voice flies across the room like a bullet. "Stop it, now!"

The blood drains out of Pepe's face; he unclenches his fist and drops his arm to his side.

"Let Eduardo see your car. Give it to him!"

His expression a mix of fear and hatred, Pepe slowly picks up the car and hands it to Eduardo, who hesitates, then takes it from him. "Thanks, *amigo*." Pepe sits silently while Eduardo gives the car a cursory examination, then puts it down in front of the older boy again.

Cheryl comes back to the center of the room, reading from her clipboard. "So we're going to change the roommates around some. "Tabitha, you're now in with Eduardo, and Shannie is rooming with Pepe. Eve, you and Alex are still together." Eduardo shivers as he looks at Pepe. *What's going on here? Boys and girls rooming together?* Pepe, still white, gives Eduardo an evil little grin. "Don't worry, compadre, I'll take care of her for you."

"Don't hurt her, man," Eduardo says, and Pepe's grin gets wider.

"Okay, Tabby, Pepe, take your new roomies upstairs and get them settled," Cheryl says. "Eve and Lex, you've got the cooking duty tonight. Dinner is at six, so don't be late."

Tabby motions to Eduardo. "C'mon." She heads for a staircase in the far corner. Pepe and Shannie follow. On the second floor, Tabby takes Eduardo's hand and leads him toward an archway in the hall, while Pepe and Shannie continue on to the third floor. Eduardo looks back in time to see Shannie give him a fearful look, but Tabby exerts strong pressure to keep him moving along with her. "Don't worry," she says. "Pepe's really a nice dude. He won't hurt her."

76

They enter a vestibule with two closed doors on the far wall. Tabby points to the left one. "That's Eve's and Lex's room. This one's ours." She opens the door and Eduardo sees a spacious chamber, with a large open window, allowing the sweet scent from the flower beds below to permeate the room. Two bureaus stand against the left wall and a large wardrobe is on the right. A queen bed dominates the center of the room. There is a desk and chair on either side of the windows and a table in front of them.

Eduardo looks at Tabby with a confused expression. "Where's my bed?" he asks.

She smiles playfully. "Right there."

"Then where are you going to sleep?"

"With you, silly. Where else?" She points to a bureau. "That one's yours, and so is the desk next to it. They have Pepe's stuff in them right now. I'm going upstairs to help Shannie, and I'll send him down to clean them out for you." She leaves the room.

Eduardo doesn't know what to think. He slept with Shannie the last few nights, but that was different. They were friends. He doesn't know this girl at all. He knows a little bit about sex, though—he's seen pictures of men and women naked together in *Penthouse*, but he's not exactly sure of what they're doing together. Will Tabby want to have sex with him? Will she laugh at him if he doesn't know how?

He hears a noise and spins around to see Pepe advancing on him with blood in his eye. He puts up his fists in a defensive posture, but the older boy just keeps coming. Backing Eduardo up, so the mattress catches the back of his legs. A push from Pepe is all it takes to send him sprawling backwards on the bed.

"Tabby is mine, you little *capullo*! You touch her and I kill you."

Even in his fear, Eduardo wonders if Pepe ever did kill anyone. He remembers shooting that man who was going to hurt *Mamá* Lupe seeing the blood gush from his mouth after the bullets struck, and he's suddenly not afraid. He can feel his features hardening as he pushes himself up on his forearms and stares into Pepe's eyes. Pepe must see something there he does not like, because he lowers his hands and backs away from the smaller boy.

"I'll do what I want, *maricon*," Eduardo says. "Sure, maybe you can beat me up, but don't you ever turn your back to me. You have to sleep sometime."

"You just stay away from her!"

Sister!

Eduardo slides off the bed and stands up again. "Just get your shit and get out of here, *cabrón*. This is my room now." He smiles. "Mine and Tabby's."

Pepe looks like he wants to say something else, but then thinks better of it. He turns and picks the laundry bag he brought with him off the floor where he threw it when he came in, then goes to the bureau and begins stuffing clothes into it. Eduardo watches him silently. When he's finished with the bureau, Pepe goes to the wardrobe and removes some clothes on hangers, which he drapes over an arm. Finally, he removes some books and papers from the desk, which go into the bag as well. He picks it up and heads for the door.

"Remember what I told you, little man," he says.

"And you remember what I told you," replies Eduardo.

Chapter 18

My dreams are chaotic, violent and full of pain.

An incessant beeping overlies everything. My eyes snap open. My phone is on the nightstand, blinking.

I reach over and snatch it up, straining my eyes to see the time in the upper left-hand corner. 10:30! It was almost 5 am when I finally got to bed. As I struggle to break through the morning fog, I realize that I hurt all over—my head, my shoulders, my back, my ass... Last night's events come roaring back into my head like a tidal wave.

I pull up a local news site on my phone, looking to see if there's any mention of an assault on a man in the East Village. Nothing, which is unsurprising given the number of shootings, rapes and muggings that happen in the City each day. I never told Irwin where I'm staying, so I'm not too worried he'll track me down or sic the cops on me. He's probably in the hospital, suffering. Serves the motherfucker right!

I get out of bed and shuffle around the room, picking up clothes from the floor and pulling them on. I get a whiff of funk and realize that I can't wear those—what I need is a shower and some coffee. The free breakfast downstairs is long over, so my choices are a ten-dollar pot of room service coffee or breakfast at Wino's across the street. I opt for the latter.

Half an hour later, I'm on a stool in Wino's, wearing my spare clothes from my suitcase. I'm sure not up for a big breakfast today, so I nix the lox and bagels and order a pot of coffee and a bagel with a schmear. That's ten bucks too, but at least I get my bagel.

Last night, I decided that I was going to try and get in touch with the woman who gave birth to my twin—Abigail Dupont. There's a phone number in the records I copied at the clinic, so after inhaling some strong coffee, I steel myself and punch her number into my phone.

It rings four times, then clicks over to voicemail. A bright female voice says, "Hi! This is Abby. Sorry I missed your call, but..." Nope! I hang up and hit redial. "Hi, this is Abby..." Once more for good luck. Ring... ring... ring... A sleepy voice slurs, "Hello..."

"Hi! I'm trying to reach Abigail Dupont?"

The voice on the other end is suddenly awake, And angry! "Bella! Is that you? You have a helluva nerve calling here after all this time!"

Sister!

"No, this is not..." The line goes dead. Shit! I try redial again. "Hi, this is Abby..." I kill the call. No way she'll answer now. And who the fuck is Bella?

What am I gonna do? My flight home leaves at eight-thirty tonight—I wanted to give myself a whole extra day in the City to follow up leads. I could book another one for tomorrow, but tonight's ticket is non-refundable. I pull up a browser and search on Sag Harbor. It's out on Long Island, near the tip, about a hundred miles from here. One hell of an Uber ride, if I can even find anyone to take me. I could go out to the airport and rent a car, but that's really not in the budget either. Danny and Lupe are already pissed off enough about me coming up here—I don't need to spend the rent. I suddenly remember that my hotel has a concierge. Maybe they can tell me another way to get there.

I slurp down the rest of my coffee and bolt the bagel, then hurry back to the hotel. After a little time on her PC, the concierge tells me there's a bus from 86th Street and Lexington Avenue that'll cost me $100 for a round trip. A car rental from La Guardia will cost just a few dollars more, but then I'd have to cope with the traffic. I decide to leave it to the bus driver.

So a couple hours later, I'm cruising down the Long Island Expressway in a ginormous bus. It's half-empty, so I've got a double seat to myself. Looking out the window, all I see is scrub brush and stubby trees beyond a battered guardrail—I could be about anywhere in the U.S.A. and it would look the same. Sag Harbor is the end of the line, so I try to sleep, but that's a non-starter. The memory of Irwin holding me down and pounding my ass last night just won't get out of my head. How could I have been so fucking stupid? I actually expected a guy who would demand sex for helping me break into his employer's office to honor a deal? I realize that my skill with Tai Chi has actually made me reckless—now I just assume that I can handle a male attacker even if he's a good deal bigger than me, as most men are. I've learned a painful lesson. I'll never let another guy get me in a position like that again. But that realization does nothing at all for the shame and anger I feel right now.

I finally do nod off, but the intense, frenzied dreams return. I relive the rape over and over again, until I feel someone shaking me. My eyes pop open and I sweep the hand on my shoulder away.

A male voice hollers, "Owww!"

I'm looking into the face of sixtysomething dude, dressed in a sober brown suit and a red-and-silver striped tie. His expression is horrified—I realize I'm glaring at him with all of the considerable hate in my soul.

"I'm sorry, Miss," he apologizes, "but I felt I had to wake you. You must have been having a terrible dream."

I'm instantly sorry for lashing out at him. "That's all right, sir. I was. Thanks for caring."

His face relaxes and he smiles. "We're just coming into town," he says, and goes back to his seat.

I look out the window again. We're traveling down a two-lane road now, heavily forested on either side. Every so often I can see houses through a break in the trees—mostly one or two stories, white clapboard or cedar shingled, each one probably worth a mil or more. This is the Hamptons, a haven for Manhattan's rich from the huddled masses yearning to breathe free. The trees begin to thin out, and houses appear more frequently, then we're traveling through an actual neighborhood, and the passengers begin moving around in anticipation of arrival. The homes are larger and more well-kept, then we're in the village itself, all extra shops, and restaurants that I probably cannot even afford a hot dog in! The bus pulls into a traffic circle and turns around, and I catch a glimpse of a windmill outside, of all things. The air brakes hiss as we stop, the front door pops open and the driver announces, "Sag Harbor, end of the line."

In a couple of minutes I'm on the pavement. A tap on my shoulder makes me turn to see the old dude who woke me jumping back out of reach. Can't blame him. "You're sure you're OK, Miss?" he asks. "I was in 'Nam. I understand bad dreams."

"I'm totally Gucci now," I tell him. "But thanks again for waking me."

He tips his hat and walks out of my life.

I check my phone for Abigail Dupont's addy, touch it and bring up a map. I'm in luck—it's only a few blocks away, on Rector Street. I cross the square and hang a right on Bay, passing a bank and a bagel shop. There's a park across the street and a marina beyond, so I cross again to enjoy the scenery. A breeze blows in off the water, bringing with it the scents of salt and fish. It crosses my mind that I totally do not have to be doing what I'm doing—who the fuck cares who my real parents are? Sean and Judy McMasters have been good enough for twenty-four years. I have my degree now and some money. Me and Danny and Lupe could live in a place like this, away from the world, where nobody gets raped or killed. Open a little shop or something. Fuck me, who am I kidding? I can no more let go of this thing than I can cut off my right arm. I've got a sister out there, and she's murdered somebody. I have to find out why!

Rector Street is just a couple blocks further on, and the Dupont house is right on the corner. It's a cedar-shingled, two-story affair with a gabled roof sporting a couple of red brick chimneys, surrounded by a white picket fence with a neatly trimmed hedge behind it. America the beautiful for sure. I press down on the latch to open the gate and follow a walkway of crushed

81

oyster shells to the porch steps. At the top, a doorbell cam is mounted beside a closed wooden door. I reach to press the button, but before I can touch it, a hidden speaker squawks, "Shit! I don't believe it!"

A moment later the door is wrenched open by a fortysomething blonde in a pink robe hanging open, a skimpy nightie beneath. Waves of alcohol wash over me as she speaks, slurring her words, "What the hell, Bella? You think you can just show up here after all this time?"

"I'm not..." I begin, but she's getting ready to slam the door, so without any thought I step into *gong bu* and pivot on my hip, thrusting an open hand to intercept the closing door. I misjudge the energy, the door flies back, taking her with it, and she lands flat on her back.

"Ohmigod! I am so sorry!"

I step into the house, reaching down to help her up, but she angrily slaps my hand away. I didn't see the drink in a plastic cup she was holding hidden behind the door—it splattered all over her as she fell. Christ, the odor of alcohol is now almost overwhelming—it must have been pure vodka!

Still sitting on the floor, legs akimbo, she hollers, "Just get out! Go back to your goddamn sugar daddy! What is it? He's not paying your freight anymore? Are you strung out? Knocked up? There's nothing here for you, girly!" She crabwalks backwards into a living room, all white furniture and shiny glass.

I follow her, and try again. "Listen, Mrs. Dupont. I'm not your daughter. My name is Natalie McMasters. I'm Bella's sister."

The rage still burns in her eyes, but at least I've got her attention. "Bella doesn't have a sister," she says. "I should know, I'm her mother. What the hell are you playing at?"

"I'm not playing at anything. New Horizons implanted your embryos in other women. I'm Bella's twin."

Her face has transformed from a mask of fury to a mask of fear. Slowly getting to her feet, her robe has slid off her shoulders and slipped down behind her. The nightie does little to hide her nakedness. Her collarbone and her shoulder blades stand out starkly—maybe there's more wrong with her than just drunkenness. I don't think I'm going to get through to her when she's in this condition. "Is your husband home?" I ask. "Bella's father?"

She's on her feet now, and the anger is back full force. "Dad's gone. Heart attack last year. Worried himself to death lookin' for you. I'd a told you if I coulda found you. Why the hell did you have to run off with that guy? I told you I was working on my drinking..."

Oh shit, we're back to I'm Bella again. I have to give it one more try. "Mrs. Dupont. Abigail. I... am... not... Bella. I'm Natalie. Natalie McMasters."

"Yeah, it just killed your dad when you ran off." She says like she never even heard me. She looks at me now with real venom in her eyes. "I know what you and him were doing!"

Shit! Now I'm hearing more than I want to. And is it even true?

"What the fuck do you want from me?" she screams.

I open my mouth to answer her, then suddenly realize that's a damn good question. Do I even know what I want from her? I guess I wanted to know about my sister, the kind of person she was, maybe see pictures when she was a kid. Try to form some connection. The shape her mother's in, that ain't gonna happen. My mind flashes back to a picture I saw of Becca, my other sister. Dead. Murdered. Cut to pieces by a crazed killer. I shake my head to get the image out of my mind.

It's obvious that this wreck of a woman has no idea where her daughter is now. I think I've gotten all I'm going to get.

Mrs. Dupont is looking around frantically now—her eyes light on a heavy crystal ashtray on an end table. She snatches it up and her arm rears back. Jesus, that motherfucker will split my head open if it hits! I scuttle backwards as she lets fly, and it smashes to a jillion pieces on the door frame, a few flying shards stinging my face.

"Get out, get out, get out, GET OUT!"

Fuck me, now she's going for a vase! I turn and bolt for the door, jumping down the short flight of stairs on the porch rather than taking them one at a time. The vase comes sailing out the door after me, smashing into smithereens. My feet hit the oyster shells and I slide like they're ball bearings—I go down on my ass and the shells cut the fuck out of my hands and forearms.

Several hours later, I buckle my seat belt on the flight home, then pick a few more oyster shells out of my skin. I checked my voicemail in the bus earlier, and saw that I had several from Lupe that I didn't even bother to listen to. But there was one from Danny, too.

"Hey Nattie, it's me. Just wanted you to know that I think I know where Eddie is. Probably going to pick him up tomorrow. But I still need you here as fast as you can make it. Lupe is going ballistic. I love you."

Love you too.

Chapter 19

Danny, Leon, and M.B. pile into Danny's truck and drive back to the homeless camp.

Danny is glad that M.B. is a small woman, because his truck does not have a back seat. The Marine could tell that Amos was not thrilled about M.B.'s decision to accompany him and Leon, but if they're going to be married, he'll just have to get used to the fact that he can't keep an active FBI agent on a leash.

"What's your plan, Danny?" M.B. asks.

"Simple," Danny replies. "We just go through the place, looking for any sign of the kids. If we don't find any, we put the screws on Thurmond again."

"If he has done something to them, it will be hard to make him talk," Leon says.

"Oh, he'll talk," says Danny. M.B. shudders visibly at his tone.

"Remember, I'm law enforcement. I can't let you..."

"Then stay in the pickup," Danny snaps. "Or I'll stop and put you out right here."

Everyone is silent for a moment. "Just don't do anything I'll have to arrest you for," M.B. says.

Danny doesn't answer. They ride for another five minutes and come to the turnoff. Danny swings the truck onto the dirt road and it jolts as it hits a pothole, They wind down into the hollow where the camp is.

"I mean it, M.B., If you're going to interfere, stay in the truck," says Danny. "I promise I won't kill him."

"And you can't testify to what you don't see," Leon says grimly.

They go around the last curve and arrive in the camp. There's a crowd here now—everybody is in a line near the firepit, facing Thurmond. One man hands the big guy a sheaf of bills, then steps aside for the next in line to take his place.

"Looks like he's getting the day's take," Danny says.

The big man looks at the truck, then reaches behind himself and comes up with a dark object in both hands.

"Gun!" hollers Danny, slamming on the brakes.

The gun cracks and the windshield explodes, showering the three detectives with tiny pieces of tempered glass. Danny throws the truck into reverse, spinning the tires while backing it up the road into the woods. "Anybody hit?" he yells, taking stock of his companions. Thankfully, he doesn't see any blood.

"Clear!" both of them yell, and Danny's heart retreats from his throat.

Throwing open his door, Danny says, "Fucker did not have that gun when I was here before." Then he remembers Thurmond rooting around in the brush, and realizes what he was looking for. He draws his 1911, saying, "Leon, go right. M.B. left." He bends low and heads straight down the road, knowing his well-trained companions will have his six.

When the camp comes into Danny's line of sight, not a person is to be seen. Likely all of them have disappeared into the woods. Thurmond's shed is front and center, but Danny has no idea if he's in there or not. Automatically, he employs BAMCIS. There's zero cover other than some long grass between Danny and the shed, which has got to be twenty yards away. He has no desire to belly crawl that distance. The smart thing to do would be to send Leon and M.B. around through the woods on the flanks, meeting at the shed in the middle. But he has no idea if anyone else besides Thurmond is armed—he doesn't want to send his companions into an unknown situation. He could lay covering fire into the shed from this position, but he doesn't want to injure unarmed civilians.

Danny's best estimate of the situation is that Thurmond has the only gun, and he's likely holed up in the shed. He raises his voice. "Thurmond! Here's your situation. It's three against one, and we're all armed. You don't stand a chance! Throw out your gun, stand down, and we won't hurt you. All I want is to search the camp and verify that the kids are not here. Let us do that and we'll leave you in peace."

Thurmond's answer comes in the form of a round fired from the doorway of the shed, which comes nowhere near Danny.

Danny holds an expert ranking from the USMC in both pistol and rifle. Sighting carefully, He returns the fire with a double tap at the area where he saw the muzzle flash. He's rewarded with a scream.

Ready to drop to the ground in an instant, Danny shows himself in the LOS to the shed. There's no return fire. He puts his head down and runs a serpentine pattern toward the building, knowing that Leon and M.B. have their weapons trained on the open door. He reaches his objective with no further resistance. Looking inside, he sees Thurmond lying on the floor. He runs in and uses two fingers to check for a carotid pulse. Nada.

Sister!

"Clear!" Danny bellows, signaling his companions to advance. Dammit! He's killed before, many times, but it never gets any easier. Why didn't the idiot just throw out his gun? He flips Thurmond over, and looks grimly at the two round holes in the center of his chest. There are no exit wounds in his back, because Danny keeps hollow point defense ammo in his pistol, specially designed to remain inside the target's body.

M.B. comes up and makes a ticking sound with her lips. Pulling out her cell phone, she says. "I'll have to call the local LEOs on this. Shit. No service."

Danny flips her his fob. "There's service up at the main road. Go do what you have to, and Leon and me will search the camp for traces of the kids."

M.B. takes off and Danny and Leon begin going through the tents and hovels. They find a few of the camp's residents hiding and ask about the kids, always getting the same answer—"They's here this mornin' when I left, but I ain't seed 'em since I been back." One fellow points out Shannie's tent and the two detectives give it a thorough going over, but find nothing inside except a sleeping bag.

"Thurmond must've been telling me the truth," Danny says. "Why did the idiot have to shoot at us?"

"Likely he was afraid of losing face in front of the others," Leon says. "So he lost his life instead."

In ten minutes, M.B. is back, followed closely by the CCPD in a brand-new Land Rover Defender, customized as a police vehicle. M.B. briefs the two uniformed officers, Adams and Stevenson, on what went down.

"What is the FBI's involvement in this, Ma'am," asks Adams, a stocky blond woman in her 30s.

"None, right now" M.B. replies. "I was accompanying these two P.I.'s as a civilian, because we had information that Mr. Merkel's missing son may have been at this location. The decedent, Mr. Jordan, chose to open fire on us and we defended ourselves."

"Who shot Mr. Jordan?" asks Stevenson, a fiftysomething black man.

"I did," says Danny.

"We'll have to take your weapon," says Adams.

Danny raises his hands and says, "Go ahead. It's holstered on my right hip. And I have a backup on my right ankle." He knows better to put his hands on a loaded gun in the presence of a police officer.

Adams removes Danny's 1911 from his holster, drops the mag and racks the slide to eject the round in the chamber, then takes the .357 revolver from the ankle holster.

"I trust you and Lieutenant Kidd are armed as well?" asks Stevenson.

"Not Lieutenant anymore, Randy," says Leon. "I've got a new job now." Leon obviously knows Stevenson from his time on the CCPD. "But yes, I'm carrying."

"And so am I," says M.B.

"We'll have to take all of your weapons until we've established which ones were involved in the incident," says Adams. "We'll take your statements, but we'll have to get homicide involved in this too."

"I know it," says Danny, mentally rolling his eyes. There goes the rest of the afternoon, and part of the evening as well.

The homicide detectives and the CSIs arrive shortly thereafter. One of the detectives is Julia Sykes, the one who arrested Nattie the other day. The group goes into action like a well-oiled machine, establishing the crime scene, taking pictures and collecting evidence, while Sykes and her partner Albert Jonas get statements from Danny, Leon and M.B., as well as all of the homeless people that they can find. The sun is setting by the time they release the 3M detectives and M.B. to go home. Sykes says to Danny, "Wow. Two times in one week I get to deal with you guys." Danny opens his mouth to retort, but she cuts him off. "Actually, this looks pretty open and shut. We shouldn't have to talk to you anymore, but please keep yourself available until we give you the all clear. You can get your weapons back as soon as ballistics is done with them, probably in a week or so."

"One more thing," says Danny. "It's pretty likely that my son Eduardo is a guest at Mr. Jay Ellis's place, but for some reason, no one there is willing to say so. His mother is very worried, and we'd like to get him home ASAP. Could you send someone out there to take care of that?"

"I'll report it, and we'll see what we can do," says Sykes.

Night has fallen by the time that the three get back to Hyacinth House. Danny was hoping that he would have a chance to talk to someone at Ellis's place before seeing Lupe, but she must've been watching for them out the window, because she comes running out just as they pull up in front of the garage,

"Have you heard anything?" she says. Danny notices a frantic tone in her voice.

"We think we might have found him, hon. We're just waiting for the cops to confirm it."

Sister!

"The cops? What's wrong? Is he hurt or something?"

Danny holds his hands in front of him like a football ref. "As far as we know, he's fine. Let me get inside and I'll call and see where they are with it." When he gets to the living room, he pulls out his cell phone and punches in the well-remembered number for CCPD headquarters. In a couple of minutes he's got Sykes on the line.

"Ellis's people tell us they haven't seen him," Sykes says.

"What! That cannot be! I traced the Range Rover that picked up the kids at the homeless camp to Ellis. Eddie has to be there!"

"I don't know what to tell you, Mr. Merkel," Sykes says.

"Send somebody over there to look for him.

"No can do. In case you haven't heard, Jay Ellis is like royalty at CCPD. If his people say your kid's not there, he's not there."

As he kills the call, Lupe is sitting across from Danny with an expectant look. "Well?"

Danny hesitates and Lupe's face falls as she anticipates what he's going to say. "The cops say that Eddie isn't where we thought. We'll just have to keep looking."

"Nooooo!"

Danny rises to go his wife, when he hears the front door chime because somebody has opened it. He and Lupe look to the archway and see Nattie standing there, trailing her rolling suitcase behind her.

"Hey, y'all! Have you found Eduardo yet?"

Chapter 20

Eduardo sits next to Tabby in the dining room, at a long rectangular table draped with a starched white cloth, a gold-rimmed soup bowl on a matching plate in front of him.

A large, clear glass tumbler stands next to the soup bowl, and metal pitchers dripping with condensation alongside matte black covered ice buckets sit in the middle of the table, available to the diners on either side.

Double doors on the far end of the room swing open, and a whiff of garlic precedes the entry of Eve and Lex, each bearing trays holding huge platters of spaghetti and meatballs, bowls of salad and baskets of bread. They split up, each walking down one side of the table, depositing the food next to the eager diners, before placing their trays on stands and taking their places at the foot of the table. Tabby smiles at Eduardo, picks up a platter of spaghetti and meatballs and holds it so he can serve himself.

"Not so fast," says Cheryl from the head of the table. "Let's say grace first. Tabby, you lead us."

Eduardo suspects that this is Cheryl's way of chiding Tabby for being too quick to go for the food. Tabby clears her throat and says, "Let us pray." After everyone has folded their hands and bowed their head, she continues, "Lord, we are gathered here this evening to share this food in your honor. Thank you so much for bringing us together as a family. We thank you for all of the gifts you've given us. Help each of us to use them to your glory. Bless this food to our bodies, and bless the hands that prepared it. We pray this in Jesus's name, Amen."

"Amen," the group intones.

Now the food is served and Eduardo finds it amazingly good. *Mámá* Lupe cooks Mexican food exclusively, and Miss M.B. specializes in Southern fare, so spaghetti and meatballs is not something Eduardo gets to enjoy very often. There's enough for seconds and even thirds—by the time he's finished, he feels like he's going to pop. Then Eve and Lex pick up their trays again, clear the plates and take them into the kitchen, returning with a plate of strawberry shortcake for all. Eduardo steels himself, plucks the bright red cherry off the snowy mound of whipped cream, and goes to town. Now he really can't eat anything else. He still can't believe his luck in finding this wonderful new home!

After the plates are cleared a second time, Cheryl taps her glass with a pen for attention. "Tonight is movie night," she says. "We've chosen a special one for you, about a group of girls who decide to start a business, like you are about to do." She picks up a remote and pushes a button, and a portal in the wall slides silently open to reveal a giant flat-screen TV—Eduardo has never seen one that big! Cheryl plays with the remote again and the lights dim. Eduardo hopes the movie is exciting, because he will surely go to sleep if it isn't, especially after all that food. The screen flickers and music begins playing—it's a rousing march performed by what sounds like a high school band. A football game appears on the screen. Hmmm. Eduardo has not seen this one before.

The boys on screen run a few plays while the girls cheer them on. Then the scene quickly shifts to the cheerleaders' locker room. In a minute, the girls are taking off their clothes and heading for the shower. So far, Eduardo isn't seeing anything he hasn't seen before. The bad man who he killed made his *abulea* and *Mama* Lupe take off their clothes in front of him, and they were very sad and embarrassed that they had to do it. Satisfaction surges through him again. He is very glad that he shot that man.

A group of football players come into the shower with the girls, and everyone begins having sex. At least that's what Eduardo thinks they are doing—he has never seen anything like this! The movie shows everything in close up detail, so now Eduardo knows what people having sex really do. He feels a vague stirring in his loins, like he does when he plays with himself, but it quickly goes away.

As the sex goes on and on, Eduardo begins to rapidly lose interest and starts getting sleepy again. But he notices that Tabby's eyes are riveted to the screen. She briefly turns her head, licks her lips and smiles at him, then takes his hand with her right one while her left creeps down below her waist and under her skirt.

The rest of the movie is sex scene after sex scene, and Eduardo struggles mightily to stay awake. Tabby seems fascinated by it, and he doesn't want to her to think he's not, too.

His gaze shifts across the table to where Pepe and Shannie sit. Like Tabby, Pepe's attention is fixed on the screen, and he's holding Shannie's hand. He turns and gives Shannie a smile that Eduardo definitely doesn't like—it's a lot like the one the bad man had when he looked at *Mamá* Lupe and *Abuela*. Shannie smiles back at Pepe and Eduardo suddenly wants to kill him.

Finally, the last scene featuring a blonde girl who looks a lot like Mama Nattie having sex with a much older man, is over, and the credits roll. Cheryl clicks the button on the remote and the screen goes black.

"Well, I hope y'all enjoyed that," she says "I know I did. Now we're going to send y'all up to bed, so you can talk about what you've learned. Good night, everyone!"

The room fills with the buzz of conversation and the sounds of chair legs scraping the floor. It seems like Tabby can hardly wait to get out of here. Eduardo is filled with great anxiety —he's not sure if it's because he knows what Tabby is going to want to do upstairs, or because Pepe is going to do it with Shannie. He feels helpless—he knows what will happen if he tries to start a brawl with Pepe. Besides, Shannie looks like she's eager to go with the older boy, which makes Eduardo sad.

Tabby reaches out and takes Eduardo's hand. "C'mon," she says. "Let's go to our room. I have a lot to show you."

He takes one last look at Pepe and Shannie disappearing up the stairs, his throat tightens as the sadness wells up. Then he thinks: *This is not how a real man should feel.* He lets Tabby lead him upstairs.

When they arrive in their room. Tabby leads him over to the bed, then lets go of his hand to go and shut the door. When she turns back to him, Eduardo says, "So, are we going to do those things now?"

She smiles shyly at him. "Is that what you want?"

"I guess so."

She crosses her arms and reaches down to grab the bottom of her t-shirt, pulling it up a little so he can see her bare belly. "Have you ever seen a naked girl before?" she asks.

"No," he fibs, then he thinks that maybe he's not lying at that. *Mamá* and *Abuela* are ladies, not girls. He's not about to tell Tabby about that.

Tabby pulls her shirt off. All Eduardo can think is, *she looks more like a boy than the girls in the movie,* but wisely doesn't say so. Tabby asks, "Would you like to touch them?"

"OK." He steps toward her and touches her, and she closes her eyes and raises her chin. *It feels just like any other part of her,* he thinks.

"Let's take all our clothes off," she says, fumbling with the snap on her pants. Eduardo does the same, and before long the two of them are staring at each other.

Now what? Eduardo thinks.

Tabby tuns down the bed sheet. "C'mon," she says. Let's do what they did in the movie."

Eduardo replies, "I don't think I can."

"I'll fix that," Tabby says, sitting on the bed and pulling him toward her. She starts rubbing him and it feels good. She begins kissing him all over and the good feeling intensifies. She stops then and lies back, saying, "Hey, this is not fair. You do me and I'll do you, like they did in the movie."

Sister!

He's never kissed a girl there before. Actually, he thinks it's kind of gross, but the people in the movie sure didn't think so. He decides if she's willing, so is he. After a few minutes, he feels a lot of pressure, like he has to pee. "You better stop," he says.

"I think you're ready," she replies. "C'mon!" She grabs his shoulder and pulls him on top of her, then everything is suddenly wet. Oh no! Did I pee on her?

"Damnit!" she says, pushing him off her.

"I couldn't help it," he says plaintively.

"I know," she replies, but now it's my turn." She kneels above his face and offers herself to him.

Eventually, she squeaks and shudders. Afraid, he stops. "Did I hurt you? I'm sorry!"

"No, silly! Didn't you hear the girls in the movie scream when they came?" She smiles and lies next to him, giving him a kiss on the mouth.

The two of them snuggle together, and Tabby goes right to sleep. Eduardo tries, but he feels like something's not right. He kinda liked what they did together, so it's not that.

Shannie and Pepe are probably doing the same things me and Tabby did.

That makes him mad. Did she even like it? He slides his arm out from under Tabby's head. She doesn't even notice—she turns onto her side away from him, snoring blissfully.

Eduardo pulls on his jeans and his t-shirt. He's not exactly sure what he's going to do, but he knows that he has to go up to Shannie's and Pepe's room and find out what's going on. Maybe he can listen at the door or something. He opens his bedroom door and the light from the hallway streams in. He partly shuts it again so the light doesn't touch the bed where Tabby is sleeping—he has no desire to wake her up and having to explain where he's going. He slides out into the hallway and softly closes the door behind him, then moves slowly toward the stairs at the end of the hall.

As he nears the stairs, he realizes that someone is coming up. He looks behind him, but there's no place to hide in the hallway. It's too late to run back to his room! He puts his back against the wall and flattens himself, hoping the person will just keep going without seeing him.

A woman's blonde head comes into view, then her shoulders. As she reaches the top of the stairs, she turns and looks right at Eduardo.

"*Mamá* Nattie! What are you doing here?"

Chapter 21

I'**m in my bedroom unpacking my suitcase when there's a knock on the door.**

I want to ignore it—it's Danny. I know his knock, and I totally don't want to talk to him right now. But he'll see the light under the door and he won't quit knocking until I answer. Marines are like that.

"What do you want?"

"Can I come in?"

You've got to love him. He's my husband, and still he asks. I'm naked— the only reason that I'm fucking with the suitcase is that I wanted a t-shirt out of it to sleep in. I grab a long-sleeved one and pull it over my head so he won't see the scratches on my arms. The bottom comes to a little above my knees.

"Come in."

The door opens and he's there, looking slightly pissed. I came up here because he and Lupe immediately started to get on my case about leaving when Eduardo was missing. Of course, I'm way ratchet that he's still not home, but I'm also tired AF, and what can I do about it at ten o'clock at night? I didn't get a chance to tell anyone about what I found out at the fertility clinic, which is fine, because I'm not totally sure about what I want to do about it yet.

"I just wanted to say I'm sorry if I gave you a hard time downstairs," Danny says. "Lupe's real upset that you chose to go away while Eddie was gone."

"I know that, Danny, and I'm sorry. I just didn't think there was much I could do. Y'all had it covered. And this thing in New York was way important to me."

"Well, there's nobody that can keep Lupe calm like you can."

"I hate to say it, but sometimes the best thing you can do for her is let her stress and wear herself out."

He frowns at that, hesitates a beat, then says, "I think I know where Eddie is."

"What! Where? Why don't we go and get him?"

"I think he's at Jay Ellis's estate, or at least he was. You remember. The moneybags who spoke at your graduation."

Sister!

"Why would he have Eduardo?"

"I'm not completely sure, but I think he's running some kind of anonymous charity where he picks up street kids and tries to improve their lot. I traced Eddie to a homeless camp not far from here, and found out he was taken out of there by a car that came from Ellis's estate."

"So why don't we go and get him?" I ask again

"I tried—the place is an armed camp—and they wouldn't let me in. I asked if they had Eddie, but they denied it."

"That doesn't make any sense," I say. I flip the lid of the suitcase closed and take it off the bed, then turn my back to Danny and reach up to put in it on the top shelf in the closet. Natch, my t-shirt rides up in back when I do so.

"Hey, what happened to you?" Danny says. I drop my arms and my shirt goes back down. Danny steps up and pulls it up in back again. "Are those bruises?"

Shit shit, shit shit, shit shit, shit! I 'm so tired that I forgot that Irwin had bruised me when he raped me. There's only one way I can explain fingerprints on my hips.

I look him square in the eyes. "Yes. I kinda fucked this dude while I was in New York."

Danny's jaw drops and his eyes go wide. This is not good, people! "What do you mean, you kinda fucked some dude? Who? Why?"

I want to tell him nunya business, but I don't. We never really talked about whether the throuple was open or closed as far as sex was concerned—it just never came up. Me and Lupe got plenty of guys off when we worked at the strip club, but I never mentioned that to Danny 'cause I didn't think it was any of his business. I never asked Danny about who he had slept with before me and Lupe, either. To me, what I did with Irwin was like what I did in the strip club—just a means to an end. Except that it turned out bad.

I explain to Danny how I needed to get a look at the records in the clinic. I can tell from his face that he's not getting it.

"Wow," he says. "So, you just screwed some random dude because you needed something from him.?"

"That's about right," I tell him.

"Didn't you even think about how I or Lupe might have felt about that?"

94

Suddenly I'm big mad. What gives him the right to question me like this? I say, "No, I didn't. Lupe wouldn't care, anyhow. And it really ain't your business."

"Not my business?" Danny is incredulous. "Even though the state doesn't think so, we're married. We even had a ceremony, with vows and everything. Doesn't that make it my business?"

"As I recall, those vows didn't say anything about who can have sex with who. They just said that we all agree to love and honor each other."

"Did you think you were honoring us when you were screwing some guy we don't even know?"

He totally doesn't get it. I knew that Danny was way basic, but I didn't think he was this deadass headass.

"C'mon Danny, it's just sex—it totally doesn't mean anything."

"I hope you used protection," he says.

WTF! Now he's totally got me hella salty. I was just about to tell him about what I found out at the clinic, but that's so not happening now. Instead, I clap back with a low blow. "Did you ever think about how Lupe might have felt if she found out you fucked me in New York City when she was missing that time? I told you I was still married to her even though she wasn't around, but you screwed me anyway."

His face goes white as an icicle and just as stiff. "That was different." he finally says.

"Why? Because you were horny and I was available? You fucking guys are all alike. You want something, you just fucking go for it. But if a woman does the same thing..."

Now his face is an iron mask. "You're right," he says. "I shouldn't have had sex with you that time. You were a married woman. I guess I'll have to apologize to Lupe after Eddie gets back. But are you going to apologize to the two of us?"

"That ain't it, chief! I did what I had to do, to get what I needed. You just need to get over it."

And I fucking paid for it, too, but I'm not going to tell you about that! Knowing Danny, he'd fly up there and kick Irwin's ass again.

"Why don't you just get the fuck out of here and let me get some sleep?"

He turns on his heel and leaves without another word.

Sister!

I cut off the lights and get into bed, but sleep won't come. My ass still hurts from what Irwin did. When I close my eyes, that feeling of utter helplessness washes over me again. I unexpectedly find myself shaking and crying, and I bury my face into my pillow to stifle the sound. I know that I need to talk to someone about what happened, and that person is Lupe. She's survived multiple rapes—I'm sure she can help me deal. But that ain't gonna happen as long as Eduardo's missing.

I know what I have to do. I'll take care of it tomorrow.

Chapter 22

Eduardo is staring at the woman at the top of the stairs.

In the low light, he can see that it's *Mamá* Nattie, but he's never seen her in an outfit like this before. She's wearing a tight, white dress with a low collar so you can almost see her titties, and a short skirt, like some of the cheerleaders in the movie wore. And she's got her long blonde hair up in a bun on top of her head—something else he's never seen *Mamá* Nattie do. As she approaches him, his nose wrinkles. She smells like his *mamás* do after a Tai Chi session, and there's a sweet perfumy undertone too.

She looks at him oddly. "Who are you, little man?" she asks. "Are you new here?"

It's *Mamá Nattie's* voice, but different, somehow. And she doesn't know him?

"I'm Eduardo. You are not my *mamá!* Who are you?"

"I'm Bella. I'm your nanny, Eduardo. Why would you think I'm your mama?"

"You look like her. But you don't look like a goat."

But you smell like one.

She wrinkles her brow, then she smiles as the light comes on. "I'm not that kind of nanny. I'm the one who is going to take care of you while you're here, like a mama does."

"I thought that was Cheryl."

"Oh, no!" Bella says. "Cheryl is just a high school student who was watching you guys while I was with Mister Jay this afternoon." She assumes a stern expression. "Now, what are you doing out of bed at this time of night, mister?"

Eduardo knows he can't tell her what he's really up to. He falls back on the old standby. "I was looking for the potty."

"Why didn't you ask your roomie?" She extends an arm and points behind him. "It's at the end of the hall."

"I didn't want to wake her," he lies. "Who is Mister Jay?"

"He's our Daddy," Bella says. "You'll prolly meet him tomorrow. Now go potty and then go to bed. I'll wait for you."

Sister!

Danny is my Daddy, Eduardo thinks, but he doesn't say so. He doesn't like this Bella. She looks like *Mamá Nattie,* but she sure doesn't act like her.

He finds the potty but he can't go, of course. He hopes that this Bella doesn't come in and check to see what he did like *Mama Lupe* does sometimes. He waits long enough so she'll think he's finished, then flushes and washes his hands, like *Mama Lupe* taught him.

Bella is there waiting for him when he comes out. "Who's your roomie?" she asks.

"Tabby."

"OK. I guess neither she nor Cheryl told you about the buddy system. While you're here, you don't go anywhere without your buddy. That's Tabby. Now get back to bed, mister. I don't want to see you again until breakfast. OK?"

"*Si, Senorá.*"

Bella comes into his bedroom with him and watches as he climbs back into bed with Tabby, who is still sleeping. After he's tucked in, she bends over and gives him a kiss on the forehead. Again, he crinkles his nose at her strong scent. She closes the door softly as she leaves.

Eduardo can't sleep—he's confused about this strange woman who looks like his *mamá* and he's still worried about Shannie up there with Pepe. But he figures that by now, they've prolly done what they were gonna do and are sleeping like everybody else. He'll talk to that Pepe in the morning and let him know what will happen if he hurts Shannie.

After a long while, Eduardo finally enters a land of troubled dreams.

Chapter 23

I slept like shit last night—the fight with Danny totally got the adrenalin pumping so I must have lain awake for at least an hour after he left, and when I did finally nod off, I continually woke up because of rape dreams.

I grab my phone from the nightstand and hit the button to see the time. 7:00. Shit. That's only about five hours of sleep.

I totally need to fix things with Danny. I should have never burned him about our sex in New York. I know that the dude loves me, and that he honestly thought that Lupe was gone for good and I just wouldn't accept it. He also just doesn't get the difference between making love and plain old sex. Sex is like breathing—it's just something you do. Lupe gets that. I need to get her back on my side to help me explain that to Danny. I'll need their help to figure out this thing about my parentage, too.

The smell of coffee creeps into the room. More shit! M.B. is prolly up. I was hoping to get out of here without running into anyone this morning. The last thing I need is somebody second-guessing my plan. I do need a cup of coffee though, so I guess I'll have to face her.

I put on my blue and red tie dye Pantera t-shirt that was a present from Danny (in case I see him) and my distressed jeans, then head downstairs. M.B.'s at the kitchen table when I come in, wearing a fuzzy red bathrobe and a towel around her head, both hands wrapped around a giant mug of coffee with that cartoon old lady Maxine on the front of it. She gives me the look, so I know she's got something on her mind. I'm sure she'll tell me what it is. She's that way.

"Couldn't help overhearing your little spat with Danny last night," she opens. "Want to talk about it?"

Easy, Nattie. Don't diss her. "Not really. We'll work it out." I grab a mug from the cabinet above the coffee machine and fill it, leaving about an inch of coffee in the pot. I take a swig. The hot, bitter black liquid burns a path to my belly and tingles run along my nerves.

I turn to go back up to my room, but M.B. shoves her cup toward me, saying "Why don't you top me off and make another pot?"

I'll look like a total asswipe if I don't do what she says. I pour what's left in the pot into her mug, then put it on the counter and open the cabinet to get a filter.

Sister!

"Danny is a real good guy," M.B. says. "You're lucky to have him in your life."

I can feel the anger growing inside me, like hot, red lava under a volcano. Please don't let me let it out! "I know that, M.B."

"And he's got traditional morals, you know. It's hard for him to be in this marriage."

"I get that too." I turn the knob on the grinder to three, to grind the right amount of beans.

"I'm really not trying to get all up in your business, but..."

"Then don't, M.B. I've got it handled. I was wrong last night, and I'm going to apologize to him." I fill the coffee pot with water at the sink.

"Sometimes an apology is not enough?" she says.

"Sure. He loves me. He'll get over it." I pour the ground coffee into the filter and slide it into the machine, then pour the water in the top.

She stares at me quietly for a few seconds—it's like she's looking straight inside me, and not liking what she sees. "Mark my words. One day you'll do something he won't be able to get over. Then what will you do?"

I put the pot where it goes and hit the Brew button. The machine starts gurgling as it works its magic.

Picking up my mug, I say, "I'll deal with that if and when it happens." I pause, then, "Look M.B., I know you're about to become part of the fam, and you mean well. But I know my husband way better than you do. I'll handle this." I turn my back and walk out.

Later, in the Jeep, I check out Google Maps on my nav system and find Ellis's compound about ten minutes away on the lake. There's a wall all the way around it except along the lakeshore. I'm gonna drive out there and demand that they let me in or bring Eduardo out. If they won't, I'll raise a stink that will make them call the cops, then holler kidnapping when they get there. If the cops won't help, I'll call the TV stations. I'll even call my friend Roderigo Hernandez, the New York shock jock, if I have to. One way or another, I'm getting my son out of there.

The road turns right and I'm next to a wall of grey stone blocks. The place is huge—it takes at least a half a minute to get to the end of the wall where the road turns left. There's a red-striped moveable barrier with a little cinder block guard shack next to it. I steel myself mentally for a fight, then pull up to the guardpost.

The guy inside is wearing a black uni with a beret, and he's got a nasty, short auto pistol with a banana clip slung over one shoulder. I guess you need that kind of firepower when you're guarding someone worth a few bil. He looks up at me, and a surprised expression appears on his face. He gives me a thumbs up, plays with a panel in front of him and the barrier raises. He smiles as he waves me through.

I do not know WTF just happened, but I know better than to look a gift horse in the mouth. I take my foot off the brake and go through the gate before he changes his mind. I drive down an asphalt road with stately oaks equally-spaced on either side and green lawns beyond—it's like a Downton Abbey ep. I come to a fork and a large black helicopter looms in front of me and there's a large, pink mansion with a brown slate roof further on.

That looks like where I'll find the boss man.

I drive past the helipad and onto an elliptical driveway surrounding a reflecting pool in front of the house. There's a garage to one side and a matched pair of Range Rovers is visible through the open doors. I pull up before an ivory staircase leading up to a massive set of double doors. Cutting off the Jeep, I jump out, ascend the steps and hunt for a doorbell. There isn't one, but there is a camera mounted beneath a balcony above the doors. I suspect that someone might show up in a minute, but I don't wait. I try one of the doors, and it's not locked, so I just open it and go inside. I stop in my tracks and just stand there dumbstruck.

I'm in a gleaming white foyer. A double staircase of white marble with black veins is twenty feet in front of me—a black runner in the middle of the stairs leads up to a gold-bannistered balcony. The faint aroma of coffee, bread and bacon comes from an immense dining room to my right, and there's an equally large sitting room to my left—neither chamber is occupied.

I walk through a passageway between the staircases into an even larger great room lit by sunlight streaming in through a glassed-in greenhouse at the back. A man and a woman are standing in the center of the room, probably forty feet away. Neither one notices my entrance. I hesitate, then steel myself and move forward. Some damn body is gonna tell me where my son is!

I pass between the stairs and under the balcony into the great room. To my left is an open kitchen where a white-clad chef is working, assisted by a black woman wearing a white dress. The man who's talking to the woman in the great room is wearing a white shirt and khaki pants, and has his back to me so he doesn't see me coming, but the woman he's talking to sure does. She's wearing a white blouse, a long, rainbow skirt and sandals with straps that come halfway up her calves. She gives me The Look over his shoulder. Touching the man lightly on the arm, she says, "Pardon me, Mr. President," and continues to glare at me. The dude turns so I can see his face and my jaw drops—that unruly thatch of grey hair, that boyish smile—the last time I saw him was on the evening news!

"It's all right. I think we've resolved the issue, Gerry," he says to the woman in his soft southern accent. He takes a step toward me, his arms extended. "So good to see you again, my dear," he says, taking my hand in both of his. A thrill goes through me as those blue eyes seem to stare into the very depths of my soul—I feel like the two of us are the only people in the room. He releases my hands and gives me that brilliant smile of his once again. A tingle starts in my belly and grows to a delicious warmth. He turns and. exits the great room thorough the foyer. I want to follow him, but I don't.

The woman called Gerry looks at me, annoyance clearly on her face. "Why aren't you taking care of the children?" she asks sharply with a slight British accent. I'm beginning to get a glimmer of what's going on here, but my expression must've given it away, because her features harden as she says, "You're not Bella. You're Natalie. How did you get in here?"

How the fuck does she even know my name?

"You have my son Eduardo here. I want him back."

The look on her face says she's not used to being spoken to like that. She glances at a table a few feet away—I follow her gaze and spy a little black, rectangular box with a speaker and a number pad, and a short antenna in back. An intercom! She reaches for it, but before she can touch it, I pull my Sig from my pocket and put the red dot of the laser on the table top. She looks at me, a hint of fear in her eyes.

"Uh-uhhh," I say. "You don't need to call anybody. Take me to my boy. Then the three of us will drive out of here. I'll let you out once we're through the gate and you'll never see me again in your life."

"I was going to call over to the children's home and have someone bring him," she says in a measured tone.

"Liar. You were gonna call for help. Let's just you and me take a ride over to where he is." I put the red dot in the center of her chest.

The tension goes out of her face. "You're not going to shoot me," she says.

"Wanna bet?"

"Yes. If you do, there'll be guards with Uzis in here in seconds, and they'll cut you to pieces. You'll never see that boy of yours again." She holds out her hand. "Give me the gun, then we'll talk about Eduardo. Or I can call the guards. Your choice."

"And she'll do it, too," says a male voice from behind me.

I wheel to see a man standing in the doorway to the foyer, with two young girls, one on either side of him. I've seen him before, at graduation. It's Jay Ellis!

Chapter 24

As usual, Danny is fully awake just after he opens his eyes.

Sorrow rushes over him like a tidal wave wiping a beach clean of everything but itself.

As far as he knows, this is the first time that Nattie has had sex outside the marriage, or it's the first time she's admitted it, anyhow. He struggles to remember the vows the three of them spoke then he opens his mouth, expelling air with an audible "Pah!" It really doesn't matter what was said that day. Marriage is all about commitment. It means that you put your spouse, or spouses, ahead of everyone else in the world, including yourself. It definitely does not include casual sex with anyone you happen to be attracted to at the moment.

Danny is also aware that Nattie and Lupe both have complicated sexual histories. Nattie began working in a strip club shortly after she and Danny made love for the first time, and Danny nearly ended their relationship because she took that job. The only reason he didn't was because he loved her, even then. He guessed that she was doing things at the club that he wouldn't approve of, so he didn't ask. And as far as Lupe is concerned, he knows she has been the victim of multiple rapes. He suspects that Nattie has been raped too, but again, he hasn't asked. He figures she'll tell him if she wants him to know, right?

Her accusation that he is a hypocrite and an adulterer really stung, possibly because it hit close to home. When they made love in New York, Lupe had deserted Nattie, vowing never to return, even telling Nattie not to look for her. Of course, Nattie didn't listen. But Danny thought that her marriage to Lupe was effectively over and that she'd come to her senses after banging her head against the wall long enough. He never actually considered that her head was hard enough to batter that wall down, and that she'd find Lupe and convince her to come back and remain as her wife. He knows better now.

Danny agreed to marry Nattie and Lupe in a symbolic ceremony because it was the only way he could have Nattie at all. But in the two years since the wedding, he has come to love Lupe too. He admires her courage and determination to make a better life for herself and Eduardo in a foreign land. An avowed lesbian, Lupe has agreed to three-way sex with Danny and Nattie—he is dimly aware of what she may be sacrificing to satisfy him, although he can never really know. But he does know that at least, he owes her an apology for what he did in New York. He made assumptions about her that he had no right to make.

Having made his decision, Danny rolls out of bed and puts on a white tank top and a pair of gym shorts with a USMC logo. He follows his nose down to the kitchen, where he finds Lupe with a cup of coffee.

She nods toward the stove, where a small sauce pan sits. "There is another cup in the pot," she says. She has made *café de olla*, the boiled, spiced coffee that is the national breakfast beverage of Mexico. As Danny retrieves a mug from the cupboard, she continues, "We are going to bring Eduardo home today, right?" She says it as a question, but Danny knows it's a statement.

"Yes," says Danny. "I am going to call out there, and if they won't talk to me or acknowledge that Eddie is there, I'm going to get Gary McDougall working and ask him to get a court order, then get the Sheriff to enforce it. We'll have our boy home by sundown." Gary McDougall is the family's attorney.

"Why will they not just let him go?"

"I don't know and I don't care," Danny answers. "Err, Lupe," he continues, "there's something else I'd like to talk to you about."

"What is it?"

Danny's always believed that the best way to broach any distasteful subject is to hit it head on. "Do you know that Nattie and I made love in New York City that time when the Albanians had you? I thought you had run away and didn't want to be married to Nattie anymore..."

"Oh yes. She told me all about that. I do not blame you. Besides, it doesn't matter now that you are my husband too."

Danny feels his throat closing and the tears welling. He turns his head so she will not see. Like many tough guys, he has a problem vocalizing his feelings, but right now, it's necessary. "You do know that I love you, right?"

"Of course, I do. And I love you too, my husband." She steps into his arms and stands on tiptoes to brush her lips against his.

A cough comes from behind the couple. It's M.B., coming inside from the garden.

"Am I interrupting something?"

"Not at all," replies Danny. "We were just talking about getting Eduardo out of Ellis's compound today." He goes on to tell M.B. about his idea to get the sheriff involved.

Sister!

"That's not a bad idea," says M.B. "The sheriff is autonomous, and actually has greater jurisdiction than the city cops do." She stops speaking and gets a worried look.

"What?" says Danny.

"I'll bet that Ellis has his hooks into the Sheriff's Department, too," M.B. answers. "Still, it can't hurt to try. If the Sheriff turns you down, maybe I can find a way to get the feds involved."

"You would do that?" asks Lupe.

"Sure," says M.B. "I'm practically family now."

After breakfast, Danny calls Gary McDougall. He explains the situation and asks the lawyer to secure a court order.

"How do you know that Mr. Ellis has Eduardo?" Gary asks. "And why don't you just call the cops?"

"Ellis has the cops in his pocket," Danny says. "They say I don't have any proof that Eduardo is there."

"Do you?"

Sighing inwardly, Danny tells the lawyer about the Range Rover, and how Thurmond sold the kids to the mysterious woman.

"So this Thurmond can corroborate your story."

"Not exactly. He's dead."

Gary's sigh is not inward—Danny hears it loud and clear over the phone. "Danny, I'm afraid that a judge is going to require the same level of probable cause that the police do before they're going to demand a search of a private citizen's residence, especially someone who's rich and powerful."

"Even if I bring the sheriff in on it?"

"The sheriff is subject to the same rules as the city cops As a former police officer, you should know this."

Danny does, but as a father, he was hoping that Gary could find a way around it. "So there's nothing we can do?"

"Perhaps we could bring a lawsuit, but that will have as much effect on a billionaire as a pinprick on an elephant. The thing to do is to get some tangible proof that he's holding Eduardo."

"That's pretty hard to do when he's got a private army guarding his estate."

"I don't know what to tell you," Gary says. "The fourth amendment makes a man secure in his home from unreasonable searches without probable cause. Call me back when you get some. Or better yet, just call the cops."

Danny kills the call and tells the ladies what the lawyer said.

"No!" Lupe explodes. "This cannot be! I come to United States so my son can be born here and be a citizen, and be safe from these things! This is just like the cartels in Mexico!" She dissolves into a paroxysm of tears and runs from the room.

Danny starts to follow her, but M.B. brings him up short. "Let her go," she says. "Other than bringing Eduardo back, there's not much you can say or do for her. Let me make a few phone calls. My agency is experienced in dealing with powerful people who think they're above the law. Maybe we can get you that probable cause. Meanwhile, why don't you go talk with your other wife? I had a little talk with her earlier and I think you might have some fence mendin' to do there. That is, if you want this marriage of yours to continue.'"

Danny's not happy that everyone seems to know his private business, but what's a guy to do? "She was the one in the wrong, M.B., not me."

"Maybe she was, but the question is, do you want to stay a family? It seems like all of you really need each other right now. Go talk to her."

Danny can't deny that she has a point. "Okay." He goes up to Nattie's room on the second floor and knocks on the door. No answer. He tries the doorknob. It's not locked, so he opens it. Nattie's room is its usual chaotic mess, but she's not there.

She must've gone out without telling me. Maybe she went to talk to Ye-ye.

The old man has become a mentor and a father figure to Nattie, so it makes sense she'd consult him if she's upset.

Shortly after they were married, Danny, Nattie and Lupe decided to install tracking apps on their phones and make them accessible to the others—a sensible precaution if you knew you were on a serial killer's short list. Amos, Leon, Ruth McMasters and Eduardo also have the app on their devices. Since Eduardo left his phone home when he ran away, he can't be located this way. But Nattie always has her phone with her.

Danny pulls out his phone and engages the app, selects Nattie's phone and activates the GPS tracking feature. After a moment, a map pops up on the screen showing the location of Nattie's phone. Right in the middle of Jay Ellis's compound.

Danny dashes back downstairs to find M.B.

Chapter 25

Eduardo is woken by the shrilling of a bell.

Sitting up in bed, he turns to find Tabby beside him, rubbing the sleep from her eyes. She smiles when she notices him looking at her, then leans over and gives him a kiss on the lips.

"C'mon," she says. "We have a half hour to shower and get down to breakfast."

She jumps out of bed naked and grabs two towels from a drawer, tossing one to Eduardo. He wraps it around his waist, but she just carries hers as she leads him downstairs to a large, open shower room. Anne and Lex are already there, soaping up under separate showerheads. They acknowledge the newcomers with a nod, seemingly unconcerned by their nudity. Tabby deposits her towel on a bench and turns on an unoccupied shower. Eduardo hesitates—he's not used to being naked in front of strangers, but since no one else seems to care, he finally unwinds his towel and places it next to Tabby's, then finds a showerhead for himself. The water is chilly at first, but quickly warms to a comfortable temperature. He finds a bottle of liquid soap in a convenient niche and is soon as soapy as everyone else.

Eduardo's upper lip involuntarily curls as Pepe, naked as a newborn mouse, walks into the shower room and lays his folded towel on the bench. In a moment, Shannie follows. Eduardo is stunned as he sees her nude. Her skin is nearly as white as the towel she carries, her expression is distressed—she has a hitch in her step and walks slightly stooped as if she has a stomach cramp. Then he sees the dried blood on the inside of both of her thighs and he goes ballistic. A primal scream bursts from his lips as he charges Pepe, bent over like a linebacker rushing the quarterback. He hits the larger boy square in the solar plexus with his shoulder, knocking the wind out of him and slamming him into the tiled wall. Both boys go down with Eduardo ending up on top, and he smashes his fist into Pepe's nose, flattening it. He draws back his arm for another punch, but a hand comes out of nowhere to grab his wrist and jerk him upward off of Pepe.

He turns his head angrily to see *Mamà* Nattie (though he knows it isn't her) holding his wrist in an iron grip, and she hauls him out of the shower room into the hallway. He flushes at her nudity, intuitively understanding that it is something he should not see, even though she is really not his *mamà*.

"Just what the hell do you think you're doing, Mister?" He opens his mouth to answer her, but she drops his wrist and backhands him across the mouth with the same hand, hard enough to knock him off his feet. Fear courses through him as she looms above him like a vengeful goddess. "Get up!" she says. "Get up and go to your room, and don't let me see you again today!" She balls a fist. "If I do..."

Thoroughly cowed, Eduardo gets up and runs, his damp feet sliding on the tiled floor so he nearly goes down again. He regains his balance and tears up the stairs, running into his room and throwing himself face down on the bed. Hatred like he's never experienced in all his short life fills his soul—it has to go somewhere or he will burst, so his crying intensifies as he pounds his fists and kicks his feet on the mattress. He can't sustain that level of emotion for long, and he quiets as sleep takes him.

Later, he wakes again. He's cold, and his skin feels tight and itchy from all the dried soap he never got the chance to rinse off. Pain lances through his forehead as he sits up on the bed and dangles his feet over the side.

The room is still and quiet. He looks at the bedside clock. 10:30 in the morning. It was 7:00 when he woke the first time, so he's slept about three hours. He feels weak, as if his strength ran out of him along with the strong emotions.

He thinks again about what Pepe must've done to Shannie—after viewing the movie last night he has no illusions about that. He feels the hatred starting to smolder again, but this time, it doesn't flare up in a rush, but glows like a slow fire, settling into his chest like heartburn. He gets up and picks up his State hoodie and sweatpants from the floor. He puts them on and the warmth is comforting, although his itchy skin is still annoying.

A painful gnawing in his stomach begins—he's hungry, but he does not dare to leave the room to find something to eat. He's afraid of the woman who looks like *Mamà* Nattie—she told him she didn't want to see him again today. He's afraid she'll hurt him if she does.

Sometimes the worst punishment that can be inflicted on a young, active boy is to force him to do nothing. Eduardo did not take his phone when he left home because he knew it could be used to track him. There is no computer, video game console or TV in his room. He did take a few of his favorite comic books though. He goes to his desk and gets them from the drawer. But he knows the stories well, so they serve only to divert him for a short time. There's some paper and pens in the desk, so he takes a sheet, puts it on top of one of the comics and tries to trace the cover picture, but the paper is too thick for him to see the lines underneath. He tries to duplicate the cover picture freehanded, but he's not artist enough to bring that off.

Sister!

Sighing, he looks around for another diversion. His eyes fix on Tabby's bureau and desk. Maybe she has some neat stuff he can play with. She won't mind—after what they did last night, it's almost like they're married or something. Opening the drawers, he finds a set of gel pens and some folders full of pictures she's drawn (she's a good artist) as well as other papers that are obviously school work. After a while he abandons the desk and goes to the bureau, but all it contains is her clothes. He gets a mild rush from playing with her underwear, but that soon fades. He closes the bureau drawers again and looks at the clock. 11:15. Will this day never end? He stares at the clock some more and tries not to feel the walls closing in around him.

The clock is a black plastic cube about four inches on a side, with bright green digits an inch and a half high in the center of one face. Looking more closely, he notices a raised plastic dimple in the center above the numbers, which seems familiar. He goes over for a closer look. It's there! A tiny piece of round glass in the center of the dimple, and a little light below it.

One day when he was with Daddy Danny in the 3M Detective Agency office, Danny was showing him some of the surveillance equipment that the detectives used in their work. There was a clock much like this one. Danny told him it had a camera inside so the detectives could watch the bad guys without them knowing. That little dimple was a camera lens, and this one was pointed straight at the bed. The bed where Eduardo and Tabby had done what they did last night. *Dios mio!* Eduardo's entire body begins burning with fear and shame at the thought that someone might have been watching!

Eduardo knows that the little light comes on when the camera is on. He doesn't remember if it was on last night when he and Tabby were doing it, but he figures it had to be. Why else would somebody put a camera there?

A knock on the door jerks Eduardo out of his introspection. Looking that way, he hears a voice from outside in the hall. "Eduardo, can I come in?"

It's Shannie!

Chapter 26

The two girls with Ellis are high school age, no older than sixteen, possibly even younger.

One has on a skimpy pink thong bikini and the other is simply wrapped in a white beach towel with her shoulders bare, so she could be wearing nothing at all underneath. Neither seems concerned that a gun is pointed in their direction—both have giggly, dreamy expressions that make me think they're on something.

Ellis doesn't seem too concerned about my gun, either. He's dressed for tennis, with an immaculate white shirt and shorts, knee socks and low sneakers. With his salt 'n pepper buzz cut, Roman nose and piecing blue eyes, he looks like he's just walked out of a Great Gatsby take. He's also wearing a snarky grin as if he's sure my Sig is an empty threat.

"Why don't you hand that gun to Gerry, and then we'll sit and have a talk," he says, looking me up and down like he's inspecting a piece of meat. "My gawd, it's amazing! There's someone else here that you really must meet."

The power of the man is obvious in his gaze. It's like an unseen aura emanates from him, drawing me in, making me want to hand him my gun. To break the spell, I move the laser around in circles on his shirt front. "Un uhh," I say. "Y'all come over here with her where I can keep you all together. Then we'll get my boy over here so we can leave."

His face scrunches up and his eyes harden. A shiver goes through me, even though I seemingly hold the power here. "You can't be that bloody stupid," he says. "Gerry wasn't kidding about the guards and their Uzis." He holds out a hand in front of him and begins walking toward me. "Now give me that popgun and we'll talk."

"Stay back!" I tell him, "Stay back, or I'll shoot!" He totally ignores me and just keeps coming, and I actually take a step back. A little voice of reason starts yapping in my head.

He's a billionaire, and I've gotten into his home under false pretenses. He's unarmed. What do I think will happen if I shoot him, guards or no guards?

Now he's standing right in front of me, his hand still extended. I take my finger off the trigger and the red dot winks out. It takes great effort on my part, but instead of giving it to him, I slide the Sig back into its holster in my pocket.

Sister!

"Now that won't do at all," Ellis says. "Get her arms, Gerry."

Gerry steps up and grips my biceps from behind, holding my arms against my sides. She's surprisingly strong, but it doesn't matter. All I'll have to do is slide my legs wide into *ma-bu*, and summon my *chi* from the earth beneath my feet. If I twitch my hips, channeling all of the power of my legs and my *dantian* through my upper body, she'll go flying away from me like a rag doll.

I slow my breathing to nearly nothing as Ellis reaches for me. What a surprise they'll get! But a thought nags.

No matter what I do, he'll never let me keep my gun, and there are plenty of armed guards around to take it from me. Do I really want to let them know what I can do?

I let my breathing go back to normal as Ellis takes my gun from my right-hand pocket. He checks the other pocket and finds my stiletto. Now he wears a totally broad grin. "Is that all? No hand grenades? Poison gas?"

Smart ass.

"Let her go," he says to Gerry. To me: "How did you get in here, anyway."

"I just drove in. Looks like your help is the WOAT."

He processes that for a sec, then presses a button on a little device on his belt. In a minute, two goons with Uzi's strapped on their shoulder enter the room. Ellis points to me and addresses them. "This isn't Miss Bella. Fire whoever's on the front gate for admitting an intruder and tell everybody else they better be checking IDs from now on. Now get out of here."

Both men salute and leave without a word.

Ellis reaches into his pocket and comes out with a sheaf of bills, a hundred on top. He peels off three of them and hands them to one of the teens, then does the same for the other. "That's all for today, girls" he says. They giggle and scamper out of the room. Looking at me, he says, "Now, why don't we go into the conservatory and get to know each other? All right, Natalie?"

WTF? I told Gerry my name, but Ellis wasn't in the room at the time. So how does he know me?

He leads the way into the greenhouse in the back. It's really an indoor garden with greenery, flowers and even trees, planted in white gravel with a brick pathway winding among them, enclosed by a glass octagonal roof. There's a blast of heat as we pass the threshold. Ellis waves us towards a white wrought iron table surrounded by chairs in the center of the room.

"Have a seat," he orders. "Brunch?"

"No thanks. You have my son here. If you'll just send for him, I'll take him and we'll leave."

Ellis cocks an eyebrow at Gerry. "You know anything about this?" She shakes her head.

"His name is Eduardo. He ran away from home," I nod towards Gerry. "She picked him up at a homeless camp the other day."

"We are trying to give back to the community by rescuing homeless orphans and finding good homes for them," says Gerry. "And I did bring in a boy and a girl the other day."

"The boy was Eduardo," I tell her.

She pulls out an iPhone and her thumbs pound the screen. "It will be just a few minutes," she says.

Looking back at Ellis, I ask, "So while we wait, tell me how you know who I am."

Ignoring my question, he says, "You sure I can't get you anything?" He presses the button on his belt again, saying, "Bring mimosas, and something to eat."

I open my mouth to refuse again, but he talks right over me. "If you want to know how I know you, you'll have to stay to hear the story. And there's someone here you should meet."

"Bella," I say. "My sister." He grins.

A sense of anticipation comes over me, followed by dread as I remember that it was likely Bella who murdered a man in cold blood the other day. I still haven't come to terms about what I want to do about that yet.

Another broad smile. "You have been busy!" he says.

We're interrupted by the black woman that I saw earlier in the kitchen, a tray with a large pitcher of orange liquid, a bottle of champagne, three tulip-shaped glasses and plates full of little baked thingees, fruit and deviled eggs, balanced on her shoulder. She sets it down on the table. "Will that be all, sir?"

"Yes, Lashonda." He picks up the pitcher and fills each glass half full of OJ, then expertly tops them off with the champagne. The little bubbles rise just to the rim of the glass without going over. He pushes one in my direction. "Here. That's not enough to get you too tipsy to drive." I ignore the glass, and he frowns at me. Not used to a woman turning you down, are you, Hunty? "You really should try it. It's Krug Grande Cuvee and it goes splendidly with the orange juice."

Sister!

He fills another glass for Gerry. She picks it up, sips and a blissful expression appears on her face. "Oh, you're right, Jay. It's just divine." I swear he sits up straighter and his chest swells at her praise. Oh, WTF. I raise the glass to my lips and taste. OMG! It's ice cold, sour, sweet, like Florida and France in the same bottle! I drain the glass and set it down, and Ellis fills it again. I pick it up and take another large gulp.

"Sylvia!" He says in a loud voice. "Lower the screen." A little noise comes from above, and I look upward to see a TV descending from the ceiling. I pick up my glass for another big swig as it reaches a convenient viewing height. "NHFC Security video, five eleven oh one hundred," Ellis says. The TV springs to life, and a picture appears—it has that particular bright green tint that indicates it was filmed using low-light equipment. It looks familiar... Holy fuck! That's me on the screen, and Irwin? We're in Dr. Thistlebottom's office at the New Horizons Fertility Clinic. "Volume seven," says Ellis, and the sound comes up.

"What did they do?" It's Irwin talking.

"It's called an Intracytoplasmic Sperm Injection, or ICSI. It's when they inject a single spermatozoa directly into a single mature ova, in vitro. Usually when they do that, they let the embryo develop like normal, then implant it into Mom when it's mature enough. But here, they let it grow, then split it into four parts."

"Why four?"

"Probably to get the same number of cells in each embryo. Then all four of them would continue to develop at the same rate. But they only implanted one embryo into your Mom."

"What happened to the other three?"

"It doesn't say here."

"Kill video." The screen goes black. To me: "You really were a very bad girl."

I can hardly speak—my sinuses feel suddenly full and there's a ringing in my ears. My words come out as a croak. "How...how did you get this?"

"The camera and microphone in that office were triggered by a motion sensor when you and Mr. Irwin entered Dr. Thistlebottom's office. There's enough evidence here to send you to prison for burglary and grand larceny, not to mention the charges that would arise from what you did to poor Mr. Irwin. I don't know how he's going to cope with his medical condition since he no longer has his job at NHFC, nor any health insurance."

I'm still clueless. "But how did you get this?" I ask again.

"I'm the principal owner of the NHFC. I am appraised of all serious situations that occur there." He takes a drink of his mimosa, then continues, "Those files you stole were my property."

"But they were my records! I should have been allowed to see them."

"And you might have been, had you just asked me."

He's kidding, right? "And how was I supposed to know to do that?"

"Well, you do work for the 3M Detective Agency..." He's wearing that fucking snarky grin again.

"So you've had me investigated!"

"I have a right to know who's been breaking into my offices."

A hot flash suddenly comes over me, and I put down my glass and wipe the sweat from my brow. "If those are your files," I begin, "Then maybe you can explain what I found in them."

"Maybe I can," he says. His eyes rise so he's looking behind me, and his smile changes from snarky to roguish. "And here comes part of the explanation now." I turn and I see myself walking towards me. My head suddenly feels like it's ten times normal size, and the room begins spinning...

Chapter 27

"**A**ny truth to the rumor that there's a task force looking into the activities of Jerome Ellis?" M.B. asks Special Agent In Charge Ezekiel Flannery.

"If I told you, I'd have to kill you," quips the SAIC. His voice, normally high-pitched for a man's, sounds positively tinny on the cell phone. "Why do you need to know?"

"It's possible he's holding a young boy against his will at his estate down here. I'd need a warrant to pay him a visit and find out."

"Was the boy taken across a state line or out of the country?"

"Not to my knowledge."

"Taken at an airport or a maritime jurisdiction?"

"Nope."

"Then it sounds like a matter for the locals."

"Yeah, well, Ellis pretty much has them in his pocket. That's why I asked about the task force. They just might need to look at him for some other reason."

"They just might," Flannery agrees. "But if they don't have a good case put together yet, the issuance of a federal warrant would tip Ellis off that something was in the works and they might never get what they need."

"There is that."

There's silence on the line for a moment, then Flannery asks. "Is this boy anyone to you?"

"He's my fiancé's foster nephew."

Is there even such a thing?

"Would it help if someone from here called your DA down there and put a bug in his ear?"

"It might."

"Then consider it done. Give me till tomorrow until you talk to her though."

"The boy's family is pretty tore up about him being missing," M.B. told the SAIC.

"Can't be helped."

Now M.B. is quiet for a moment before she says, "Well, thanks for trying, Zeke. I'll owe you one."

"And you'll pay up, too," the SAIC says. "I collect with interest. Be well, Maribeth."

"You too, Zeke."

The SAIC kills the call. He looks up at the ceiling, closes his eyes and pinches the bridge of his nose for a minute. Then he opens them and dials a number on his desk phone.

"Mr. President, we have us a situation," he says.

Chapter 28

"**C**ome in," Eduardo says.

The door opens and Shannie slips inside, closing it softly behind her.

"You shouldn't have come," Eduardo says. "If that lady finds you, you will get in trouble."

"I don't care," Shannie says. "I wanted to see you. I was worried about you."

Her words send a chill through him. She comes over and sits next to him on the bed. Scared, he looks to see if the camera light is on. It isn't.

"You shouldn't have hit Pepe," she tells him.

"He deserved it. He hurt you."

"No, he didn't."

"Yes, he did!" Eduardo insists. "I saw the blood. He hurt you down there."

"Well, maybe it did hurt a little," Shannie concedes. "But he didn't mean it. He did it because I told him to."

"What do you mean, you told him to?"

"What I said. He didn't want to. He said Tabby was his girlfriend and it wasn't right for him to do it with me. But I told him I wanted him to. After I saw the movie, I thought it would make me a grown-up. A woman, I mean."

Eduardo can't believe what he's hearing.

"I would have rather it was you, but you were doing it with Tabby," Shannie goes on, and Eduardo winces at her words. "So it was okay for him to do it with me. He really didn't want to, but I started to play with him like the girls in the movie did. Finally, he did it."

Eduardo can't look at her. After a while, he says, "But I thought you liked me."

Taking his hand, she says, "I do, silly. But you were with Tabby. I didn't think you would mind."

I do mind. I guess you don't.

He pulls his hand away from her. "But what about the blood?"

"Pepe said that's because it was my first time. It won't happen anymore after this." She smiles. "Now I want to do it with you."

Eduardo reddens, then he suddenly remembers the camera. Other people shouldn't be hearing this! He says, "Why don't we go outside? C'mon." He takes her by the hand and leads her to the door.

"I thought you were supposed to stay in your room."

"I am. C'mon"

If they're watching, we'll get busted before we ever make it downstairs.

They go out into the hallway, then he lets her hand go and leads the way downstairs, quivering as he awaits *Mamà* Nattie's, that is, Miss Bella's voice screaming out his name. But no scream comes. He beckons Shannie to follow him past the bathroom and the showers toward the back door, wisely staying away from the dining room and the classroom where people may be working. Going outside and down the steps into the rear garden, Eduardo looks around furiously for a place where they can talk unobserved.

There!

His eyes light upon a flagstone path that winds around the shrubbery and disappears into a copse about fifty feet away. He heads that way and is rewarded when he sees a bench in the center of a lawn, surrounded by a thicket. He leads Shannie there, saying, "Now it will be safe to talk."

"Safe? What do you mean?"

He tells her about the camera upstairs. "If I've got one in my room, I bet we all do."

"Somebody was watching us?" She sounds incredulous.

"It sure looks that way."

"But why?"

Eduardo has a terrible thought. "Maybe they were making a movie with us in it."

Shannie looks horrified. "You mean to show to other people?"

"I guess. Why else would you make a movie?"

Both kids are quiet for a moment, trying to process. Finally, Shannie says, "What me and Pepe did was private. It isn't right that somebody else should see."

"The people in the movie we saw last night sure didn't care," Eduardo says.

"That's different," Shannie replies. "They knew they were in a movie."

Sister!

Eduardo notices the tears welling up in Shannie's eyes. "Hey, don't cry." He takes her in his arms.

"It isn't right," She says again. She pushes him away from her and looks him in the eyes. "We need to get away from here."

He gives a nervous laugh. "Have you seen the men in black with guns out there? And the wall? The wire on top?"

More tears flow, but Eduardo can tell that this time, they are born of anger. "Well, we at least need to stop doing sex so they can't make any more movies of us." She wrinkles her brow, thinking. "I want you to make up with Pepe," she says. "Let's you me, and him try to get together. Maybe the three of us can think of a way to get away from here."

"What about Tabby?"

Shannie frowns. "OK, I guess she can come, too."

Eduardo hesitates, then, "This could be dangerous. I was out of my room last night and that lady caught me."

"What lady? The one who brought us here?"

"No, the blonde lady from this morning." He hesitates. "She looks like my *Mamà* Nattie."

Shannie looks at Eduardo like he just grew a pair of horns. "You think she's your Mama?"

"No, I know she's not. She sure looks like her, though."

"She said her name was Bella after you left," Shannie tells him. "If you're afraid..."

"I'm not afraid!" Eduardo says.

Shannie opens her mouth and covers it with her fist. "Oh no! What about the cameras? They'll see that we're gone!"

Eduardo replies, "The cameras aren't on all the time. There's a little light in front that comes on if the camera is on."

Shannie relaxes. She thinks a second, then says, "We had school downstairs this morning. When lunchtime came, I told Miss Bella that I didn't feel so good and wanted to lie down, then I came to see you instead. School's gonna start again soon. Maybe if you came in with me and apologized to Miss Bella, she'd let you stay. Then maybe we can talk to Pepe and Tabby at recess."

Eduardo considered Shannie's idea. "I guess the worst thing that could happen is that she'd yell at me again and make me go back to my room. Let's try it."

"Sounds like a plan."

Chapter 29

Ailín Greene is sitting at his computer at work, watching a video of a couple of nude high-school girls engaging in a vigorous sixty-nine.

His swelling manhood pushes hard against his trousers as he savors the thought that he'll be joining them shortly.

A buzzing sound comes from his lower desk drawer, and a lump of uneasiness suddenly gnaws at his belly. He opens the drawer and takes out a phone, setting it on his desk before he picks up the receiver.

"Yes, sir."

He listens a moment.

"OK, give me that address."

A voice murmurs in his ear.

"Right. I'll take care of it." Silence, then, "We're still on for tonight?"

The voice speaks again, and a smile creeps over his face. "Great!" He hangs up the phone and replaces it in the drawer.

He reaches for his desk phone and hits a speed dial button.

"Detective Sykes? It's Deputy Chief Greene. I have a job for you..."

Chapter 30

Danny, M.B., Lupe, Leon and Amos are in Amos's office. Amos is behind his desk in his wheelchair, while the other four sit in a semicircle in front of it.

Danny does not want Lupe there, but she simply would not be excluded. She's way too emotional—Danny has told her if she starts wigging out, she's gone, even if he has to carry her and lock her in her room.

M.B. tells the group about her call to Quantico. "The SAIC promised to call the DA and get us a warrant to go get Eduardo, but we'll have to wait until tomorrow..."

"Why we have to wait?" Lupe hollers in the broken English that she reverts to when she's stressed. "That man Ellis, he has no right to keep my son! He's a billionaire—why does he want him?"

Danny sidles over to Lupe and put an arm around her to calm her down. "Lupe's right. Why can't he just get us a federal warrant to go in there?"

"Couple of reasons," M.B. answers. "In this instance, kidnapping is not a Federal crime. Eduardo wasn't taken across a state line, nor did the abduction occur in a Federal jurisdiction."

Lupe is now as white as a bedsheet. "We have to get my son away from him," she says in a low voice that Danny thinks is even scarier than her earlier yelling.

"Look," says Leon, "we have a leg up in that Ellis knows that we know he has Eduardo. Anything bad done to him will be laid right at Ellis's door."

"But why won't he let him go?" Lupe wails again.

"He's obviously a narcissist." M.B. says. "They have huge egos. It's a point of honor that no one tells them what to do. Maybe this warrant will allow him to save face, let Eddie go just to save himself the hassle of getting it quashed. Let's give the DA a chance and wait till tomorrow."

A buzzer sounds in the office. "Somebody coming up the driveway," says Danny. He goes to the window for a look. "Hmmph. Police. Two cars... and a SWAT vehicle?"

The vehicles pull into the circular driveway and stop in front of the house. The doors spring open and cops pour out

"They've got ARs and a battering ram!" Danny says. "What the hell?"

Sister!

He can't see the front door of Hyacinth House from the window, so he runs into the hallway to look over the balcony. A loud thump echoes through the house, followed by calls of "Police! Daniel Merkel! Show yourself!" in a woman's voice.

Danny starts for the stairs, but a hand on his shoulder stops him. "Go into the office," M.B. says. "Disarm, and put your guns on the desk. I'll go meet them." Danny goes into the office and does as she told him.

In a minute she's back, two tactically-garbed SWAT officers behind her. "Everybody! Show your hands!" One of them yells. "Daniel Merkel! We have a warrant for your arrest for the murder of Thurmond Jordan. Turn around!"

As an ex-cop, Danny knows the drill. He places his hands on top of his head and turns his back to the officer, who slaps a handcuff on his right wrist before bringing it down behind his back. The left hand follows and Danny is secure.

The other officer notices the guns on the desk and scoops them up. "Everybody else! We know you're armed. Get up and keep your hands raised while we confiscate your weapons!"

Kidd looks at Lupe and says, "Do as they say."

Amos shouts, "We have permits for these guns..."

"Not anymore, you don't," a woman says. Detective Sykes pushes past the two enormous SWAT dudes. "You too, ma'am."

"Go to hell!" says M.B.

"What?"

"You heard me. I am Supervisory Special Agent Maribeth Woodrow of the Federal Bureau of Investigation, and you have no jurisdiction to take my weapon. If you lay a hand on me, I'll arrest you for assaulting a federal agent. I'm now reaching for my credential." She withdraws a black leather wallet from her rear pocket and lets it fall open so Sykes can see the contents.

"Now let me see that warrant."

Sykes glares at her, but knows better than to touch her. She pulls a piece of paper from under her vest and gives it to M.B., who scans it, then tosses it back to her.

"You're too late," she says. "I'm taking Mr. Merkel into custody as a person of interest in a federal investigation. She reaches behind her and comes out with a set of handcuffs. "My arrest trumps yours. Take your cuffs off him. I've got my own."

"This is bullshit..." Sykes begins.

"Want to take that chance, shug? Interfering in a federal investigation is a felony."

Sykes's eyes are slits, and her lips a thin blue line. "What are you investigating?" she hisses.

"You don't need to know, now do you, honeychile?" M.B. tells her, her voice dripping icicles. "Now get those cuffs off, him or I'll confiscate them."

Sykes fixes M.B. with an angry stare, but thinks better and removes the cuffs. "I'm keeping his guns," she says.

"What for? You've already got the one used in the shooting. You know, the one that you said looked open and shut, if you've forgotten. And as far as I know, his CCH is still valid."

"Thanks for reminding me," says Sykes. She removes another paper from beneath her vest. "This is a letter from the Sheriff, revoking the CCH's of Mr. Merkel, Mr. Kidd, Mr. Murdoch, and Natalie McMasters until further notice."

"You don't need a CCH to keep a pistol in your home," M.B. says. "And last I knew, open carry is legal in this state. Leave the guns."

"Fine," says Sykes. She looks at Amos. "By the way, you'll be getting a registered letter from the Attorney General that your private investigator's license has been revoked as well."

Sykes skewers M.B. with one more dirty look, which the agent seems to be totally unconcerned about. The detective says to the SWAT officers, "C'mon, y'all, we're done here," then backs out of the room and heads for the exit, the SWAT guys trailing her like robocops.

"We'll send y'all a bill for our door!" Amos hollers after them, then he looks at M.B. "That's my gal!" he says with a broad grin.

Chapter 31

The first thing I notice is a warm, floral aroma, like roses in a steambath.

I open my eyes onto a pure white world—white light, white ceiling, stark white walls. I see myself in a mirror, propped up on an elbow, blue eyes wide open, pink nipples peeking out above the white sheet... wait a minute! That's no mirror, that's...

"Bella?"

She gives me a dazzling white smile. "You gonna sleep all day?"

There's pressure in my forehead, like I'm trying to think through cotton. I remember now. "Ellis! The mimosas! He drugged me!"

"Jay said you threatened him with a gun. He was just trying to calm you down."

I'm lying in a big, soft bed. Naked, under white sheets and a white quilt. Bella's naked too, or at least topless.

"What are you doing here?" I ask her.

"Waiting for you to wake up."

I feel my face wrinkling into a frown. "You know what I mean. And why are you naked?"

She throws the covers off, revealing that she is, in fact, nude. "I just wanted to see if we really looked alike. Everywhere. Her hand travels downward toward the thatch of dark hair in her crotch, then points to a mole on her belly just above it. "See? You have one, too."

I know I do—it was the reason for a never-ending fight with Daddy when I was a teenager. I wanted to get it taken off so I could wear a two-piece bathing suit. He said no.

"Big yikes! You stripped me naked just to check out my bod?" This is beyond savage!

"I didn't take your clothes off. Jay did. Don't worry, you can wear some of mine. That's what twin sisters do, wear each other's clothes, y'know?"

A shudder runs through me.

That Zaddy took off my clothes?

Bella must see it on my face. "Don't worry, he didn't do anything else. He won't fuck you unless you ask him to. At least, that's how he was with me."

So Ellis is fucking her? Big shock, that.

I think of my Pantera shirt, the one that Danny gave me. "Where are my things?"

"Don't worry about it."

"I am. That was my fave t-shirt."

"I said don't worry. You'll get it back. Eventually."

I'm silent for a minute, then, "What are you doing here?"

"I just told you..."

"Not here with me. I mean here with ol' moneybags."

"Don't call him that! His name is Jay and he's a super dude. He's gonna get me a job. In Hollywood. As an actress!"

Right.

I suddenly remember what started this whole mess for me. I ask her, "Why did you do it, Bella? Shoot those people, I mean."

She doesn't miss a beat. "I told Jay that I'd do anything for him. 'Prove it,' he said. 'Kill somebody for me.' So I did. Gerry helped me. She even picked out the convenience store."

Now my heart is a ball of ice. I totally can't even.

She must see my reaction on my face. "C'mon! Those dudes don't matter! The only reason you need to do something is because you want to. That's what Jay says."

I totally cannot believe this babe!

She offs two people just to get in good with her Zaddy? And she's my sister?

"You totally believe that?" I ask her.

"Sure! Why not?"

Because they were fucking people, you cray bitch!

"Jay says, 'There are people who do, and people who get done.' I know what kind I am."

Yeah, me too. You're a fucking cold-blooded murderer.

But I can't let on I have those feels. Not if I want to get Eduardo and get the fuck out of here.

127

Sister!

"Jay wants us to have dinner with him," she goes on. "He'll tell you about your son. I've met him, by the way. Cute kid."

She knows where Eduardo is? I rocket across the bed, grab her by the shoulders. She rolls over on her back with me on top.

"Take me to him! Now!"

Smiling, she snakes her arms around my neck, pulls my face to hers and kisses me, sticking her tongue in my mouth.

This cunt is totally warped!

I push away from her. She's still grinning.

"What the fuck!"

"Chill, Sis. Your boy is fine. He's having the time of his life." An evil smirk on her face makes me wonder just what she means by that. "Come and have dinner with us. You'll see him later."

All of me just wants to roll her out of this bed and stomp the total living shit out of her until she takes me to Eduardo. But I have a strong feeling that if I do, the boys with the Uzis will be back here in a minute. Odds are Zaddy Jay is watching us right now, getting his rocks off. I try to keep my face bland.

"Gucci. Dinner it is. But ol' moneybags better take me to my boy afterwards."

Red anger flashes in her blue eyes. "I said not to call him that! One thing you better learn, Missy. Jay calls the shots around here. Don't piss him off."

"What about that woman, Gerry?"

She looks at me like she just stepped in something warm and wet. "Her too. She's his main squeeze." A smile. "But I'm workin' on it."

I think maybe he ain't watching after all, if she's willing to be so real about that. Maybe this is something I can use. "What do you mean?"

Now she's wearing a roguish smile. "You know damn well what I mean." She hops out of bed. I have to say that my titties tingle as I check out her naked bod. A lump wells up in my throat as I remember another woman who looked just like us. She turned me on, too. But she's dead now.

"C'mon!" says Bella. "Let's go to my room and pick out some clothes to knock Jay dead." She opens the door and strolls out into the hall, tots nude. I look around for something to put on, but seeing nothing but the bedsheets, I follow reluctantly.

There's an Uzidude out in the hall who gives us a big grin as we walk by him, but he says nothing. Bella opens a door at the end of hallway and beckons me inside.

Chapter 32

Eduardo and Shannie sneak back into the house the same way that they left, then proceed to the classroom like they've just come from upstairs.

Eduardo mentally steels himself for another tongue lashing from Bella, but she's not there. Looks like Cheryl has the duty instead.

Class is awkward, as Pepe, his nose sheathed in a large, white bandage, keeps throwing Eduardo shady glances when Cheryl's not looking. *Just wait till I get you outside,* they seem to say. But Eduardo's not nearly as worried as he would have been yesterday. Maybe it was a sucker punch that did all that the damage to Pepe, but maybe not. Eduardo is not a big dude, but what he lacks in size, he makes up for in heart. Besides, Eduardo's pretty sure that Pepe never killed a man...

After a couple of hours, Cheryl calls recess, and the kids are allowed outside. They head for the fenced playground next to the house. Once there, Pepe makes a beeline for Eduardo, but the smaller boy just stands his ground with his arms hanging at his sides, his fists balled up, throwing him a stink eye. The bigger boy stops outside of arm's length and glares at Eduardo, saying, "You better watch out!"

"For what?" Eduardo claps back. "Nice nose, asshole. How'd that happen?"

Pepe reddens, but before he can wade in, Shannie lays a hand on his arm and Tabby puts herself between the two boys.

"Pepe, you need to back off and listen to what Eduardo has to say," Shannie says. Pepe's face says that he doesn't like that a bit, but he's not gonna go through the girls to get to Eduardo.

Eduardo looks around the playground, and seeing that Cheryl is absent, jerks his head toward the rear gate, then walks off toward the back garden where he and Shannie talked earlier, trusting the girls to convince Pepe to come along. Once at the bench, Shannie gets Tabby and Pepe to sit on it along with her, leaving Eduardo standing in front them like a lecturer. Eduardo notices that Pepe takes Tabby's hand protectively as soon as they do. Maybe Shannie was right about him after all...

Eduardo tells Pepe and Tabby about the cameras. The two of them are just as p.o.'d as he and Shannie were.

"You sure?" Pepe asks. "This ain't no jiveshit?

"You can go to your room and check it out yourself. There's a little lens on the front of the clock with a little light underneath that comes on when the camera does."

"So why they be watchin' us fuck?"

"We think they're making movies," says Shannie.

Pepe's jaw drops and he can't speak for a sec. Finally, "That shit is fucked up!"

"So what do we do about it?" Tabby asks.

"For starters, stop giving them a show," Shannie says. "No more sex for the camera."

"We gotta be chill, though," says Eduardo. "We don't want them to know that we know about the cameras." A beat. "What we really gotta do is get the fuck out of here."

"Right," Pepe sneers. "You see all them mothas with guns, dude? And all them fucking walls fulla bob wire?"

"There's got to be a way," says Tabby. "You been here the longest, Pepe. How 'bout the lake? There's no wall there."

"No, but there's a ton of guards. And we were told to stay away from there."

"You always do everything you're told?" scoffs Eduardo, and Pepe gives him a dirty look.

"No man, I'm not you. But they catch us, they'll lock us down, and that's the end."

"If you were going to escape at the lake," Shannie presses, "how would you do it? Swim? Steal a boat?"

"I can't swim!" whines Tabby.

"Then we don't," says Eduardo. "Everybody goes, or nobody goes. Who knows how to run a boat?"

No answer.

"What about Eve and Lex?" asks Shannie.

"No!" Pepe and Tabby exclaim at the same time. Pepe continues, "Those two'll snitch."

"So what's the plan?" Shannie asks.

"Let's check out the lake tonight," says Eduardo. "The wall has to end at the shore. Maybe we can get around it somehow."

131

Sister!

"What about the fuckin' cameras?" asks Pepe.

"They don't watch us twenty-four seven," says Tabby. "They turn them off after we go to sleep."

"Miss Bella caught me out the other night," says Eduardo. "I don't know if she saw me on the camera or not, though."

"So let's wait until the light's off," says Shannie. "If they catch us anyway, we're hosed."

I think we're fucking hosed.

"Okay," Eduardo says. "Lessdoodis tonight."

Chapter 33

A fter the exhilaration generated by M.B.'s deft handling of Sykes wears off, a pall descends on the detectives.

The loss of their licenses may well be the death knell of the 3M. Detective Agency. Amos is not paying rent for the office space in Hyacinth House (though he wanted to), so there won't be a problem keeping the lights on, but once the insurance companies who are their principal clients take their business elsewhere, it may be well-nigh impossible to get it back.

"Is there any kind of appeal process with the Attorney General's office?" Danny asks.

"I 'spect so," Amos replies, "but what do you think our chances are, since he's the one who lifted our licenses?"

"It should be possible to take him to court," says M.B.

"Sure, but who's gonna pay for that? I've always run 3M on a shoestring. As long as people kept claimin' worker's comp, it was never a problem. But now..."

"Our fam is pretty well-heeled since Nattie's inheritance," says Danny.

"No!" says Amos. "I'll not let my niece piss away her money on a lost cause." A beat. "What I want to know is just who this Ellis is, that he can do sumphin' like this."

"That's a really good question, sweetheart," says M.B. "Jerome Ellis is one of the richest men in America."

"Where'd he get all that money, anyhow?" asks Amos.

"Another great question. The short answer is that he worked in arbitrage on Wall Street for a while, selling everything from stock options and commodities futures to currency. Eventually he formed his own hedge fund, and made headlines by not allowing anyone worth less than a hundred million or so to invest with him. Doing that, you don't have to make too many good deals to amass a whole lot of money very quickly."

"But that's not the end of the story." M.B. goes on. She looks at each person in turn. "What I say next does not leave this room." After getting a nod from each one, she continues, "The bureau routinely investigates billionaires. Those people scare them—a lot of power comes with that kind of money. A few organizations like the IRS and the Bureau thought that Ellis had a lot more money than could be explained by his Wall Street activities."

Sister!

Danny perks up his ears at that. "So there is an ongoing federal investigation of Ellis?"

M.B. purses her lips. "I think so, but I don't know for sure. If they're not ready to go to a federal grand jury, the bureau would play their cards close to the chest. That's probably why Zeke Flannery, the SAIC I talked to up there, told me to get a local warrant from the DA instead of a federal warrant, so as not to tip Ellis off that he's under investigation."

She goes on, "The Bureau would have opened an investigation to make sure that, among other things, Ellis isn't laundering money for the Mob or for drug cartels. But Ellis is smart. He started making the best investment of all—buying influence. He made friends with a lot of important people, simply by throwing parties and wining and dining them. He's famous for his social gatherings, many of them for worthy causes—charities, the Arts, et cetera. It's become a mark of distinction to get an invitation to one." She hesitates. "But then, there's a dark side. Ellis bought himself his own Caribbean island, which isn't controlled by any government, and rumor has it that he throws real Bacchanals down there, involving drugs and underage girls."

Danny: "How much underage?"

"High school, for sure, maybe even younger. He'd fly groups down south for the weekend or longer on his private jet. You can assume that he has plenty of videos of the goings on, so it isn't hard for him to pick up a phone and request favors. Some of his pals include a former U.S. president—guess which one—a member of the royal family, Senators and Congressmen, a couple of governors, etc. You already know that he's been donating money and goods to the local police around here for years. He could have a lot of dirt on a lot of people, and that makes him dangerous as hell."

"But isn't that kind of influence peddling illegal?" Danny asks.

"Only if you can prove it. And Ellis is damn careful about who he talks to and what is said."

Leon Kidd: "How about FBI agents? Does Ellis have dirt on any of them? All due respect, M.B., but don't you think it's a helluva coincidence that you talked to a SAIC up in Quantico this morning, and this afternoon, the cops are here to arrest Danny for a shooting that they said would cause no trouble, and the AG has lifted our licenses? Ten to one they've gotten to the DA, and there ain't gonna be no warrant tomorrow, nor any other day."

Lupe howls, "Noooo!" and buries her face in her hands.

134

M.B.'s face looks as if it's carved in marble. "I've known Zeke Flannery for a lot of years. We went through the academy together. I'd hate to think he's dirty..."

"What's the alternative?" asks Danny. "And more importantly, what are we gonna do now?"

M.B. looks like she's lost her best friend. "I don't know," she says.

Chapter 34

Bella's bedroom is pink—my all-time, least fave color.

And when I say pink, I mean loud, deep, eye-hurting pink. The walls are pink. So is the ceiling. The room is carpeted wall-to-wall with a plush, furry pink carpet like you'd find in a cheap whorehouse. The round bed features a quilted pink coverlet and lots of pillows sheathed in pink pillowcases. Even the fucking furniture is pink.

Of course, the room does contain some things that are not pink. Like the dozens of stuffed animals that litter every available surface. The chandelier that dangles from the ceiling in the center of the room is white, but when Bella turns it on with a wall switch, it becomes obvious that the bulbs are pink. A pink, neon sign in the shape of a reclining nude woman hangs on the wall behind the bed, making me wonder if Bella likes girls. She slipped me some tongue when we were in my room a while ago, so I think that's likely.

Could I really do it with my sister?

The wall opposite the bed is taken up by a pair of pink, louvered folding doors. She opens them to reveal a closet full of clothes on hangers, many of which are gowns and dresses. My usual clothing choice is t-shirts and shorts or jeans, so I shudder when she waves an arm in front of the dresses and says, "Jay will expect us to be decked out for dinner. We're the same size. Pick one." When I don't respond, she rummages inside and comes out with two pink gowns, which she holds up. One is bright, flamingo pink and the other is a more understated, lighter hue. "Which one do you like?"

"Err, I don't know how to break it to you, Bella, but I hate pink. Have you got anything else?"

Her lips collapse into a deep pout, but she puts the gowns back and rummages some more. "Ah!" she exclaims, and comes out with two cocktail dresses, one gold and the other silver. They're barely longer than a nightie. "I couldn't decide between them, so I got both," she says. "Which one is you?"

Neither, I think, but it's obvious that I ain't gonna get outta this unless I'm wearing some kind of fancy shit.

"I'll wear the silver one."

When she hands it to me, I can see that it's semi-transparent so it won't be hiding much. Having worked as a stripper, I'm not shy about showing off my bod, but I wonder if that's the right move if I'm trying to get Ellis to give back Eduardo. Maybe. If a fast fuck will get me my boy back, bring it on. It's just sex, right?

I wiggle into the silver dress. It fits like a second skin. The cloth is scratchy, making my nipples harden as I move. Ol' Moneybags will prolly get off on that.

Bella puts on the gold dress and finds us some matching shoes in another closet. They're high heels, which I don't wear much, but I used to dance in them on a stripper pole, so I get used to them again pretty quickly.

Bella brushes her hair, then sits me down in front of the mirror on her pink vanity and does mine. Looking at the two of us is spooky—we look exactly alike, except for the color of our dresses.

She casts an eye at a clock on the nightstand. "We better get down there. Jay doesn't like it if you're late."

Big whup.

We go out in the hall to the big double staircase that leads to the first floor. Food smells waft up from below, and my mouth waters—I suddenly realize that I'm starving, having had nothing since breakfast. It's a little dicey doing those stairs in the heels, but I manage. Bella, on the other hand, skips down them like she's wearing sneakers.

At the bottom of the staircase, I can hear convo from the front of the house. We turn and walk under the staircases and turn left toward the dining room. I start to follow Bella inside, then I see who's sitting at the table and stop dead in my tracks, just staring.

Two men are sitting with their backs to me at the large rectangular table, but across from them is our former president, engaged in an earnest convo with someone else I recognize. The last time I saw him was on TV, dressed in a bright red uniform with a powder blue sash and gold decorations, standing on a balcony next to his mother in her big, floppy hat.

The two guys with their backs to us become aware of our presence by the reactions of the Pres and the Prince, and turn so I can see their faces.

I recognize the one of them as the anchorman for the evening news on a major TV network. The other one, I've never seen before. He's an ordinary-looking fiftysomething dude with a military haircut.

"Hi, everybody!" says Bella. She turns to look at me, then waves me forward. "Nattie, come up here so I can introduce you!" She takes my hand and drags me up beside her, putting a protective arm around my shoulder. "I'm sure you recognize our former president and his royal highness. And this gentleman is Andy, and this one is Al. Guys, this is my sister, Natalie."

Sister!

All of the men rise to greet us. They are wearing black tuxes with tails and white bow ties, making me feel totally underdressed. I shake hands with Andy and Al in turn, hoping that I'm not drooling all over the floor as I do so. Andy is *très* hot for an older dude! There's an empty chair next to the head of the table, which Bella takes, pointing to another one on the opposite side where the Prince and the Pres are.

The tables are set with gold-rimmed service plates, several different knives and forks on either side of the plates and three wineglasses at each place.

"It was you that I met earlier, right?" the Pres asks. I nod—I'm still not quite up to speaking to him yet.

The Prince takes my hand and bends low to kiss it. "Charmed, I'm sure," After his highness releases me, the Pres steps behind my chair and pulls it out for me, scooching it up to table after I sit. I'm not usually the type to get star-struck, but damn Gina, this is totally extra!

The four dudes are just staring at me and Bella, like they can't believe what they're seeing. I feel my nips getting harder and harder as they stare, both from the scratchy dress and the cool temperature of the room. The grins on the boys' faces tell me that they're totally aware.

"It's bloody amazing," says the Prince. "If it wasn't for the dresses, you couldn't tell them apart."

"Are you exactly alike even under those dresses?" Al asks, with a lecherous smirk.

"Sure!" says Bella, crossing her arms as she takes the top of her dress in both hands, as if she's gonna pull it over her head. "Wanna see?"

"Time for that later," says the Pres. He looks to his right. "Now here come our hosts."

I turn to see Jay Ellis and Gerry entering the room. Ellis is decked out in white tie like the other guys, and Gerry is wearing an immaculate, floor-length white evening dress. It's strapless, showing ample cleavage below the diamond-studded choker round her neck.

"I hope we haven't kept you waiting too long, gentlemen," says Ellis, but his tone says he doesn't give a damn.

Walking right past the Pres and me, Ellis takes his place at the head of the table, leaving Gerry to sit at the foot. The Prince performs the same service for her as the Pres did for me, and she rewards him with a smile full of promise.

138

"I can't speak for the rest of you," says Ellis, "but I'm starved." He pushes a button next to his place setting. In a moment, four girls enter, a blonde and three brunettes, topless, in miniskirts, knee-high white socks and black heels. Not one looks older than sixteen. Two of them carry trays— one is empty and the second contains salads. Another one has a bottle of wine in a two handled silver ice bucket. The girl with the empty tray visits Ellis first, removing his service plate, while the second one steps up behind him as soon as the first girl moves away and places a salad in front of him. He smiles slightly as the girl's titties swing in front of his face and looks right in my eyes as he does so. I suppress a shudder. The girl with the ice bucket is next, and the last girl removes the bottle from it, wrapping it in a towel, then pouring a sample in Ellis's glass. He picks it up by the stem, swirls and sniffs it, takes a sip, then nods at the girl. She fills his glass half full and he nods.

The young ladies make their way around the able delivering a salad and wine to everyone. I notice Al, on the other side of the table from me, reach up beneath the blonde girl's skirt as she serves him. She starts a little when he touches her and I'm afraid she'll drop her tray, but she makes a nice recovery before favoring him with a smile that looks forced.

Once all of the plates are delivered, the girls leave the room.

The salad looks like small chunks of cantaloupe on curly greens with chips of hard cheese scattered around and drops of brown liquid over everything. The smell of vinegar rises to my nostrils. That's a prob—I hate vinegar. I guess no salad for me.

Ellis sure likes it though, scarfing it down like he hasn't eaten in a week. He looks at me.

'Something wrong with the salad, Natalie?"

"I don't do vinegar," I say.

"But this is balsamic vinegar, from Modena in Italy. Seventy-five years old. I'm sure you've never tasted anything like it before."

"Vinegar's vinegar, dude."

Ellis rolls his eyes and goes back to his salad, then I catch a glimpse of Bella's face across the table, looking at me like a bird at a cobra. Guess I must've done something wrong. Oh, well, he'll get over it.

"Leave it to Jay to serve us vintage vinegar," Al says, chuckling.

"Only the best at this table," agrees the Prince.

Ellis raises his head, reminding me again of the snake, and his eyes travel from the actor to the Prince. "It is apparent who is royalty and who is not," he says. "Blood will tell."

Sister!

Al's eyes narrow and he purses his lips. "Surely, you don't believe that tommyrot, Jay. You're a self-made man. Nobody ever handed you anything."

The Prince stiffens at that last, and spits Al with a glare. "Meaning that I was handed everything?"

"Now I'm sure that's not what Al meant," says the Pres to the Prince, while Jay looks on with a snarky grin. "Your ancestors risked their lives for everything you now have."

"But he didn't," says Al, clearly pissed.

"Now that's not fair, Al," says the Pres, cutting off the Prince's retort. "His highness actually went to war for his country. Came under fire. Didn't you?"

The Prince, looking somewhat more chill, agrees, "That is correct, Mr. President, I did indeed."

"I got my start in a warzone, too, you know," says Andy, puffing his chest out.

Wow. You can smell the testosterone in here.

The salad course over (I didn't eat mine), Ellis pushes his button again, and in a moment the girls return, six of them, this time. Four are carrying trays containing plates topped with metal domes, which they put down on stands. Two more are there to serve the wine, this one a rosé. They remove the salad plates, replacing them with a domed plate. When the cover is removed from mine, I find that I have a grilled filet mignon, a lobster tail, asparagus and a loaded baked potato. The wine girls do their thing, and after Ellis's approval, I take a sip of mine. It's surprisingly light and fresh and will go well with both the beef and the lobster.

As I dig into the steak, Ellis turns the table talk to politics. The Pres's party is in power right now, and Al and Andy seem to support it as well, so when Ellis starts criticizing some of the current policies, things start to get heated.

"You can't run a country on borrowed money forever," Ellis says. "Sooner or later the reckoning will come due. The U.S. either pays up, or China will own the whole fucking place. And the U.S.A. simply doesn't have the money."

"It's not the paying up that's important," says the Pres. "It's that we never let them realize that we have no intention of ever paying up."

"We British had the perfect solution to that a century ago," says the Prince. "We just addicted the lot of them to opium, then made them pay and pay to get it from us."

140

"And fought a war over it too," says Andy.

"Two wars," the Prince claps back. "Won 'em both!"

"Maybe that's the reason that China hates you now," I say. "And us, too."

As one, the four men turn to look at me, slack-jawed. Bella and Gerry too.

"What?" I say. "I'm not allowed to have an opinion?"

"Not when you're spewing absolute bullshit," says Ellis. "What do you know about it, anyway?"

"Plenty," I clap back. "We studied the Opium Wars in college, in European History."

Ellis pushes his chair back, stands up and bows from the waist. "Do pardon me, gentlemen, I forgot. We have a scholar in our midst," he says with a broad grin.

The chuckles and snickers that pass around the table really piss me off.

"You've got to admire the absolute brass of her, though," Ellis continues. "Sitting at a table with a prince of the realm, an elder statesman, a respected newsman and a titan of finance who never graduated college, she dares to venture her own paltry opinion."

"What about me," says Al.

"What about you?" returns Ellis. "You're just a damned cop. A lackey!"

The other three men roar with laughter, and Gerry sits silently, gazing adoringly at her man. Al springs up, turning his chair over in the process, and stomps out.

"He'll be back if he wants Suzie and her little friend later," says Ellis. He looks at me. "As for you... the next time I want your opinion, I'll give it to you."

I open my mouth to deliver a response, but Bella beats me to it. "Stop it!" she hollers. "Don't treat my sister that way!"

We all gape at Bella in amazement. Where the fuck did that come from?

"The mouse that roared," laughs Ellis.

"I mean it, Dad. Don't treat her like that!"

Dad?

Chapter 35

The twin odors of bruised leaves and earthworms invade Eduardo's nostrils as he cowers among the shrubbery.

The foliage of the surrounding trees is periodically illuminated by the bright yellow beam of a searchlight dancing among them.

Por favor, Jesucristo, do not let me sneeze!

The light is mounted on the back of a Jeep parked in the road next to the woods. The kids heard the vehicle coming and got off the road, taking refuge in the woods. But it may have been too late. Else, why are the soldiers searching this patch of trees with the light?

Sweat streams down over Eduardo's forehead and his neck tickles in back as something with legs works its way inside his hoodie.

Shannie lies quivering beside him, quiet as a ghost. Tabby and Pepe are nearby, but he cannot see them.

She gropes for his hand in the darkness, touches it, but he pulls away. Then he thinks better and allows her to take it.

This is not her fault.

He is momentarily blinded as the yellow beam sweeps across the bushes hiding them.

Dios mio! Did they see us?

***

The evening began simply enough with a fine dinner of hot dogs, baked beans, cole slaw and apple pie. Afterwards, Cheryl showed the kids another sex vid.

This time, the actors were kids their own age.

I knew it! They are making movies of us!

Thankfully, the film was shorter than those they'd seen before. Eduardo's face burned with shame when the lights came up. He hoped the others couldn't tell how he felt.

"There now," said Cheryl. "Wasn't that great? We're going to call it an early night—I'm sure you have plenty to do upstairs in your rooms. See you in the morning."

Once in their room, by unspoken agreement, Eduardo and Tabby stripped to their underwear and slipped into bed. A glance told Eduardo that the little light on the clock, and so too the camera, was on.

Tabby snuggled close and brought her lips to his ear. "We'd better give them a show," she whispered, "so they don't figure out we know they're watching."

He grunted his assent, then she put her mouth on his and kissed him. He didn't kiss her back—this was supposed to be for show, right?

Her kisses became more insistent, then she reached down and slipped a hand into his shorts.

Oh well, at least this will be the last time...

When it was over, Eduardo saw the little light wink out.

"Let us wait a little while, and then we'll go get the others," he said.

Twenty minutes later, the foursome of Eduardo, Tabby, Pepe and Shannie slipped out the back door of the kid's house into the darkness. The air was warm and humid, and smelled of car exhaust. Nevertheless, everyone wore long sleeves because the mosquitos were fierce at night. Pepe led the way, as he knew in which direction the lakeshore lay. He had on an orange and blue State University hoodie just like the one Eduardo had, over blue jeans and sneakers.

"It's *muy fácil*, Pepe said. "We'll just follow the road right to the docks."

Eduardo disagreed. "Perhaps we should keep to the woods," he said. "That way no one will see us. Especially you, wearing a bright orange shirt. I left mine upstairs. What were you thinking, *amigo?*"

"It's too thick in the woods," countered Pepe. "It will take us all night to get there. And this is the only long-sleeved shirt that I have."

Eduardo had come to realize that he could never be right as far as Pepe was concerned.

"Ok. We'll do it your way."

***

Sister!

As the searchlight beam plays about, Eduardo regrets his decision not to fight harder against Pepe's insistence about staying on the road.

The men's voices carry easily through the night air.

"I'm sure I saw somebody run in here, Sarge!"

"Well, I don't see 'em now. Do you?"

"No, but..."

"But nothing! This perimeter is secure. A mouse couldn'ta got inta this compound from outside without we'd know about it. I am not goin' stomping through those woods in the dark. Do you want to?"

"I guess not..."

"Okay then. Back inta da Jeep and let's finish this sweep."

The men climb in the car and the light dies, plunging the woods into darkness once more. All Eduardo can see is the white pool in front of the vehicle as it rapidly moves out of sight. The noise of the engine dissolves into the darkness—soon only the high-pitched drone of crickets remains.

"Let us wait until we can see again," says Eduardo, "then we will go the rest of the way in the woods." This time, Pepe does not object.

It turns out that Pepe was probably right though, because it takes the kids another thirty minutes of bushwhacking before they arrive where woods end near the water. Eduardo's heart drops as he sees the eight-foot chain-link fence topped with razor wire. On the other side, a group of squat wooden buildings illuminated by white, shining light bulbs hanging on strings between poles is nestled on the shore. The sepia waters of the lake itself shimmer beyond.

"Sheeit, man!" exclaims Pepe. "How we gonna get past that?"

"Let's go this way," says Eduardo, pointing right. "Maybe we'll find a way."

They come out of the woods and walk toward the road. When they get there, they see it's blocked by a double gate in the fence.

"Think we can slide between those gates?" Eduardo asks.

"We can try," says Shannie.

Walking up to the gates, Eduardo can see there's only a couple inches of space between them. He grasps them and pulls, but they don't budge.

"Fuck!" says Pepe. "We came all this way for nuthin'!"

"Let's keep going to the wall," says Eduardo. "Maybe there's a way in there."

The kids cross the road, and follow the fence for about a hundred feet until they reach the wall. The fence lies tight against it, coils of concertina wire forming an unbroken barrier on top.

"Would have been nice if you had mentioned this fence when we talked about this," says Eduardo to Pepe.

"Hey man, don't put this on me! I told ya there was guards. I don't remember even seeing the fence when I was here."

"It's not Pepe's fault, Eduardo," Shannie says. "We can't get out this way, is all. We'll just have to go back and try something else."

Eduardo can feel the tears of frustration welling up in his eyes. They'd come too far, risked too much to quit now!

"Fuck, no!" he spits, worming out of his black hoodie. "Let me see if I can cover up that wire."

He holds the sweatshirt by the hood and the bottom, steps back and swings his arms back and forth, simulating a throw. He knows he's only got one shot at this—if the hoodie doesn't land just right, he'll never be able to get it back.

Here goes nothing...

He rocks his arms back, then forward, letting go of the cloth at the end of the arc. The sweatshirt flies up, up, up, goes clear over the fence and catches on the wire as it comes back down, covering the last third of the wire on the back side of the fence.

Damn it! The wire on this side is totally bare. It would cut to dogmeat anyone who tried to get over it.

"C'mon everybody!" says Pepe. "Take off your coats. Let's get the rest of it covered up." It's not long before a section of wire eighteen inches wide is blanketed with cloth.

Pepe is still holding his State hoodie, which he was obviously reluctant to sacrifice. He pulls it back over his head. Seeing that the section of wire that's covered is small, Eduardo says, "Hey Pepe. Throw your hoodie up there too!"

"You don't need it, man! We can get over that."

Maybe, if I'm really careful.

Not wanting to argue with Pepe again, Eduardo grabs the chain link with his hands and pulls himself up, sticking the toes of his sneakers through the holes in the fence. When he reaches the concertina wire, he levers himself up with his arms so he's standing on the bar on top, then he attempts to bring his leg over the wire while holding on to it with the cloth protecting his hands. He gets one leg over and places his foot on the bar on the other side, then tries to bring his other leg over. Once he has, he carefully reaches down to grasp the bar between the wire, then lowers his feet to climb down, jumping the last three feet or so.

"Wow! Pretty easy, man! C'mon Pepe—you're next."

Pepe tries to emulate Eduardo, and he does fine until he's bringing that second leg over the top. He's bigger than Eduardo and his legs are longer, so his jeans catch on the wire where there's no cloth. He has to jerk his leg to free it, and the razor wire parts the denim, slicing through the flesh beneath. Pepe yipes and loses his grip, and is left hanging on to the cloth, dangling from the fence. It rips with a rasping sound and Pepe drops six feet to the ground. Now the razor wire is completely uncovered again and the cloth in Pepe's hands is in shreds, unusable.

"Smooth move, *amigo*," Eduardo says angrily, and Pepe wheels around on him with his fists balled.

"Don't fight!" shouts Tabby from the other side.

"Go and do what you came to do," says Shannie. "We'll go back to the house. We'll be expecting you to come and get us."

"Hey, wait…" says Eduardo, but the girls disappear into the darkness.

"*Muy bien, gilipollas.*" All right, shithead, says Pepe. "The girls are counting on us. Let's go." He heads off along the wall toward the lake shore.

Eduardo shakes his head.

No matter what I do, he just will not be my friend.

He follows the older boy.

The lake is only a hundred yards away. The wall ends at the shore, but another chain link fence festooned with concertina wire abuts it, extending at an angle out into the water for another couple hundred feet. On the other side of the fence, the shore is built up and a large horizontal drainpipe empties into a culvert leading to the lake. On this side, it's about a ten-foot drop onto jagged rocks.

"What do we do?" says Pepe.

"We have no choice," says Eduardo. "We must get on the fence and climb down. Can you swim?"

Pepe looks like a deer staring at a shotgun. "No, man. Can you?"

Eduardo can—Daddy Danny taught him a couple summers ago. The thought of his Daddy brings tears to his eyes. What an *imbécil* he was to ever run away from the family that loved him. He realizes that *Mamá* Lupe hadn't meant to hurt him like she did—she was just scared he'd be taken away from her again.

He says to Pepe, "It doesn't matter. We'll climb down and get into the water. You can hold on to the fence while we go around to the other side. Then we'll be outside of this place and can go for help."

Pepe looks warily at the sharp grey rocks below. "You go first."

"Okay."

Eduardo grabs the fence, gets his toes in the holes and scootches sideways until he's beyond the rocks and over the water. He knows better than to let go and jump in—that water is as black as sin and there's no telling how deep it is. So, he just scoots down like a monkey until he's immersed.

"It's not too cold, but it smells like the sewer," he hollers to Pepe. "And it's over my head. But remember, it don't matter how deep it is, because you can hold on to the fence."

A wailing siren splits the air, making Eduardo jump. A yellow beam slices through the night and settles on Pepe, starkly illuminating him, frozen on the edge of the wall ten feet above.

"Stay where you are!" A voice blares through a bullhorn. "Don't move or we will shoot!"

Unthinking, Pepe spins around to face the voice. An Uzi rattles. Pepe's foot leaves the wall and dangles over open air. As if in a slo-mo replay, his body tilts backwards until the other foot comes off, and he falls, fully stretched out, onto the wicked rocks at the base.

"Noooo!"

Chapter 36

For once, I'm totally at a loss for words.

"Well, well!" says Ellis. "The cub finally shows its teeth. I was really wondering if you had any, Arabella. Your sister certainly does."

If Bella's my sister and he's her dad, then that makes him...

"What do you mean?" says Bella.

...Sperm donor 001?

"I mean, you've been falling over backwards to impress me with your filial devotion ever since I apprised you of our relationship."

So who is egg donor 001? My eyes drift to the end of the table where Gerry sits, a half-smile on her face as she watches the exchange between her man and Bella.

OMG! No way!

"So, these two are your little girls?" asks the Pres.

Ellis answers him with a broad grin. He turns to look at me. "Cat got your tongue, Natalie? This is not how I wanted you to find out, but..."

For lack of a reply, I cut a piece of lobster and cram it into my mouth. I'm not sure if I want to cry or to get up and wipe that fucking grin off his face. My muscles tense as I prepare to do the latter, but then I remember the reason I'm here.

Eduardo.

Picking up his knife and fork, Ellis says, "Well, we shouldn't let this surprise cause an excellent dinner to get cold." He turns to the Pres once more. "Now, Mr. President, when do you think your successor is going to put a stop to this profligate spending?"

A lively discussion between the three men follows.

Bella looks at me with tears in her eyes, then begins mechanically shoveling her food into her mouth. I remember Ellis's reaction when I wouldn't eat the salad, and think that I'd better do the same.

I wonder WTF Ellis expects from me? Did he take Eduardo just to get me here? That seems unlikely—it was Lupe who was responsible for Eduardo running away. But now that he has my son, is Ellis going to use him to get something from me? What could he want?

The main course is finished and the girls appear to take our plates and deliver *crème brûlée* for dessert. Al returns while they are serving, and the scowl he's wearing vanishes when he sees Suzie again.

Ellis delivers a monologue on international finance while dessert is being consumed. The shock after Bella spilled the tea is fading—I find it interesting that even the Pres isn't speaking up to contradict him anymore.

"I want to thank all of you for a most interesting evening," says Ellis, as the dessert dishes are cleared. "I'd offer coffee and an after-dinner libation, but I know there are other activities you would rather pursue."

The girls return, along with a boy of about sixteen with dark, curly hair and oversized glasses who goes to stand behind Andy's chair. Al crooks a finger at Suzie, whom he's been harassing all evening, and she reluctantly comes to take his hand. Another girl joins them. A girl of no more than fifteen approaches the Prince, while the other two girls, looking much more cheerful, go to the Pres. It becomes pretty real about what's going to happen upstairs.

"Until morning, gentlemen," says Ellis, and the men leave the room with their fuck buddies in tow.

When they're gone, Ellis turns to me. "Now Natalie, I'm sure you have questions."

"Just one." I say. "Why?"

"Why did I make you? Simple. For the good of mankind."

Yeet! This is one thoroughly fucked up dude!

"In the early twentieth century, eugenicists such as Alexis Carrel and Charles Lindbergh believed that mankind could better itself by selective breeding—encouraging people with good genes to procreate and discouraging the breeding of those with inferior traits. The greatest flaw in their thinking was that they did not understand the scale of the problem. There are so many menials and so few exceptional men that such a program could never succeed. The elite would simply constitute a drop in very large bucket, and be overwhelmed by the rampant proliferation of the rabble. Ever since the failure of our friend Mr. Hitler, governments have been loath to enact the measures necessary to see such a program to fruition. Of secondary import, but just as crucial, is the difficulty of identifying those with desirable genes. Success and wealth are good indicators, but a close look at our friend the Prince shows that they are not infallible. Still, the presence of even one *ubermensch* cannot help but enrich humanity, and since I knew of one, I resolved to create my own program to perpetuate him."

He's talking about himself?

"So, I acquired New Horizons as a vehicle to carry out my plan. My approach was twofold. First, I endeavored to spread my own genes throughout the population as much as I could. I'm proud to tell you that the number of my descendants is in the thousands. Secondly, I decided to attempt controlled inbreeding to concentrate my superior genes in other individuals, much as a selective breeding regimen for champion race horses or show dogs works. The first step was to acquire a suitable mate—he looks to a beaming Gerry at the other end of the table. Next, I had to create some suitable breeding partners. You and Arabella are some of the results."

"You want to have kids with me? No fucking way, motherfucker! Why don't you just clone yourself?"

"Actually, I think daughterfucker is a more precise locution. And cloning technology is not yet sufficiently advanced to make that foolproof. Cloned animals suffer from a plethora of health issues such as bodily deformations, organ dysfunctions and early death. Besides, the world is simply not ready for another me. On the other hand, directed inbreeding has been employed for thousands of years to produce superior stock. There is the problem concentrating deleterious genes in the progeny, but that is what culling is for."

Culling? You mean killing those who don't measure up. I look at my sister. "You're okay with this?" Her broad smile is all the answer I need.

"I knew I had dear Bella on board when she actually agreed to murder someone to impress me," Ellis says. "Having become acquainted with you through the frequent coverage in the media that you seem to attract, I anticipated some difficulty in bringing you on board. The threat of violence is always an option, but I find that unpalatable. So imagine my surprise and delight when fate took a hand to bring me exactly what I needed to encourage your participation."

Now I'm scared. I think I know, but I ask anyway. "What do you mean?"

He pauses, and looks to the ceiling. "Sylvia! Lower the screen."

As before, a slot in the ceiling opens and a screen descends into the room. When it has reached a level for comfortable viewing, it stops. Ellis consults his watch, which displays a list of numbers rather than the time, then he says, "Schoolhouse video 86-a."

The screen flickers and a picture takes shape. A guy and a girl in bed, making love.

Wait a minute, those are kids!

Holy shit! That's my son!

"Eduardo!"

I stand up so fast that my chair falls over backwards, intending to dive at Ellis and beat him to a pulp. Then I see the Tazer in his hand.

"I said I found violence distasteful, but I never said it doesn't have its place."

I stand quivering for a moment, every part of me urging me to damn the stun gun and go for him anyway. But reason prevails. "What did you do to him?"

"Not much, actually. Just set up the proper conditions and let nature take its course. But now you have something to consider. I can destroy that video and send your boy back to his family, or I can sell it to a distributor who will have it all over the dark web in a day. Which one would you prefer?"

"You know which one."

"And you know the cost."

Unexpectedly, Gerry is behind me, picking up the chair that I knocked over, so I can sink back into it. I look at Bella across the table. She's smiling at me, like she could care less.

Did she even know about this?

"What made you even think that you could do this?" I say to Ellis. "It's totally fucked." I don't expect an answer, but I get one.

"Thomas Carlyle, the great historian and philosopher, promulgated a theory in 1840, which held that all of human history is simply the history of a few great men—everyone else is simply the supporting cast. Great men do not seek sanction from others before acting—they follow their instincts, which always results in the best outcome. So, I don't question what I can do. I know that I can do anything I want to, and that it will always be the right thing because it was I that has done it."

"But I'm not a monster," Ellis goes on.

Coulda fooled me, asshole.

"You've had a number of shocks this evening, Natalie, and frankly, I'd like to have you as a willing participant when we do the deed. Why don't you go upstairs with Bella, do what sisters do, and get your head wrapped around your new reality. You've got a new family now."

"When are you going to let Eduardo go?"

Sister!

"As soon as you've convinced me that you're totally on board with my program," he says. "And there's one more thing." He presses the button next to him on the table.

A young girl comes out, carrying a tray containing a small plate with a metal dome on top, and a knife and fork. She places them in front of me, and removes the dome. The odor of vinegar makes me queasy.

"Eat your salad," Ellis says.

Chapter 37

Back in the pink bedroom, Bella says to me, "Natalie, I'm so sorry you had to find out that way."

You sure didn't look like you were sorry when we were downstairs.

"Find out what?" I respond "That Jay Ellis is an entitled prick?"

She puts on a serious pout. "Of course not. And he isn't. He's our father."

"Not mine. My daddy was Sean McMasters and my mom is Judy Murdoch McMasters. I want no part of that asshole!"

"Stop calling him names! He's our father, and he loves us!"

I can't believe that she believes that shit.

"Loves us? Bella, he conned you into killing an innocent man. The cops've fucking got you on tape! If they get their hands on you, they'll throw you in jail for the rest of your life! And Ellis has got a vid of my little boy having sex with another kid, which he's threatening to sell to a bunch of pedos. You call that love?"

"He's just testing our faith in him. He won't let those things happen to either of us."

She pulls the tight gold dress over her head and throws it on the floor. Underneath, she wears nothing at all, and her little puss is shaved bare. Just like her Zaddy likes it, I bet. She turns down the shocking pink coverlet on the bed and pats the mattress. "Here. Let's sleep together tonight, like sisters do. It'll all be better in the morning."

"I've got a better idea. You know where Eduardo is, right?" The way she cocks her head a little says she does. "Why don't you take me to him? Then the three of us can get out of here. I'll help you with the cops. We can play you as some kind of brainwashed cult victim. You'll be free of those two maniacs!"

She raises her hand to her mouth and chews on the nail of her little finger. Her eyes are wide. "I can't do that," she says. She pats the mattress again. "Please, Natalie. Take off your dress, get into bed with me and let's cuddle." Her tone is almost pleading.

When I worked the strip club, I was proud that I could get a guy to do just about anything I wanted. Give him a look that promised him the world,

Sister!

show him a little more skin, convince him that another ten dollars would get me to go home with him and spend the night having hot, raging sex. Earlier, I got a vibe that Bella was into me sexually. Maybe I can use that now. Crossing my arms in front of me, I grab the top of the silver dress and pull it over my head. Bella's eyes are glued to my bod. I spread my legs a little and push out my titties like I'm getting ready to strut my stuff on stage. Her eyes get a little bigger and she licks her lips. Oh yeah, she likes girls, all right.

I stand in front of her as she sits on the bed, put my hands on her shoulders and bring my tittie close to her face. She can't help it, her mouth pops open and her little pink tongue snakes out. She leans forward to kiss my nipple, but I pull back at the last sec so she gets nothing but air.

"This isn't right," I say.

"What isn't right?"

"This. Having sex. We're sisters."

She smiles at me. "Sisters shouldn't love each other?"

She raises a hand to touch my pussy. Unlike hers, mine has a dark thatch that both Lupe and Danny like to play with. A thought arises unbidden.

Should I be doing this? To my spouses?

The answer comes.

Yes, I should, if it will get me to Eduardo.

I step closer and let her run her finger through my hair, and a tingle runs from there up to my belly button.

"See," she says. "You like it."

Her hands move to grip my hips and she leans forward, her tongue flicking out again. I step back once more. She looks up into my face with doe eyes.

"Please," she says. "Let me do you. Afterwards, I'll take you to Eduardo. I promise."

Gotcha!

I let her pull me toward her, put her mouth on me, part my lips with hers and swirl her tongue inside me. I grip both sides of her head and press her mouth into me. I think about what Danny would say, then blank it out.

It's just sex. It means nothing. It will get me what I want.

154

And it feels so, so good, her warm tongue circling, the pressure building in my loins, spreading up into my belly and down into my legs. I lean forward as my knees give way and she falls backwards, then we're both in bed, with me on top and her still tonguing me. Her hands move to my ass and she spreads my cheeks, her finger strokes that sensitive spot between my butt and my cunny. I start grinding into her mouth, but now she pulls away.

"Turn around," she says. "Do me too!"

Totally on auto now, I do as she says, stretching myself out on top of her, my head between her legs. I lean down and apply my tongue—a muffled moan comes from beneath me as she doubles down on me. The warmth in my underparts has grown as big as it can and I know I'm gonna come. I raise my head and arch my back, and a scream bursts from my lips as I let go. It seems to go on forever until I'm finally drained, collapsing on top of her again.

She opens her legs wide. "Finish me!" she says, her tone no longer pleading. I do as she asks, and she grips my head with her hands and thighs, shuddering and screaming so the whole place will hear.

When she's finished, she says, "C'mere." I turn around and slide into the comfort of her embrace, her face in mine.

"Hey you," she says, stroking my hair. "You're me."

I kiss her gently, then again more intently. "I love you, Sis."

She smiles. It's what she wants to hear. I close my eyes.

I must have passed out, because the next thing I know she's kissing me again, short little nips on my lips followed by a full-on tongue kiss that gets my pussy stirring again. She rolls me so I'm face up and she gets on top, kissing my mouth non-stop until she begins working her way down. She spends a few minutes on my tits, licking and biting the nipple, each touch of her hot mouth sending electric shocks to the end of my fingers and toes. She goes further down to my belly button, swirling her tongue there until I can't take it anymore and put my hands on top of her head to push her where I really want her. She licks me again, getting me nice and wet, but then stops.

"No," I murmur, "please. Keep going."

"Just wait," she replies, sitting up and grabbing my ankles, pushing my legs upward like she's going to mount me like a man.

"Hold your legs," she says, and I do, and she moves up so we're joined in the middle. She begins moving, rubbing herself on me. At first, the sensation is soothing, but as she continues, I feel myself opening up, and so

Sister!

does she. I slide my hands up to grip my ankles, hold my legs widespread while she looms above me, stroking, stroking, stroking, and the tension builds in my loins until I think I'll go cray with want. I see her with her head thrown back, long blonde hair streaming down, eyes shut and her mouth half-open, nipples erect, sweat streaming down her naked bod, and suddenly the absolute wrongness of it all hits me—it's me, fucking myself, the height of narcissism.

It's just sex, Nattie.

But is it, or is it something else, dangerous and powerful?

Which one of us just got played?

Once again, my insides spasm in ecstasy and Bella collapses on top of me, driving the breath from my lungs. She pushes her face against mine, nuzzles my ear as she whispers, "I love you, Sis."

My nose buried in her long blonde hair, I inhale her sweet, sweaty scent. "I love you too, Bella."

Cold fear rushes through me as I realize that this time, I mean it!

Against my will, my eyes begin to close again.

No! I can't fall asleep! Not now!

I jerk my head to wake myself, and my eyes fall on the door to the hallway. The knob slowly turns...

Chapter 38

The door opens and Gerry floats into the room, resplendent in a red kimono covered with cranes and palm trees.

Leaving nothing to the imagination, it hangs open at the top to reveal her drooping, cow-like breasts, ending just below her belly-button where her dense black bush is clearly visible.

Behind her comes the man himself, jaybird naked, sporting a shameless erection.

Bella sits up next to me with a big smile of anticipation. As a former stripper, I'm totally used to just about anyone seeing my goods, but this is just totally fucked. But it is just what Ellis said he wanted, now isn't it?

Gerry sheds the kimono and sits on the bed next to Bella, placing her open mouth over Bella's. Ellis comes round the bed to me. I want to move away, but that would take me right into the mother-daughter scene next to me. This is beyond creepy!

Ellis skips any preliminaries, taking me by the shoulders and pushing me backwards on the bed. Once again, my martial training is useless, because I can't get my legs under me to draw power from them. I kick at him, but he simply grabs my ankle, pushing my legs apart so he can get between them and slip into me. I'm open and wet from Bella's earlier ministrations, so he has no problems.

"No!" I holler as he begins thrusting. All of the powerlessness and anger I felt in Irwin's flat in New York comes rushing back. Not again!

Ellis doesn't last long at all—his eyes close and he grits his teeth into a skeletal grin. The thought occurs that I haven't taken my pill since I got back from New York on Wednesday.

Still flailing with my legs, I knock him backwards and he slips out of me. As he reaches for me again, I roll out of bed, get my feet on the floor, then grab his wrist and use his forward energy to pull him completely out of the bed, sending him flying face first into the wall. He lets out a pitiful "Owww!" as he collapses to the floor.

Both Gerry and Bella are looking at me as if I've just sprouted horns and a tail with a spearpoint on the end. "Jay!" shouts Gerry. "What did you do to him, you little bitch?"

"Gave him what he fucking deserved," I say.

Sister!

Gerry gets out of bed on the other side and jerks open the door to the hall. "Guard!" she yells.

Bella, all teeth and claws, comes at me across the mattress. "You fucking bitch! You hurt my Dad!" she snarls.

I don't want to injure her like Ellis, so I settle for an open-handed slap across the face before stepping back out of her reach. She falls face first onto the bed, bawling like a child.

The hall door slams open, taking a chunk of plaster out of the wall as it hits. A thug with an Uzi stands there, mouth agape as he takes in a room full of naked people.

Pointing to me, Gerry hollers, "Get her!"

I step into *gong-bu*, my hands rotating in the reciprocal circular pattern called cloud hands, ready for the guard to accost me. He takes one look at Ellis, who's still trying to get up from where I tossed him, and levels the Uzi at me saying, "On the floor, Lady, hands behind you." Smart man.

Will he really shoot me if I come at him?

I decide I don't want to find out, so I assume the position. He moves next to me and places a knee on my neck, shutting off my breathing. I try not to panic as I feel a zip-tie go round my wrists and tighten painfully. The knee is removed so I can breathe again, but the thug grabs the tie between my wrists and jerks me painfully to my feet. I let out a yell, because it hurts, but also to distract him as I set my feet in *gong bu* again. I feel to detect which way his weight is shifted, then abruptly rotate my hips in that direction, taking him completely off his feet and tossing him into the bed with Bella. The bed gives way as his 200-pound plus frame hits it and crashes onto the floor. I run for the open door, but Gerry sticks out a foot to trip me, and my face slams into the doorframe as I fall forward.

As I struggle to my feet once more, I feel the barrel of the Uzi at the base of my neck.

"Try that one more time, girlie, and I'll take your head off. Now get up."

I do as he says. At least I've convinced him to keep his hands off me.

Ellis has finally gotten to his feet. He's got blood running down the side of his face and the beginnings of a glorious black eye, and I see with satisfaction that his member is shriveled up like a prune. He walks right up to me and throws his right fist into my belly. I see it coming, so I tighten up the muscles of my *dantian* and his fist bounces like he hit a board. His eyes open in surprise, but then he recovers and backhands me across the face. That one hurt.

158

"I've got just the place for you, you little cunt," he hisses. To the guard: "Take her downstairs and lock her up."

Chapter 39

M. B.'s eyes pop open and travel automatically to her bedside clock. 4:58. Shit.

Short sleep is the blessing and the curse of advanced age. More time to spend in the world before you leave it at the expense of being sleepy all the time.

Like everyone else, M.B. is worried about Nattie and Eduardo being in Ellis's compound. On the other hand, she just can't see the billionaire doing them any actual harm. He's been put on notice that others are aware that Nattie and Eduardo are there—he's got powerful friends that can shield him from a lot of things, but murder and assault are likely not among them.

In the kitchen, M.B. puts on the coffee pot while considering what else she can do to rectify the situation. The FBI has a lot of power, but even it is subject to oversight. Most agents don't want to do anything that would be a career killer. Pissing off a billionaire could be one of those.

M.B.'s phone begins playing *Strangers in the night* and a tinny voice announces "Unknown caller."

She hits the button. "Woodrow."

"Be at the Confederate Cemetery downtown in half an hour," says a heavily disguised mechanical voice. "I have some poop for you about Jay Ellis."

"Wait! Who..." M.B. realizes that she's talking to herself.

Half an hour! If she just throws on some clothes and doesn't worry about prettyin' up, she'll just make it. As an FBI agent, she's got a lot of experience at that.

The sky is going from indigo to rose as the sun is just crawling above the horizon, when M.B.'s bug pulls up in front of the old graveyard. A sign on the gate says it isn't open yet, but the gate is cracked. One of the perks of a federal agent is that you don't get arrested for trespassing, so she locks the car and slips inside, heading for the domed structure in the center of the cemetery that serves as a memorial to the Confederate dead.

The cobblestone pathway winds among pointed grey tombstones engraved with the names, units and dates of the men interred there, some of them decorated with little confederate flags and flowers. M.B. thinks the air here is heavy, with a faint smell of sulfur, but that might be her imagination—she was never fond of buryin' grounds because she's been uncomfortably close to occupying one herself a few times.

The memorial structure is simple, just a stone dome supported on pillars, with the flag of the CSA flying on top. Inside is a pedestal containing a green copper plaque engraved with the names and dates of the soldiers buried here. The place has become a bone of contention lately, with some protesting that it memorializes a bunch of racists and traitors, which should be torn down to put in a safe space for some politically popular group. M.B. shakes her head—used to be there was respect for those who fought for something bigger than themselves, even if one didn't happen to espouse their cause. That, among many other things that used to hold people together, is slowly withering away.

Passing between the pillars, she notes that the place is empty. She walks to center and sees a disposable cell phone known as a "burner" lying on top of the plaque. It begins humming as she picks it up.

"Woodrow."

It's the same disguised voice she heard earlier. "You don't know me, but I was a friend of JV's." JV was M.B.'s former supervisor and mentor, now deceased and greatly missed. "He asked me to look out for you when he retired."

"That's nice," says M.B., meaning it. "But what's that got to do with all the tradecraft?"

"I hear you've been asking about Jerome Ellis. I just thought you should know you're about to walk into a minefield."

"How so?"

"You must know that Ellis has got a lot of friends in high places, including the Bureau. You might also guess that he's got enemies, too. Well, his friends and enemies are in a war. And this is a war you really don't want to take sides in, because you stand an excellent chance of becoming a casualty no matter which side you're on."

"Some friends of mine have become involved with Ellis, through no fault of their own. I just want to make sure they can get uninvolved, without getting hurt."

"Unfortunately, that may not be possible."

"What do you mean?"

"When this thing started, the main goal of Ellis's enemies was to put him away on federal charges."

"For what?"

Sister!

"A whole raft of things. Various and sundry financial crimes including manipulating markets, insider trading and money laundering. Extortion. Exploitation of minors. Enough to see that he becomes a permanent resident of a federal prison somewhere. But it's gone way beyond that now. Ellis has let it be known that if he goes down, he's going to take a lot of folks with him. He's got a lot of dirt on a lot of very important people. Career-ending dirt. Now, the smart money says that the only way to get rid of Ellis is to get rid of him, permanently. Problem is, he's got a private island and a private army, and connections everywhere from cartels to terrorist states. So, like I said, there's a very good chance that a lot of folks are going to get hurt when this thing plays itself out. For JV's sake, I just wanted you to know what you're getting into."

Earlier, M.B. thought that Nattie and Eduardo were in little danger because people knew that they were with Ellis. Now, she's not sure at all.

"So, what do I do?"

"Unless those friends of yours are very special, cut 'em loose."

"No can do. Actually, they're not friends. They're family."

"Then you better get them the hell out of there. Fast. Word is, something big is going down, soon."

"What..."

"I've said enough."

The line goes dead.

Chapter 40

Eduardo never sees Pepe hit the rocks.

At the rattle of gunfire, he ducks under the tepid water and starts swimming toward the center of the lake like a seal. He knows that he could never make it across—that lake must be half a mile wide—but if he can stay mostly submerged, they can't see him to shoot at him.

Can they?

He swims and swims until his lungs feel like they're about to burst, then he surfaces and sucks in a big breath of sewerstench. Looking back at the shore, he sees two dudes standing at the top of the wall about fifty feet away, shining their lights down at the rocks below. He sees no sign of Pepe, for which he's grateful.

He ducks under again and continues swimming out into the lake. The further he goes the colder the water's gets. When he surfaces again, he's about twice as far from the guards, who are now aiming their lights outward, white ovals skimming the water's surface.

One more good swim ought to get me out of range.

He's just about to duck under when the entire shore blazes yellow with floodlights—it's like he's in a swimming pool in broad daylight.

Down he goes again, arms and legs churning for all he's worth. The time he's able to stay under is getting shorter with each swim—he rolls over on his back when he feels his chest constricting and sees light on the water above, so he turns over again and tries to go as far as he can. Finally, he just can't even, so he surfaces to the sound of a siren blaring in the compound. There's a lot of activity on the shore now, but no one is looking his way, so he stays on the surface and starts swimming parallel to the lakeshore. He figures he's about fifty yards out.

He makes it out of the light, then turns back towards shore. His strokes are getting weaker and the water's getting colder—fear wells up in his belly as he realizes he may not have the strength to make it. He tries not to think about what it will be like to slide beneath the surface, to suck the smelly black water into his lungs. His Daddy is a Marine and he's told Eduardo a thousand times that Marines never give up.

I won't give up until I cannot swim another stroke.

The sound of a giant buzzsaw splits the air—it's got to be a boat!

Sister!

Oh no! They're taking to the water to hunt me down.

It changes nothing, though. He's got to keep on swimming for shore or drown, a fate that he's pretty sure would please his pursuers.

Finally, his limbs ache so bad that they just freeze up. A cramp lances across his back from shoulder to shoulder. His head is going under!

Dios mio, I'm going to die!

He lets his legs drift downward to keep his mouth and nose above water, but fails. He holds his breath one last time as his nostrils go under, then his feet hit something solid and sink into it. He pushes upward, but the mud sucks at his feet, holding him back, then all at once he's bobbing like a cork on the surface, taking a deep breath through his mouth, inhaling a good gulp of the oily water along with the air. Choking, he stumbles forward until he falls on his face, but now the water is shallow enough that he can make it rest of the way on his hands and knees. He pulls himself out of the lake onto a muddy shore, then blackness descends upon him.

It's the cold that wakes him. He's never been this cold, not in all of his ten years. A stiff wind coming off the lake makes it feel like a block of ice is lying on his back—of course, it's just his wet clothes plastered to his skin. Shivering, he tries to stand, but his legs fail, so he crawls like a worm toward the bulk of the woods looming on the shore, a primal instinct telling him it will be warmer once inside. He can't hear the boat on the lake anymore, so maybe they've given up looking for him. Sure enough, when he reaches the sanctuary of the trees, he feels warmer out of the wind and finally stands up with help from a tree.

Zeeee... A high-pitched whine next to his left ear. He swipes with his hand and it stops. *Zeeee...* The other ear this time. Mosquitos! Covered with lake water, he smells just like home. He makes the buzzer go away again, then a tiny needle pierces the back of his hand. He swats it with the other one and something squishes, then he feels the pricks on his arms (the little *cabrones* are biting him right through his clothes), on his face, the back of his neck.

He's deadly tired, but he knows he's got to get moving, get out of here before all the blood in his body is drained. It's dark, but the moon provides just enough light for him to see silhouettes of trees. Daddy Danny taught him a trick to walk a straight line in the forest—stand next to a tree, find another one in the direction you're going and walk straight to it. Do that over and over until you're out for the woods. Sooner or later, there'll be a road where he can flag down a car and a kind driver will take him back to his family. Then he'll call the police and tell them to get Shannie and Tabby out of that terrible place where they make kids have sex with each other.

Sweet, resiny pinescent mingles with the sewer smell on his clothes. Thorny plants grow between the trees on the forest floor and catch his legs as he plows though the woods, while branches rake his face leaving behind a coating of what feels like spiderwebs. He chuckles inwardly—Mamá Nattie is deathly afraid of spiders—she would hate it here. But Eduardo is a man.

I killed somebody and I'm not afraid of no fucking spiders.

The thought of killing someone brings Pepe into Eduardo's head without warning.

Is Pepe dead? I hope not. He's an asshole but I hope he's not dead.

He feels tears flowing down his cheeks—what's up with that? Pepe and him weren't even friends or nothing. He realizes that doesn't matter. They were working together to escape. Pepe did not deserve what happened to him. Now Eduardo is very afraid.

If they'll shoot Pepe, they'll shoot me, too.

He goes from tree to tree for what seems like hours. The buzzing mosquitos are constant companions now, and his hands alternate between pushing branches aside and grabbing saplings for balance and brushing the hateful little buggers off his exposed skin. He stops for a sec to dig at a particularly insistent itch. Looking up, he wonders, are the woods just a little bit lighter now? Is morning finally here? Near as he can figure, it was sometime after eleven when the kids left the house last night, and it took at least a couple of hours to get to the fence. Another hour to get over it, so that made it about two o'clock when Pepe got shot and Eduardo went into the lake. He lost all track of time after that. He hopes the sun is rising, because it will greatly speed his progress through the woods.

Sure enough, the forest becomes progressively brighter as he travels, but as the air warms, a mist rises from the forest floor. The groundfog that clings to the tree trunks gives the woodland an otherworldly feel, like he's in *The Hobbit* or something. He remembers that when the woman brought him to the walled compound, there was a road that ran in front of it. If he can just make it there, he can flag down a passing motorist and tell them he's been kidnapped, and to call the cops.

The trees ahead become brighter still, and it's not because of the sun, it's because the branches are thinning out—he must be getting near the road! He no longer has to move from tree to tree, he can just focus on heading for the brightness.

In a minute he's pushing through the briars and bushes at the forest's edge. Because of the hot sun, the fog is lifting, and he can see the dark strip of asphalt in front of him! As he starts to run for it, a little yellow VW bug zips by him.

Sister!

He knows that car!

"*Mamá* Lupe!"

Chapter 41

When she got into work this morning, Detective Third Grade Julia Sykes realized she had a problem.

A Capital City Police Department detective for only a few months, Julia knows the importance of doing the Job by the book and striving to satisfy the demands of her superiors, if she wants to reach the lofty position of Detective First Grade someday. She's had few problems so far, but this case involving Natalie McMasters and her odd family could cause all her good work to be for naught.

She can understand why any family would be bent out of shape if one of their children was missing. Since Danny Merkel is an ex-cop and a private detective, it's understandable that he would want to investigate his son's disappearance himself. He did excellent work linking Eduardo to Jay Ellis. The shooting of the homeless man Thurmond Jordan was unfortunate, but justified in her eyes, and the higher-ups at CCPD seemed to agree with her when she first filed her report. Then all of a sudden, they didn't.

It's no secret around the CCPD that Jay Ellis is sort of an unofficial mascot. The billionaire shows up at department celebrations and funerals, and has contributed a helluva a lot of money and equipment to the department over the years. He's even established a fund to support the families of fallen officers to keep them in their homes or provide college for their kids. It would take some serious probable cause to get anyone in the department to execute a search warrant on the Man.

Deputy Chief Greene was livid when Sykes returned to the precinct without Danny Merkel. "I can't believe you let that FBI bitch walk all over you, Sykes. That's not the kind of chutzpah we expect out of our Detective Firsts."

"What do you want me to do?" asked Sykes.

"Nothing!" said Greene. "I'll call up to DC and find out if that investigation into Merkel is real. When I find out she was bullshitting you, I'll send a man over there who can handle the job."

For of all her outward audacity, Julia Sykes is a young woman with all of the diffidence, inexperience and lack of self-confidence that can accompany her tender age. To have a deputy chief tell her that she disappointed him is devastating.

Sister!

There must be something she can do to salvage the wreckage of her career! If she could only get Merkel to turn himself in before Greene sends anyone else to bring him in.

Her mind made up, she thinks; *Better not to do this on a department phone in case it doesn't work.*

She rises from her desk and goes outside to the park across the street from headquarters. Sitting on a bench next to the statue of the unknown confederate soldier, she takes out her cell and starts punching in numbers.

***

At Hyacinth House, Danny is at breakfast with M.B. and Lupe. The two of them are trying to convince the distraught mother that Ellis can't afford to hurt Eduardo.

"Whether they'll admit it or not, the cops know he's in there," says Danny. "Ellis doesn't need the kind of grief he'll get if anything bad happens to him."

"He's a rich white guy!" says Lupe. "Everybody knows that those kind of people can do anything they want in America."

"That's not true, Lupe..." begins M.B.

Danny's phone chimes. *Unknown Caller.* The Marine is about to punch the button to kill it when something in his head warns that might be a bad idea. "Sorry ladies, I have to take this."

He gets up and goes into the mudroom. Sitting on the bench in front of the wardrobe, he answers the call.

"This is Danny."

"Mr. Merkel, this is Detective Sykes."

Now he's really sorry he answered. Resisting the impulse to just cut her off, he says, "What can I do for you, Detective?"

"My chief was furious yesterday when I didn't bring you in like he ordered me to. He claims he's got a contact with the Feds who can verify whether that investigation Agent Woodrow claimed was real. If he finds out it isn't, there'll be a whole 'nother slate of charges lodged against you, as well as a formal protest to bureau regarding Agent Woodrow's actions."

Danny says nothing. His eyes wander to the wardrobe across from him where the winter coats and muddy boots reside.

Sykes goes on. "Honestly, I think the best thing you can do is to come downtown and turn yourself in to me. I'll do my best to help you get a fair shake on this thing."

Sure you will.

When he was a cop, Danny employed a hundred versions of the same spiel to get a perp to incriminate himself.

If you don't turn yourself in and tell me what happened, I can't help you...

"If you truly want to help me, Detective, help me get a search warrant for Ellis's compound. I'm sure my son is in there. I have no idea why Ellis would want to keep him. But..."

Danny's eyes flick to the top of the wardrobe, where the drone is resting. His throat tightens and tears well up as he remembers the good time he and Eddie had with that thing.

Sykes cuts him off. "Mr. Merkel, let me stop you right there. It would take an act of Congress to get a search warrant for that compound. Unless you have pictures of your son walking around in there or something else equally compelling, no judge in this town will ever issue one."

"What did you just say?"

"What? I said if you had a picture of your son..."

Rocketing up from the bench and reaching for the drone, Danny kills the call.

Chapter 42

Danny is in a small motorboat in the center of the Green Lake.

There are plenty of fishermen and sailboats on the lake, so I'll never be noticed.

Danny really doesn't have much of a plan. Put the drone up and fly it around Ellis's compound to get the lay of the land, see if he can figure out where they might have Eddie. He might spot Nattie, too, but that wouldn't do much good for probable cause, because he'd have to convince a judge that she was being held under duress.

Now if somebody was holding a gun on her...

He shivers at the thought.

Danny brings up his call list on his cell and touches M.B.'s number. Luckily, there's a good signal here, probably because the billionaire has made sure there are plenty of cell towers nearby. She's back at Hyacinth House, in front of a PC, ready to monitor the vids from the drone.

Wonder if Ellis can tap into my calls? No matter, this is our only shot.

It only rings once before she picks up.

"Woodrow."

"Hey, M.B., I'm about to send her up. Let me know when you've got a visual."

"Roger that." The older lady voice doing military speak makes Danny smile. M.B. is worth her weight in gold.

Better get started.

Soon the little bird is in the air. Danny has chosen an altitude of a hundred meters—high enough so the drone will be virtually invisible from the ground but low enough to provide clear pictures which can be electronically enhanced if they spot anything interesting. Flying manually, he directs the bird to the northeast corner of the compound, where the wall abuts the lake, stopping at the edge of a ten-foot cliff above the water. A chain-link fence begins at the cliffside and extends at an acute angle out into the water for another couple of hundred feet. Large grey rocks are piled at the base of the cliff. Further from the edge, a cluster of single-story clapboard buildings is bunched on the clifftop. A wooden staircase leads down to a dock where a couple of powerful-looking motorboats are moored.

MBs voice crackles over the phone. "Got a good clear visual now. Go for it, Danny."

"Roger."

Danny flies the drone above the cliff near the wall. He almost misses it—a compact mass of orange cloth bunched up among the gray rocks. *Orange cloth?* He suddenly has an overwhelming desire to pee. *Doesn't Eddie have an orange State hoodie?*

He angles the camera and zooms it to center the mass in his screen. "M.B.! Are you seeing this? What does it look like to you?"

At Hyacinth House, M.B. is viewing the scene on a 32-inch monitor. She tweaks a few keys and the image blows up, then she moves her mouse to scan it. Black sneakers with white soles. Blue jeans. Dark hair. "Oh my God, Danny, it's a body. It looks like the body of a young man... or a boy!" She clicks the mouse to get plenty of pictures.

"Have you got what you need?" Danny asks MB.

Her voice is hushed. "I think so."

Danny hits a button to recall the drone, then puts down the controller and goes to the pilot's seat. On the deck beside it lies an AR-15 with a full mag. He turns the key to fire up the engine and points the prow at the dock.

"Call backup, M.B. I'm going in."

Chapter 43

L upe is at the end of her rope.

As a little girl in Culiacán, Mexico, Lupe was no stranger to violence perpetrated on children by evil men. She was raped by *siccarios* of the infamous Sinaloa cartel—one of them became Eduardo's father. At thirteen, the pregnant and fed-up Lupe decided she would ride the beast for the United States in the hope of a better life. Repeatedly raped during the journey, even by a police officer, Lupe now has no illusions about what a rich and powerful man can do. Her only son has been with such a person for days now. And it's all her fault.

Right after Eduardo went missing, Lupe was willing to trust the fam, especially Danny and M.B., to find him and bring him home. But that trust ebbed as the days wore on. She has seen this before. A wealthy and connected man like this *Señor* Ellis, who has his hooks into the police, the district attorney and who knows how many other government officials, can do anything he wants to anybody. She's encountered men who like young boys before—it's a sickness that cannot be denied, and why would they even, when they have the money and means to satisfy their urges?

Danny said that Eduardo was a prisoner in Ellis's compound. The police know it, but will not do anything, hiding behind the shield of probable cause. She's waited days for Danny, and M.B., a member of the all-powerful FBI, and even her beloved Nattie to act, but nobody has. Nattie even deserted her but then returned to become the only one to breach the villain's walls. But it's done no good. The *cabrón* still has her boy.

Now it's up to me!

Going into the gun room on the first floor of Hyacinth House, Lupe chooses a small semiautomatic pistol from the weapons stored there. A firm believer that in a house with guns, everyone living there should know how to handle and use them, Danny has taught her. She finds an extra magazine and tucks it into her purse with the pistol after filling it with hollow point .380 rounds.

I'm gonna drive over there and tell them they have to give me my son back. If they will not listen, well, that's what the gun is for.

Making sure that no one sees her, Lupe goes out front and gets into her little yellow VW bug. She loves that car. It's an older model that Danny found and lovingly restored. *A wedding present,* he called it. She turns the key and the little engine fires up, sounding like an oversized lawn mower. She steps on the clutch and throws it into gear, then sets off. Ellis's compound is about a ten-minute drive from Hyacinth House.

Soon the grey stone wall of the compound comes into view. *What was that?* A motion from the roadside catches her eye, but whatever caused it is gone by time she can look. *Probably a deer or something.* The double cast iron gates at the corner of the wall stand open. The road will funnel her into a lane next to the guardhouse, beyond which a red-and-white-striped metal barrier blocks access.

If I stop to talk to the guard, he won't let me in.

Her eyes travel around the inside her beloved little car.

Danny will understand. Eduardo is our son.

The guard looks up with a bored expression as the bug approaches the gate.

Lupe mashes the gas pedal and the engine noise goes from a clatter to a whine.

The guard's eyes widen and he raises his Uzi when he realizes the bug shows no signs of stopping.

Lupe is thrown against her seatbelt as the car hits the barrier, which snaps at the impact—luckily, it has not been reinforced to stop a vehicle. There are other means for that.

The guard regains his cool and throws a switch on the wall inside the guard shack.

In front of her, Lupe sees a section of the road flip up, and row of six-inch spikes pops into the sunlight and rotates a half-turn so they're pointed directly at her tires.

¡Ai Caramba! What is that hijo de puta?

Seconds later, she finds out.

POW! POW!

Her front tires explode like IED's, followed by the rear ones a second later. The bug starts careening like a car on a crazy amusement park ride. The two driver's side wheels leave the pavement, and come crashing back down. Lupe hauls on the steering wheel, trying to get the car back under control, but that's exactly the wrong thing to do. The bug flips and the roof is crushed like an egg as it slams into the pavement. It bounces, flips again, and comes to rest on its roof in the middle of the road.

***

173

Sister!

A phone on the wall of the guard shack overlooking Green Lake buzzes. A uniformed QRF guard picks it up.

"Smitty, here... What! OK, we're on our way."

As he hangs up, his partner looks at him questioningly.

"Some crazy broad just tried to ram the main gate." Smitty says. "She wrecked, but they're calling all hands in case she has company. Let's go."

The two guards rush outside, jump into a Jeep, and drive off toward the main gate.

They do not notice the motorboat approaching the dock below.

Chapter 44

Danny steers the boat with one hand, the other holding the AR-15 by the pistol grip, while scanning the top of the cliff for unfriendlies as he nears the dock.

No one appears as he pulls up next to the pier. He cuts the engine, tosses a loop over a convenient pylon, and disembarks, taking the AR along. He makes it to the wooden stairs unobserved and looks up, still holding his rifle at instant readiness. Still no guards.

Pretty shoddy security if you ask me.

He walks along the border of the rocks at the base of the cliff and is soon forced to wade in the lake when the beach disappears. He can see the orange mass where the rocks meet the fence.

It is a body. And it is a boy!

He wades as fast as he can, splashing furiously, throwing great gouts of water in front of him. He spots the boy's head. His brown hair.

Oh no! Please God...

He puts the rifle down on the rocks so he can use both hands to clamber up to the body. He grabs the head, turns it toward him so he can see the face.

It's not Eddie! Thank Christ! I don't know how I could have faced his mother if it was.

He lays a couple of fingers on the carotid artery on the boy's neck. No pulse.

Danny's vaguely ashamed that he feels joy rather than sorrow at the death of a young man, but it is what it is. Sitting on the rocks, he pulls out his cell.

"M.B.? It is a body. It's not Eddie, but it is a teen-aged boy. He's dead. I call that probable cause, don't you?"

"Yes I do. I'll get on the horn Judge Kirk in Capital City. He's a federal judge."

"I thought you said this is not a federal case?"

"I'm going to tell Kirk that he has to issue the warrant because we don't know which of the locals Ellis has his claws into. He owes me a favor—he'll do it. Then I'll call the local SAIC and tell him to meet me out there ASAP with a team."

"Why don't you loop Detective Sykes in on this too?"

"I thought we couldn't trust the locals?"

"Sykes is good police, M.B. She won't rat us out."

"If you're sure..."

"I'm sure. Loop her in."

"OK, consider her looped."

Danny kills the call. Once again, he stares at the broken body of the teenager on the rocks, trying to summon up a modicum of sadness. He has to settle for anger. It just as easily could have been Eddie. Somebody needs to pay for this. And now, more than ever, he has to find his boy.

Picking up the rifle, Danny slides off the rocks into the water and wades toward the wooden staircase.

Chapter 45

I'm freezing.

I've been sitting on this cold concrete floor in the nude for hours, my arms embracing my knees and my back against a cold stone wall. Light is provided by a wire-encased fluorescent fixture—the low whine it produces is doubtless the cause of my whanging headache.

The room is about ten by ten and sealed with a metal door. There's a little barred window in the center of the door, blocked by a cover on the outside. It could be one of those trendy escape-room puzzles except there's not a goddamn thing inside to use to get out. Who the fuck would lock you in a room then give you shit to escape, anyway? Apparently not Jay Ellis.

I hear a clank and the squeal of hinges, I look up. Light from outside is now coming through the barred window on the door.

"Well, you've really done it this time!" A female voice says.

Bella!

"What do you mean?"

"I've never seen Jay so mad. He says he's gonna take you to the island."

"The island?"

"He has his own island in the Caribbean. He's gonna take you there and deal with you."

"What do you mean, deal with me?"

"I don't know exactly, but whatever he's got in mind, you won't like it."

We're both quiet for a minute. Then I ask, "Why are you letting him do this, Bella?"

"Do what? Punish you? You fucking hit him. That's on you, not me."

"That's not what I mean. Why do you let him fuck you? He's your father."

"So? He's good to me."

"Good to you? He let you kill somebody for him! The cops have it on video!"

Sister!

"It doesn't matter. Jay won't let anything happen to me. He loves me. He'll take care of you too, if you'll just let him."

"I don't need him to take care of me. I've got my fam for that. And Jay's got my little boy. He's teaching him to have sex. He's only ten years' old!"

"Eduardo? Yeah, I met him. Seems like a cool kid. And hey, you gotta start screwing somebody sometime."

You met him? You know where he is!

"Bella, you've got to do something for me. Get Eduardo out of here! I don't care what happens to me. Just don't let Jay hurt him anymore."

"Hurt him? The kid's prolly having the time of his life!"

You just don't get it!

"No, Bella, he's not. We studied this in college. Kids who start having sex early have a lot of emotional problems later on. What's worse, Jay is making vids and putting them out on the net for any pedo to see. What happens if Eduardo finds out about that? What if one of those lowlifes who see them come looking for him? Would you want your sex life on display for the whole world?"

"I wouldn't care."

No, I guess you wouldn't.

"Fine. But that's your choice. Eduardo isn't getting a choice."

Bella doesn't respond to that..

I go on, "And I don't know what his mother would do if she finds out. She's a recovering addict. She's got a lot of problems because she was abused herself as a little girl. This might just kill her."

"That's not on me, Natalie. Those people will just have to fend for themselves."

Like you did? She doesn't say it, but I hear it loud and clear. I suddenly remember what Abigail Dupont told me.

"Who abused you, Bella? Was it your daddy?"

"Jay's my dad and he doesn't abuse me!" she says angrily. "I want to do it for him!"

"I meant the guy who raised you. Did he fuck you when you were a little girl?"

She doesn't answer.

Abigail Dupont was telling the truth.

178

"When we were upstairs, you told me you love me. Prove it! Get me out of here! Help me get Eduardo away from Jay Ellis!"

Clank! The little door on the bars is closed again.

So much for playing her.

My chin sinks back down on my knees.

A deep CLUNK! comes from the door as the latch is withdrawn, and it slowly opens...

Chapter 46

Sporting a black eye that covers nearly half of his face, Jay Ellis is as mad as he's ever been.

"The ungrateful little cunt! Just look at what she did to me!" he says for the tenth time.

Gerry McCauley, sitting across from him at the breakfast table, is wisely silent.

"I was going to make her part of our family," he goes on. "Give her things she never could have imagined. All I wanted in return was for her to bear me a child. One child! Is that too much to ask?" He glares at Gerry, obviously waiting for an answer.

"No, Jay, no. Not at all." Gerry says hurriedly.

"You're goddamn right, not at all! Then what the fuck does she do? She fucking hits me! Throws me into a wall! I won't be able to show my face in public for weeks!" He takes a large swig of coffee, laced with 30-year-old scotch. "I'll teach her a lesson she'll never forget! I've contacted Muhammed. He's going to meet us down at Isle Bleu. We'll see how she is after six months or a year in his harem. He'll teach her respect."

Footsteps in the doorway announce the Pres's arrival at the breakfast room. He asks, "Who'll teach what to who?" then stops short when he gets a look at Ellis. He smirks, "What happened, Jay? Run into a door, did you?"

Ellis wheels on him like a rabid dog. "You think this is funny?" he snarls.

The Pres stands still, obviously aware that he's just poked the bear. He's trying to control his facial muscles so he doesn't break out into a grin, but he fails miserably. "Actually, yes," he says. "It is pretty amusing."

Ellis silently stares at him. The anger in the air almost shimmers between them like the presence of an evil spirit.

Finally, the billionaire says, "I wonder how funny it would be if a video of your antics with Beverly and Sara last night was leaked to the Internet."

The Pres goes white. "You're recording us? You told me you would never do that."

"Are you really that naïve? I lied. I think you owe me an apology."

180

His expression changing from cheerful to deadly serious, the Pres does not reply immediately. Then he says, "That would really be unwise, Jay. Really unwise."

"You think? Apologize!"

The Pres says nothing for at least ten seconds, glaring aggressively at Ellis. Then, "I'm sorry I offended you, Mr. Ellis. It won't happen again."

Sounding somewhat mollified, Ellis responds, "It better not. Now sit down and have your breakfast."

Turning to leave the room, the Pres says, "I think I've lost my appetite."

"I said sit down and have your breakfast!" Ellis barks.

The Pres slowly faces Ellis again, disbelief rife on his face. He moves to take a chair at the table. Ellis smiles with satisfaction as the expression in his eyes slowly becomes neutral.

***

Later, the door to the Pres's bedroom opens and a black-uniformed QRF guy comes out. He closes the door, looks left and right to ensure he's unobserved, then hurries downstairs and outside.

Chapter 47

Ascending the stairs, Danny hears a car engine fire up above.

He drops into a kneeling position, training the barrel of the AR at the clifftop.

After a moment, the sound of the engine grows fainter, then disappears altogether.

Danny stands and hurries to the top of the cliff.

He's looking at a small, single-story wooden building with a gravel driveway adjacent, now empty. Danny checks his three and nine o'clock, then hurries across an open area to the door to the house. He presses his ear against the door, and hearing nothing, tries the doorknob. It's open so he goes inside.

He's in a sparsely furnished room smelling of burnt coffee, which contains a wooden desk and swivel chair, a couple more wooden armchairs and a file cabinet. There's a phone on the desk. The coffeepot i on a low table against the wall. The pot is empty, but the light on the switch below it is still on, which accounts for the odor. On the wall next to the table is a wooden coat rack containing a couple of jackets with QRF in block letters on their backs. A black beret hangs on a peg above one of the coats.

It's a warmish day, but Danny would rather be seen in a QRF coat than in the clothes he's wearing. He dons a coat and the beret. The hat is a little too small, but it'll do. He'd rather have an Uzi than his AR, but it is what it is.

He goes outside and around the back of the guard shack where a gravel road runs parallel to the cliff. Looking left, he sees the wire-topped wall about a hundred yards away. To the left, the road turns into the heart of the compound. A haze of dust still hanging in the air indicates that the vehicle he heard probably went in that direction. Slinging the AR over a shoulder, Danny takes off that way in a ground-eating trot.

Rounding the bend, he sees a formal garden on his left, surrounded by a low stone wall. Beyond is the rear of a large mansion built of rose-colored stone, with a brown slate roof. Danny continues on, watching carefully for anyone out and about, but he sees no one. He passes the house, and the road forks into a circular driveway in front of the house, and continuing on toward the front of the estate. He passes a copse of trees and pulls up short at the sight of a black helicopter sitting on a white concrete pad in the center of a circular green lawn. Beyond, the road forks again, one side going right to the opposite wall of the estate and the other to the left toward the state road that runs in front of the place.

Danny realizes that he's been lucky to have encountered no one so far. He moves more carefully now, going to the side of the road and taking the fork going toward the front of the estate. As he comes round another bend, a scene of chaos comes into view. A couple of Jeeps bearing the QRF eagle are parked in the road and half-a-dozen guards are milling around what appears to be a car wreck. Looking more closely, Danny sees a small car turned over with the tires pointing skyward and its roof crushed. Wait a minute, he knows that car...

Lupe!

Unthinking, Danny unlimbers the AR and trains it on the QRF guys, then sanity strikes. He is trespassing. If he fires on that group, he's not only committing felonious assault, he's likely toast because he's massively outgunned. He puts his gun down and pulls out his cell, hitting the speed dial for M.B. It's ringing. Come on, come on...

A sound arises. Sirens, low at first and increasing in volume as they near the estate.

"Woodrow. Danny? We're nearly there!"

"M.B.! Call a bus. It's Lupe, she's here and she may be hurt."

"We've got one with us in case of casualties. Hang on, we're coming in!"

Blue lights flash as a black Suburban comes through the gate followed by a white armored Humvee with the letters FBI emblazoned on the hood. A CCPD police car follows and finally, a green and white ambulance with red lights blazing.

***

Inside the mansion, the Pres is in his bedroom, watching his valet close a suitcase, when his cell phone buzzes in his jacket.

Downstairs, a topless, young girl brings Jay Ellis a phone on a silver tray.

"Ellis."

He listens.

"OK. We'll deal with it."

Sister!

***

As the police vehicles pull up on the accident scene, red and blue lights flashing, the QRF dudes take their hands away from their weapons. The doors to the suburban open and M.B. gets out, followed by Leon Kidd and two FBI agents in blue jackets. The Hummer disgorges more officers in combat gear and black helmets. The QRF boys raise their hands; Ellis is not paying them anywhere near enough to fight U.S. government agents and cops at close range.

Detective Sykes and two more CCPD officers exit the police car.

Danny heads for the group at a run. A SWAT dude, seeing him coming, raises a rifle, but M.B. looks that way and orders, "Put it down, Mister, he's one of ours."

Coming up on the stricken VW, Danny can see a body inside in the driver's seat through the crushed window, held in place by the seat belt.

Lupe! Oh God, oh God...

Danny throws the AR aside and hits the pavement on his belly, thrusting his arm through the window, feeling for the pulse in her neck.

Please God, let her be alive, let her be alive...

It's there! It's slow and it's thready, but it's there!

As Danny rises to his knees, a young voice sounds behind him.

"*Mamá* Lupe!"

Danny stares incredulously as Eduardo runs up to the wrecked car, snatching him up in his arms before he can get a clear look inside. Standing, he pushes the boy's face into his shoulder and kisses the top of his head.

"Hey, Eddie, Mama's ok, she's gonna be ok..."

***

Another black Suburban coming from the mansion rounds the curve near the helicopter pad, turning away from the accident scene towards the far side of the estate. Spotting it, M.B. hollers, "Hey! Stop that car!"

Somebody trips a siren in one of the police cars and the Suburban stops. M.B. grabs one of the FBI agents and runs over to the SUV. The windows are heavily tinted, so she can't see inside, so she draws her sidearm as a precaution. The driver's window hisses down as she walks up on it, and a black man in chauffeur's livery jerks his thumb toward the rear of the vehicle. The back window lowers and M.B. goes slack-jawed as she comes face-to-face with the former President of the United States.

"It's inconvenient for me to talk with you right now, agent. I assure you I will get in touch with your director forthwith to make myself available at another time."

As a government employee, M.B. makes the only response she can.

"Yes sir."

The windows glide back up and the SUV drives off.

***

M.B. returns to the accident scene. A fire truck comes through the gate, pulls up near the ruined bug, and firemen get out, carrying equipment to remove Lupe from the wreck. In short order the driver's door is lying on the pavement. A fireman cuts the seat belt and pulls her out of the car. An EMT standing by begins an examination.

After a moment, Danny asks the EMT, "How is she?"

"Alive, and lucky as hell" she replies. "She has no head injuries that I can see. Apparently she's so short that the crushed roof didn't come in contact with her head."

The EMTs place Lupe on a stretcher, raise it up and take her to the waiting ambulance.

"Where are you taking her?" Danny asks.

"University Hospital. Want to ride along?"

Danny is torn. On the one hand, he wants to be with his wife in her time of need. OTOH, Nattie is still somewhere in the compound and may need him as well. He makes his decision.

"No. I'll get over there as soon as I can."

As the ambulance takes off with lights flashing, Eduardo tugs on Danny's sleeve.

"Is Mamá Lupe gonna be OK?"

"Yes." Danny can tell from Eddie's face that he has something else on his mind. "What?"

Sister!

"Two of those guys in the black shirts shot my friend Pepe by the lake."

"Do you know which ones?"

"No. It was dark."

"And?" prompts Danny.

"There's a woman who looks just like Mamá Nattie inside the house."

Danny calls M.B. and Detective Sykes over. He says to Eduardo, "Tell them what you just told me."

When he's finished, Sykes says to M.B., "That woman must be the one who killed the convenience store clerk. I hope you're not going to interfere with my collar."

"Nope," says M.B. "I am going have a talk with Mr. Ellis about his security people, though."

A chattering noise fills the air, rising in intensity as it changes to a buzz. A helicopter!

"Oh no, you don't," says Sykes, motioning to a couple of uniformed officers and running toward the house. M.B. and two FBI agents follow.

Danny tells Eduardo, "Stay here with Mr. Kidd," then trots after them.

They come into view of the helipad in time to see a group ascending the stairs on the chopper—A man and a dark-haired woman, and a short blonde female wearing a blue-and-red t-shirt and jeans. The door closes behind them as the girl disappears inside.

Danny knows that shirt.

"Nattie!" he hollers, but his voice is drowned in the wind from the chopper.

The storm from the rotors has whipped up in earnest now, almost impeding forward progress. The chopper's nose raises the small front wheel off the concrete, and the two rear wheels follow as the bird leaps skyward. In a moment the chopper is a hundred feet above the ground, flying toward the lake at a forty-five-degree angle. Danny has a sinking feeling in his stomach as he watches it. One of his wives is heading for the hospital in uncertain condition and the other one who-knows-where as a prisoner of a rogue billionaire.

The engine noise ebbs as the copter gets smaller and smaller as it rises above the lake, until it resembles the little drone Danny bought Eduardo for his birthday.

CRUMP!

An orange ball of flame erupts, obliterating the aircraft. Black smoke ascends into the blue sky as metal rains down into the water. The compression wave hits, and Danny's ears are suddenly ringing as the heat from the blast sears his face.

OMG! Nattie was on that chopper!

Chapter 48

Danny, M.B., Sykes and the cops and agents walk slowly to the main house after they recover from the shock of the blast.

There isn't much reason for Danny to go with them, but if he doesn't, he'll have to deal with what he's just seen, and he simply isn't ready. And he still has the rest of the family to care for. He knows that Lupe is not going to take this well at all. His own grief will have to come later.

Nattie! I can't believe she's gone.

"I'm sorry for your loss," Sykes says, and Danny winces at the canned phrase. "You should go and be with Ms. Ibáñez and your son. But my murderer may still be here, and I'm going to arrest her."

"I'd like to see this through, if you don't mind," Danny says.

"I don't," says M.B., looking pointedly at Sykes. "Stay as long as you need to." And that settles it.

The group enters the house without knocking or ringing the bell, coming into the gleaming marble foyer. The staff is milling around in confusion. Nobody seems to realize what just happened—they'll find out later that they're all out of work. Bypassing the marble staircase for now, Danny and the cops proceed into the sunlit great room. The chef and his assistant are working in the kitchen, seemingly oblivious to the carnage outside. A man sits in the breakfast room, his back to them, a topless high school girl standing nearby. The man doesn't look around as Danny and company approach—he's too busy eating.

Sykes and her cops are the first to come into his field of view, then he turns so everyone can see him. Danny's jaw drops to the floor as he realizes who it is.

Seeing the uniforms, the Prince says, "I think you'll find that I have diplomatic immunity," then calmly goes back to his breakfast.

***

Later, the cops are searching the bedrooms on the second floor. It has become obvious to Sykes that there are many underage girls in the mansion and she wants all of them rounded up. She's also still hunting the murderer.

The entire estate has been sealed and Sykes has requested more manpower to search the outbuildings—it's just a matter of time before the culprit is apprehended.

Sykes opens a door to an opulent bedroom. The odor of alcohol and sex is heavy in the air, and loud snores indicate that canopied bed is occupied. As the detective approaches, two girls sit up—one is bare-breasted while the other holds a sheet to her chest in a nod toward modesty. Neither looks older than sixteen. The bare-chested girl pokes the snoring man between them in the ribs. The snores stop as he wakes and struggles to sit up.

Sykes does a double take, then smiles. "Chief Greene! Imagine finding you here."

As the girls exit the bed, revealing that both are nude, an empty liquor bottle rolls out on to the floor. Sykes reaches to unsnap her cuffs from her belt.

"Can you get out of bed on your own, Chief, or do you need my officers to help you?" Sykes asks.

Greene asks the stupid question of the day. "Just what do you think you're doing, Detective?"

"Arresting you, of course, for child molestation, statutory rape, giving alcohol to minors, and other things I'll think of later..."

***

M.B. takes charge of gathering the staff in the great room and getting any half-clad girls decent. To his dismay, she relieves the Prince of his breakfast and orders him off the premises.

"Maybe I can't arrest you, but I can and will get you out of here for your own safety," she tells him.

"Give him a ride to where he wants to go," M.B. tells an FBI agent.

To Danny: "There's really nothing for you to do here, hon. Why don t you go to the hospital and be with Lupe and Eduardo. And tell Leon not to say anything about Nattie to Amos and her Mom. I'll break the news to them later."

"Ok." Danny moves like a zombie to follow the agent. M.B. goes with him. She has come to like this young Marine a great deal, and can't imagine the depth of his grief.

Sister!

They reach the front door and Danny opens it to see a short blond woman coming up the stairs, herding a group of kids. She stops for a second when she sees him, then leaps forward, throws her arms around his neck, and gives him a long, deep kiss.

"What the fuck was all that noise before?" says Nattie, after she comes up for air.

Chapter 49

I still haven't got my head straight about the tragedy at the Ellis estate.

The worst thing is Bella's death, of course. It's the second time that I've lost a sister, and it's even worse than the first time because I truly did fall in love with her. I know because of the size of the hole her death has left in my heart. And the WOAT is that I feel partly responsible for it.

Ellis told Bella that he was going to turn me over to an Arab sheik at his private island, who would place me in his harem and "teach me how to behave." Apparently, Bella loved me too, so she proposed a simple plan. Having stolen the code to unlock my cell, she would pretend to be me. She swore she wouldn't tell Ellis and Gerry until me and Eduardo were safely away. When he came to get her, Ellis brought her the clothes I was wearing when I entered the compound. She was sure that, while the billionaire would be angry when he found out she'd tricked him, he wouldn't really hurt her. I wasn't so sure about that, but my fear for my son overrode my reservations, so I agreed to her plan. Turned out that what Ellis would or wouldn't have done didn't matter after all.

M.B. told us that the FBI thinks that there was a bomb with a barometric trigger on Ellis's chopper. When it reached a predetermined height, boom! The bureau has no idea who planted it, but there are many suspects. Jerome Ellis was not a man who endeared himself to others.

I'm still trying to come to terms with the fact that Ellis and Gerry were my biological parents. They were both terrible excuses for human beings and I'm not sorry they're dead, but I do have to cope with the idea that I share their genes. I also have another sister out there somewhere (that embryo was split into fourths!) that I want to track down if I can get access to the NHFC records again—M.B. has said she might be able to help with that. I guess the bottom line is that I'll always consider Sean and Judy McMasters as my parents and trust the upbringing they gave me to counteract any bad vibes from Ellis's and Gerry's genes.

My grief for Bella is lessened by the fact that Lupe survived the car wreck and is on the mend. But everything isn't Gucci with her, either. She's currently in a wheelchair, and while she's expected to leave it soon, it's a constant reminder that she's not well. Her withdrawal symptoms have returned because it was necessary to give her opiates for pain when she was recovering from surgery. She's back on suboxone, a maintenance drug she had been successfully weaned off of some time ago. Even though it wasn't her fault, she feels like she's backslid and has to work very hard to get drug-free again. The wheelchair makes it hard for her to go to meetings, because many of them are for addicts only, meaning that me or Danny has to take her and wait outside until the meeting is over before we can take her home. She can't cook, she can't do housework—it's even hard for her to go to the bathroom on her own. Lupe is a very independent, strong-willed woman, and having to depend on us for such things has made her totally ratchet.

We're also not unaware that Eduardo now needs more help than ever. The early sexualization of a child can have many bad effects. He's seeing a shrink to deal with his experiences in Ellis's compound, as well as the effects of having taken a life. While the doctor is cautiously optimistic that everything will be all right in the end, it's not certain. Because of Lupe's disability, Danny and me have to step up our involvement as parents, and that's not a bad thing.

A few days after Lupe returns home from the hospital, Danny calls a meeting.

"I know our wedding vows didn't say so," he begins, "but I think we should agree not to have sex outside of our marriage."

"I do not think I would want to," says Lupe, "so I am fine with this."

Danny looks pointedly at me.

I've done a lot of thinking since getting away from Ellis. "I'm okay with it, too," I say. Danny's eyes widen with surprise. "I guess Jay Ellis showed me the trouble that sex can cause when you use it as a tool to get what you want. I think that the three of us have something really special, and I totally do not want to be the one to screw it up."

Danny goes to Lupe in her wheelchair to give her a hug, and opens an arm to invite me in. I'm crying when we're finished, and so are both of my spouses.

The events that occurred in Ellis's compound have dominated the news cycle for what seems like forever. I've been thrust into the spotlight again, because the vid of the convenience store murder finally went public. Betsy Kiefer wrote an article in the The State of State alleging the killer was me, but Chief Trevelyan and M.B. convinced the new DA that I had a lookalike who was responsible. The old DA was arrested for conspiracy after Deputy Chief Ailín Greene implicated her and many other high-placed dudes in the criminal justice system in Ellis's schemes.

Ellis had about two dozen high school girls who came in and out of the mansion as well-paid prostitutes, as well as the homeless kids he'd picked up for his budding kiddie porn enterprise. When asked why Ellis would have even considered such a thing, a certain disgraced network anchor man went on the record to say that, while toxic narcissists outwardly radiate total confidence in themselves and their abilities, most of them have to continually prove that they can do anything they want to, to bolster their fragile egos.

Somehow the Pres and the Prince managed to stay out of the news. I guess both have people who see to such things. I have no interest in outing either of them right now, but what I know might prove useful in the future.

The homeless kids who were rounded up by the cops are going into the foster care system. When he hears about that, Eduardo comes to me and Danny to ask if we can do anything for Shannie.

"I promise you, she will hate foster care and she will keep on trying to run away until she makes it," he says.

So Lupe, Danny and me put in a petition to adopt Shannie as co-parents. Not surprisingly, we're turned down. Seems that the system ain't woke enough yet to consider a fam with two wives and a husband as suitable to adopt a child.

That's when M.B. steps in. Her marriage to Uncle Amos will occur soon, and she plans to move into to Hyacinth House after the wedding. "A child of our own will make us a real family," she says. "It will be a whole lot harder for Child Services to turn down an FBI agent and a decorated Marine as foster parents, even if we are a couple of old farts. Besides, we all know who her real parents will be."

After that petition is approved, Eduardo is beyond stoked. It looks like somebody is going to gain a sister out of this tragedy after all.

Epilogue

A motor launch cleaves through the waves of an impossibly blue summertime sea, a foamy white wake streaming behind it like a tail.

The weather is glorious in the Gulf of California in June—mid-eighties with a fresh breeze that make it feel ten degrees cooler.

The driver of the launch is an older Hispanic man in a straw hat, a dirty white shirt and faded red shorts. Three passengers occupy a bench behind him—a fiftysomething white guy with his hair in a ponytail, an elegant dark-haired lady who's a little younger, and a short, pretty, twentysomething woman with shoulder-length blonde hair and a bulging tummy. All of them wear expensive sunglasses and are dressed like typical monied tourists out to enjoy a day on the water.

Approaching a rocky cay, the driver aims for a break in the cliffs where a white wooden pier can be seen. A path winds upward from the waterfront to a large house on top of the island.

The rhythm of the engine changes as the pilot throttles down when turning to line up his craft with the dock.

He cuts the engine and lets the boat's momentum carry it alongside the quay. Standing, he tosses a loop over a convenient pylon and heaves on the line until the side of the vessel bumps on the pads tied there for protection. After making the rear end fast as well, he steps out on the dock and offers a hand to help the passengers disembark—first the gentleman, then the dark-haired lady, and finally the blonde *chica*. He hops back into the launch to retrieve their luggage, which he brings out onto the pier as well.

Finally, he turns to the Señor, holding out his hand to receive the payment he was promised to bring them here. He does not see the blonde reach into an open canvas bag sitting on the dock and withdraw a small, flat black semiauto pistol.

CRACK! CRACK!

The old sailor collapses to the boards, never having heard the shots that killed him.

The man acts like nothing unusual has happened, turning and following the pathway to the house, leaving the luggage for someone else to take care of.

A deep red pool spreads from beneath the corpse, soaking into the wood of the dock.

"I'm sorry about the mess, Ma'am," the blonde says.

"These things happen, Dear."

---The End---

Did you enjoy Sister!? Have you read the other Natalie McMasters Mysteries? If not, get your copy of the first book, Stripper! from Amazon now by visiting the link below:

https://www.amazon.com/gp/product/B07C87Y2FH?notRedirectToSDP=1&ref_=dbs_mng_calw_0&storeType=ebooks

And be sure to sign up for my email list at:

https://www.3mdetectiveagency.com/contact/

Follow me on:

Facebook:
https://www.facebook.com/groups/541595279667727

Twitter: @3Mdetective

Blog:
https://www.3mdetectiveagency.com/blog/

Instagram: 3mdetective

Goodreads:
https://www.goodreads.com/author/show/17956517.Thomas_A_Burns_Jr_

Bookbub
https://www.bookbub.com/profile/thomas-a-burns-jr

Tumblr
https://www.tumblr.com/blog/nataliemcmasters

About the Author

Thomas A. Burns Jr. writes the Natalie McMasters Mysteries from the small town of Wendell, North Carolina, where he lives with his wife and son, four cats and a Cardigan Welsh Corgi. He was born and grew up in New Jersey, attended Xavier High School in Manhattan, earned B.S degrees in Zoology and Microbiology at Michigan State University and a M.S. in Microbiology at North Carolina State University. As a kid, Tom started reading mysteries with the Hardy Boys, Ken Holt, and Rick Brant, then graduated to the classic stories by authors such as A. Conan Doyle, Dorothy Sayers, John Dickson Carr, Erle Stanley Gardner and Rex Stout, to name a few. Tom has written fiction as a hobby all of his life, starting with Man from U.N.C.L.E. stories in marble-backed copybooks in grade school. He built a career as technical, science and medical writer and editor for nearly thirty years in industry and government. Now that he's a full time novelist, he's excited to publish his own mystery series, as well as to write stories about his second most favorite detective, Sherlock Holmes. His Holmes story, *The Camberwell Poisoner*, recently appeared in the March – June 2021 issue of *The Strand Magazine*. Tom has also written a Lovecraftian horror novel, The Legacy of the Unborn, under the pen name of Silas K. Henderson—a sequel to H.P. Lovecraft's masterpiece At the Mountains of Madness.